D1823845

My Lady, Rich And Fair

Margaret Carradus

ISBN:9781973409748
ISBN-13:

DEDICATION

To Sara Wilson, thanks for the encouragement.
Diolch cariad!

As ever, to my dearest husband Laurence, for showing me
how nothing else matters.

My family, near and far, who give me such an insight into
how families work, whatever the weather!

ALSO IN THIS SERIES

My Lady, Rich and Fair

Chapter 1

Bitter, the wind blew from the North East and swept across the fenland unhindered. Snow clouds tumbled across the sky, driven by the Arctic blast, and began to shake free the little white feathers of snow they carried within. The air smelled of salt and marshlands as it forced its way past the rags the shepherds had tied around their faces for a little protection. It was eye watering weather, sending scurrying home the few folk out and about on their business.

Down by the side of a narrow waterway, a child was crouched, poking a stick into the oozing mud on the bank. She was as fair as the sky was dark, her hair whipping across her face in the wind. She pulled it back crossly and tucked it back behind her ears. Solitude suited her. She liked being out here on her own, away from everyone and their silly little rules. Girls were supposed to sit and sew, or read, or learn to look after men. How insufferably boring. She would much rather sit here by the waterside, playing around in the mud, hiding in among the rushes, helping the eel catchers make their baskets and then pulling the thick, tough skin down the snake -like bodies of their catch. It was too miserable today for even the fishermen to be about but that wouldn't keep her at home. She wriggled her bare feet in the mud, feeling the satisfying oozing between her toes ; slippery and slimy and very, very smelly.

"Hello Edith." The voice seemed to come from nowhere and yet it was all around her. The girl looked up, searching with eyes as bright as ice for the speaker fool enough to be about in this weather. To her right she saw a tall, elegant woman. She was swathed in a gown of brilliant blue and wore a veil of white, draped across her head and flung across one shoulder. Anchoring it in place was a sliver of gold, encircling the crown of her head. To the child she seemed familiar, although she knew they had never met before. The woman stretched out her arm and placed her hand lightly on the child's shoulder. A warm, tickly feeling ran through her slight frame. Edith squinted at the lady's face, puzzled as to what she wanted. "Remember, Edith, remember." The wind swirled harder, blowing snow into the child's eyes. She blinked, trying to regain her focus. By the time she could see straight again, the lady was gone.

Edith stood, pulling her feet free of the cloying mud. She wiped her hands down the sides of her gown and, realising that the short winter day was almost done, pulled up her skirts and hared as fast as she could back towards the cluster of buildings huddled on the patch of high ground. She hurtled past the hovels and service buildings towards the great hall which dominated the site. Pushing through the doorway, she ran towards the curtained area at the far end of the building. If she was really quick , she would be able to tidy herself up before her mother found her.

She hooked back the heavy tapestry that served to give privacy to the family and felt her heart sink. Standing in the middle of the room was her mother, looking very severe and not a little put out. She grasped the girl by the arm, and despite the howling protestations hauled off her clothes and dumped her into the bath of warm water which had been prepared for just this eventuality. Edith wailed furiously as she was scrubbed from head to foot, the water in the bath quickly turning opaque with mud. The shrieking halted for a moment as her head was ducked under the water to rinse her hair clear, then she bobbed up again, spluttering but much more subdued. Climbing out of the tub she stood sullenly while the maidservant rubbed her dry and roughly pulled her clean undershift and gown over her body. Edith pushed her away crossly, wriggling into her hose by herself then lacing up her shoes. She was pushed down onto a low stool while the maid and her mother attacked her hair with combs, picking out tangles and smoothing it down until it lay around her shoulders like a cape of burnished silver.

"I told you, this morning, that we had guests

arriving today. Keep clean, I said. Do not go playing by the dykes, I said, but what do you do? You come back looking like some raggle taggle hovel dwelling urchin!" At this point, Edith had the sense to bite her lip. It was not the time to make her mother any more irritable than she was already. "What escapes me is how you can come in looking like that and yet now you stand there looking as like an angel as you could find on Earth." Edith risked a glance from under her eyelashes and grinned cheekily. No one ever managed to stay angry at her for too long.

"You said we had guests? Is it the lady that I saw down by the water? The tall one with the blue gown and the gold coronet." Edith's mother looked at her, perplexed. There was no one in the party of visitors that fitted that description. In fact, there were no women at all. Sometimes the lady Cyneburg despaired of her wayward daughter and her vivid imagination. It was a miracle that she could ever unpick the real world from the one that she spun in her head.

CHAPTER 2

To be visited by someone as prominent as Earl Godwin created a flurry of excitement in the normally quiet household. Cantwareburh was not the busiest town in the Fens, and the little settlement at Hintone was even quieter. Cyneburg had raided the food put by to sustain them for the winter in order to feed the Earl and his entourage in a manner they were accustomed to. Her husband, Eadfrid, had been out hunting to provide fresh meat for the table. It was hard for him. Since he was injured in a Viking raid he had found it difficult even to walk and harder yet to ride. He had to rely so much on his wife nowadays that it made him feel less of a man, so it was important to him to at least provide something towards the feast.

He was standing outside, lantern in hand, awaiting the arrival of his guests when the freshly laundered Edith ran up to him, hugging him fiercely. He stepped back, assessing her by the light of the lantern. For once she looked neat , tidy and presentable. Thank heavens for that, he sighed. It was vital that she looked every inch the noble mistress if his plan was to come to fruition.

Eadfrid's chain of thought was interrupted by the sound of hooves clattering on the cobbled way which lead up to the gates protecting the compound. Servants dragged the gates back to allow the party to enter. Several men, on stocky little ponies, rode up to the doorway followed by a covered cart bearing chests and feed for the animals. Alongside the tall man who seemed to be in charge there were two young boys, mounted on the shaggiest ponies Edith had ever seen. They both looked extremely serious, as if their father had given them orders to be on their absolute best behaviour. Eadfrid would have tried to do that with Edith, but it would have been a lost cause; she would do as she wanted, whatever was said so he might as well save his breath and avoid the argument. The grooms came forward to lead the ponies off towards the stables as the riders dismounted stiffly. It had been a cold day for riding, and the weather would cut to the bone on days like this. Eadfrid bowed in welcome, hampered by his bad leg, and he glared at Edith for her to do the same. She resolutely refused and stood upright and proud in the glow of the candlelight. Earl Godwin helped Eadfrid upright and, laughing, tousled the girl's hair. She crumpled up her face in reply, causing him to slap his leg and laugh all the harder. "She is indeed a lively little minx, just as you said."

The group went through into the Great Hall, to be met by Edith's mother. She smoothed her gown as she curtseyed and lowered her eyes in respect. The Earl gave his hand and raised her up, kissing her on the cheek as he did so, "It is wonderful to see you again , my lord. It has been too many years since our paths crossed. How is your lady Gytha? Well, I hope."

"She is indeed, and ready to bear me another child any day now; hopefully another boy to join this pair." He beckoned the two boys forward and both bowed elegantly. As they raised their heads the younger one cast a glance in Edith's direction. She crumpled her face at him, and he responded by sticking his tongue out at her. She turned away, arms folded. What a horrible boy, she told herself in irritation.

Cyneburg called to the household steward, and ordered him to take Godwin and his party over to the guest chambers so they might freshen themselves ready for the feast that had been prepared in their honour. The boy turned his head towards Edith, sticking out his tongue again as he scampered to catch up with his father. "For the Lord's sake child, will you behave like a lady just for once?" Cyneburg had decided that her daughter needed a warning before she helped serve at the feast, "Your father has arranged for this, and you know how difficult things are for him now. He wants to be able to be proud of you, as his heir, and acting like an ill bred skivvy is not going to make that happen." She tilted the girl's chin upward with the tip of her forefinger, "Just for once, child."

Nobody could say that she didn't try. All through the evening she trotted back and forth, pitcher in hand, pouring mead into the upheld beakers. She smiled, answered questions politely and generally behaved like the perfect little lady. Gradually, her mother began to relax and enjoy the company. Earl Godwin was more than happy to regale them all with tales of life at Cnut's court. There was always some or other intrigue , it seemed to her, and delicious as it was to hear the gossip it was much safer being tucked away here in the wilds of the Fens. At least it was for as long as Cnut was strong enough to dissuade any other Vikings from attacking the English shores. Edith carried on with her task, carefully carrying the heavy pitcher from place to place. Eventually, she came to the table where the Earl's sons, Swein and Harold, were picking apart perch with their knives, popping the tender flesh into their mouths greedily. She brought their beakers towards the edge of the table and began to pour , biting her tongue in concentration. She half filled the beakers then reached for the water to weaken the strong brew.

"Here, leave off that!" Swein reached forward and stopped her hand.

"I was told to give you half strength, and that is what I will do. Children do not drink their mead unwatered." Swein made to stand up, annoyed at being called a child, but Harold pulled him back to his stool. By the look of it he had already drunk far too much of the powerful liquor. His face was flushed and he was starting to slur his speech. Father had warned them, more than once, that they had to behave themselves on this trip. Swein had behaved like an idiot before and Godwin had been livid; so much so that he had taken his belt and beat him across the back until it bled raw. Swein needed saving from himself and young Harold was unfortunately the nominated guardian.

Angrily, Swein shook off Harold's warning hand. He made a grab for the mead jug, sending Edith toppling over backwards as he pushed. She scrambled back to her feet and lunged towards the table, grabbing the knife which Swein had dropped. He leapt towards her, diving over the table and grabbing her wrist . He twisted her arm backwards until she yelped and dropped the dagger to the floor. Harold had by now hurtled across the table in her defence, tussling with his brother as he reached for his knife. Edith threw herself into the fray, and feeling her fingers around the weapon's hilt she thrust blindly in front of her. There was a squeal of pain and Harold dropped to his knees, clutching his side in agony. Edith had plunged the knife through his tunic and caught him along the ribs; not once but twice. She was standing frozen to the spot, her hands to her mouth in horror and face as pale as her silvery hair. Swein had pulled himself upright and staggered back to the table, panting with exertion, and was pouring the mead straight from the jug down his throat. The whole room sat in silence.

Edith was trembling now, tears springing from her eyes from the shock, "I didn't mean it. I'm sorry, I didn't mean to do that: not to you." Harold had pulled up his tunic and undershirt to survey the damage. The knife had sliced his side, twice, and the mark of the cross it had left was leaking blood down his side. By now Cyneburg had run to fetch warm water and a cloth and was gently wiping away the gore. Harold looked her in the eye, "It was not your daughter's fault, my lady, rather it was caused by the foolishness of my brother. I fear that your mead has caused him to lose his senses." And not for the first time, he muttered under his breath. Godwin had joined them and sent Swein away to his bed with one of his men for escort. He hugged the girl, a smile on his face, "Well tried, little mistress. It is about time my sons learned manners, especially that one."Godwin jerked his thumb in the direction of the retreating Swein's back. Smiling, he returned to his seat, clapping Eadfrid heartily on the shoulder as he went, "She is as brave as any son, and as bloodthirsty too. This country will need wives of such strength soon , I fear." He lifted his beaker, encouraging everyone to resume their feasting while Cyneburg lead the two remaining children to the private area behind the tapestry curtain.

"I'm so sorry. I didn't mean to cause you any trouble. Does it hurt much?" Edith was dabbing shakily at the wounds while her mother sought out a bandage and some healing unction to smear across the wounds.

"Only a little bit," Harold was trying not to cry. He bit his lip at each touch of the cloth, "My brother is an ass. He should not have behaved the way he did. He thinks he's so grown up, just because he is a year older than I am, but he is an idiot who cannot hold his liquor."

"I think your father might have a few strong words for him in the morning."

"Oh, more than words, you can trust me on that. Look, don't be upset about this. It's only a little scratch, really." Harold managed a smile. Edith reached for his hand and squeezed it in thanks. Her mother ducked back into the room, hunting for a particular small pot fashioned from stone which contained a soothing ointment heavily scented with herbs and spices. Dipping her finger into the pot, she began to salve and bind the wound,

"I fear there will be a scar. In the shape of a cross at that." She caught site of the children sitting hand in hand and smiled. It was good that they had made their peace.

CHAPTER 3

"Which one?" Edith's eyes were wide with shock at the news. "Not that Swein, he's awful!" Her hands were on her hips now, foot tapping angrily.

She is a miniature version of her mother, Eadfrid thought, bossy, nosy and as stubborn as an ox.

"No, not Swein. Harold. Earl Godwin and I have discussed it and are in agreement that you should be betrothed to one another. It is an excellent match for you, my child, so please do not even contemplate arguing about it. You are to marry Harold, when you are both of an age."

If she had to marry either of them, which was a repulsive thought, then she supposed that Harold would be the better bargain. He was much more likeable, and he had been so kind to her about the stabbing incident. She stopped for a moment, trying to recall his features. He was fair, blonde fair not silvery haired like her. His eyes were very blue, and had a twinkle of fun in them , especially when he stuck his tongue out at her. Better not think too much about it though. Time and again betrothals came to nothing, victims of the flow of politics and power.

Before long all such thoughts were driven out of her head. Years before, Eadfrid had been sorely wounded by Viking raiders who had swooped down onto the East coast in their Dragon ships. As Thegn, he had called out his fyrd men to protect their homes and families, and successfully so but not without a high cost. Edith had a brother, rather older than her, named Eadwyn. It was hard to recall him clearly, but he had been a fine youth, tall and powerful and by nature gentle as a lamb. He was fourteen when the raiders struck and he had leapt to the defence of his lands, accompanying his father as his squire. Barely had they faced the Vikings when he was killed, stuck down by a hulking warrior with his axe. Eadfrid had spun around at the sound of his son's scream and had himself been wounded, a glancing blow breaking his leg and as he fell his side was pierced by a sword. He had passed out, only coming round when he felt himself being dragged from the field of battle by some of his men.

He had never really got over that terrible day. For months afterwards he had woken screaming and in a cold sweat, overtaken by nightmares. His leg healed crooked and ached all the time in damp cold weather. But that was not the worst of it. The wound in his side had never really healed properly. The skin would close and seem to heal but time and again it would break down into a suppurating mess. Cyneburg's mother had been a healing woman, and she used many of her potions to try to fix the problem but nothing seemed to work and each time it happened it took longer and longer to settle back down. Now it was winter again and the aches in his bones meant that Eadfrid didn't want to get up from his bed. He lay there until the afternoon, when Cyneburg's pain relieving potions started to have their effect. The wound had opened again too, stinking and foul and deeper than ever before. Even the honey plaster seemed to have lost its healing power. Eadfrid stopped eating, existing on sips of mead Cyneburg fed to him from a spoon. He was fading away to a shadow before her, and there was nothing she could do to stop it.

In the month of After Yule, he finally closed his eyes for the last time. All the pain slipped from his face as he joined his precious boy, but Cyneburg felt it all and more. She crumpled before Edith's eyes, shrivelling in her agony. It was just the two of them now, and Edith knew that her mother would much rather be at rest with her father than having to carry on alone.

The body was laid out in the Abbey church, washed and sweetened with fragrant herbs and sweet flowers to disguise the smell of corruption. The night before the funeral service, Edith was kneeling in vigil by the coffin, praying for the soul of her father. The wind was howling, blowing the winter rain hard against the strong stone walls. Candles were lit on the altar and around the coffin, throwing curious shadow creatures against the walls. Suddenly she realised that the rain had stopped and the wind had ceased its blowing. The whole of the church felt beautifully warm, like being wrapped in a woollen blanket. There was a hand on her shoulder, she was sure of it. Slowly turning her head, for fear of who might be there, Edith felt a presence, a familiar one. The soft blue gown was the same, the white veil, the sliver of gold. She smiled gently at Edith, stroking away the tears from the girl's face with her slender hand. She quietly moved towards the coffin and gazed at the body within. Her dark brown eyes seemed to be filled with all the sorrows of the world as she bent forward and kissed Eadfrid on the forehead. "I will care for him now, for him and for your brother. They are safe where they cannot feel hurt any longer. I will do this for you, but you must make a promise to me. One day you will remember me and you will build a place for me and my own that is safe and as welcoming to strangers as God is to those who love him."

Edith felt a terrific light enter her head, so powerful that it made her screw her eyes tight shut and cry out in pain. Then, as it subsided, the sound of the rain blowing hard on the stonework began again. She opened her eyes slowly, searching for the lady but she was gone, enveloped by the shadows. Had she imagined the whole thing? She had heard of hallucinations caused by hunger and she hadn't eaten since yesterday morning. But she had seemed so real; so human somehow. Edith stood, shakily making her way to the side of the coffin. Her father's face was wreathed in a beatific smile, a smile that almost glowed. There was something on his forehead that she was sure had not been there before. Edith leaned forward to pick it away, then stayed her hand. There, where the lady had kissed him, was a little pile of blood red rose petals. Edith reached uncertainly forward, lifting one of the petals to her nose. It smelled sweeter and more heady than any flower she had ever known. The girl sat down on the altar steps deep in thought. No earthly rose petal ever smelled like this one, nor did they flower in the depths of winter. Thoughtful, she tucked the little petal into the scrip that hung from her belt, intending to keep it forever.

CHAPTER 4

Life was difficult after Edith's father died. Edith inherited his lands as the only living child, but Cyneburg had the task of managing them until she came of age. Although Cyneburg had always ruled the household with a rod of iron, she now had a task which was a completely different challenge. Slowly but surely she began to get a grasp of the situation and found that, rather than being beyond her, she had an aptitude for the role. It took her mind off her loss, for which Edith was grateful. Cyneburg had always known that they were comfortably off, but when she saw the figures of how much land they had, how much it was worth and how much income was generated each year the slow recognition dawned on her that she and Edith were very wealthy indeed.

Money was the most powerful aphrodisiac of them all, and as soon as the unwed lords of East Anglia and

Wessex realised how much they were worth then both Cyneburg and Ealdyth would be in danger. Too many times, women had been spirited away from their families and found themselves wedded to some avaricious brute by dint of forcing themselves upon them. The thought was terrifying. Sooner or later it was bound to happen, if they two of them did not take action to prevent such trouble.

Godwin heard of the death of his old friend with real sorrow. Trustworthy thegns were hard to find, and Eadfrid had been one of the most honest. He thought that he ought to visit the widow to pay his condolences, and to check on the general situation. Godwin was always concerned when any change of events might affect his plans. Taking his wife and Harold with him, he set out from Bosham , heading towards Hintone.

Harold was not in the finest of moods. It irritated him immensely when his father dragged him about like one of his hounds on a leash. He was a man now, at least as far as the law considered, and as such his father really ought to take his views into account. But no, not Godwin. When Harold had raised the subject of staying in Bosham with his brothers he was made to understand, by the use of the Earl's heavy belt, that he would do as his father told him for as long as he,

Godwin, lived. And that was why he was trotting along now, behind his father and mother, making rude gestures behind his back. He had to have some sort of revenge even if only he could see it. Snatches of conversation kept drifting back to him, blown about on the wind. It seemed he was the subject and his parents were talking about their plans for his future. Wouldn't it be lovely to have some sort of say in the matter, he grumbled to himself. He hadn't seen that girl in years. From what he could remember she was a fiery little witch. Supposing she had grown to have a face like an ox and a body to match! He would still be expected to wed her and bed her and , oh heavens, sire children on her. He went pale at the thought. It wasn't as if he had ever *done* it before, let alone with a complete stranger. Swein had. He had tumbled one of the brew house maids last summer, out in the fields under the starlit sky. He couldn't wait to brag about it to anyone who would listen. The blow by blow account almost frightened Harold to death. And here he was about to be parcelled off to some female he could barely recall.

Their arrival in Hintone was met with a sense of relief by Cyneburg. It didn't matter how capable a woman she was, it would be good to be able to discuss business with someone as knowledgeable as Godwin. They were shown over to their lodgings by the steward, who informed them that someone would be along shortly with drying cloths, should they wish to wash after the long ride. Harold was at least happy about his lodging. It was across a narrow alleyway from the building his parents would be sleeping in so at least he could escape the misery of listening to them planning his future. He stretched wearily, working out the knots in his back with his hands. He was damp and sweaty, in no fit state to dine with his hostess. He pulled his tunic and undershirt up and over his head, dropping them to the floor as he heard the knock on the door. It must be the maid with the water and drying cloths and about time too. He shouted to her to enter as he sat down on the bed to undo his footwear.

"Put the water on the chest and bring me the cloths. Hurry up about it!"

"I am glad to see my lord in such sweet temper!"

Harold turned, prepared to tongue lash the ill-mannered skivvy and then he stopped in his tracks. Standing before him, illuminated by the rushlight , was someone who most certainly was not a common servant. She stood tall and slender, her figure beginning to show the curves of womanhood at hips and breast. Her hair was plaited, reaching down below her waist and the most wonderful shade of silvery blonde.

Sparkles danced in her icy blue eyes and her full lips were curved in amusement.

"I see you still bear the scar I gave you."

Harold leapt up, pulling his tunic up to cover his nakedness. He could feel his cheeks glowing scarlet,

"You are Edith? You have changed much since last we met."

"As have you, my lord. I apologise if I startled you. It was not my intention to cause you such... discomfort."

She backed out of the room, biting her lip to stop herself from laughing out loud, then leaned against the wall, bent double in silent laughter. The look on his face had been utterly priceless, when he realised who had entered the chamber. He could hardly cover himself quickly enough. Wiping tears from her face, she lifted the hem of her skirt to walk back across the wet courtyard towards the Great Hall. He certainly had changed from the little boy she remembered. Thick fair hair still flopped over his brow, shading his deep blue eyes, but his jawline was that of a man now, strong and angular. He was much taller too, taller even than she was, and his body rippled with athleticism. How shy he seemed, though, so unsure of himself. She hadn't been looking forward to the visit of her future husband at all, but now she was willing to suspend judgement, at least for a little while.

The chamber bed creaked as Harold eased himself back onto the pillows. He threw his hands behind his head and whistled softly to himself. In his head, Edith had stayed a little child, awkward and feisty, but she had grown like a rose in the time that they had been apart. Such a lovely rose, on the point of blossoming. He reached for the drying cloth and began to rub his tousled hair dry. A grin crossed his face as he remembered the sight of her body. The gown she was wearing was not new, it was obvious, as it clung a little too tightly to her body, giving a hint of what might lie beneath. Easing himself from the bed, he crossed to his clothes chest which had been brought in from the cart. He lifted the lid and began to rifle through the clothes packed within. For some reason, he found himself wanting to make a good impression that evening. He pulled out a clean undershirt and tugged it over his head and down, the fabric sticking where he was still damp. Then he lifted out a dark blue tunic, trimmed with green and yellow braid. It couldn't fail to impress, he mused, clipping together the gold cuffs given to him by his mother on his coming of age. Pulling on moss green hose, he tied them to the hem of his braies, then fastened his shoes and belt, pouching the tunic fabric over the top to show off a little more of his trim calf muscles. He picked up his dirty clothes, hanging them on a peg to dry before he grabbed his cloak and pinned it closed with a plain annular brooch, heavy and shrieking wealth in its simplicity. How could she resist, he considered, when he looked like this?

There was a sharp rap at his door,

"I presume you are ready, boy. Out here now! It is the worst of manners to delay the meal for others because you are too lazy to get a move on." Harold rolled his eyes heavenward. His father was a clever man, politically astute and cunning, and actually very fond of his family despite what they might have thought, but sometimes just the sound of his hectoring voice set Harold's teeth on edge. The youth sighed, and with one last hitch of his belt he stepped out to meet his parents.

The room was buzzing with conversation as the Godwins took their seats. Cyneburg insisted Godwin sat in the place of honour, with her seated on one side, his wife on the other. Harold went to sit at one of the long side tables but his father hauled him up onto the dais and seated him next to Cyneburg.

"Do your best to impress her," Godwin hissed in

his ear, "she's a wealthy woman now, and so will her daughter be. The girl will have the choice of men, boy, and a betrothal means nothing now her father is dead. Make her see that you are the best of the bunch or I will make sure you regret your loss."

Harold gulped and nodded rapidly. His father's wrath was not something to be dismissed lightly. Fortunately, the Godwin men were blessed with natural charm which they could switch on and off at will. Women seemed to find it irresistible. At least that was what Swein would say when he went to meet his brew house girl. In fact, Harold was indeed a likeable lad, which his potential mother in law was relieved to discover. She adored her daughter, truly, and would never willingly marry her to a boor or a bully. The reality was, though, that Cyneburg needed the protection of being part of the family of the strongest nobleman in the South of England and whatever the character of her husband to be, Edith would have to be the sacrificial offering.

The adults were deep in discussion with each other, leaving Harold prodding at a slice of venison on his trencher when Edith shimmered towards the dais, a jug in one hand and a cloth in the other. She smiled at the youth as she poured out the mead,

"Thank heavens that it doesn't need to be watered this time"

Harold threw back his head and laughed, his eyes glittering with fun,

"Perhaps this time I will be able to enjoy it without interruptions."

It felt good to be able to share a personal joke and it broke the ice between them. Harold shifted along on the bench and beckoned to Edith to be seated beside him. He reached across the table, cutting some more meat to offer her. She pulled her knife from her belt and speared the morsel, thanking Harold for his attention. While they talked, Harold took a longer look at the young woman Edith had become. She had changed into a gown which was obviously new for the occasion. The pale blue suited her to perfection, the slit neckline offering tantalising glimpses of her creamy white throat. She was easy to talk to, listening intently to what he had to say and laughing in all the right places. She was impressed by him too. The way that he fixed his gaze on her, as if she was the only person in the room, sent spangles of excitement down her spine. Not only that, he had grown into the kind of handsome lad that the servants would be swooning over for days. If she had to marry, but only if, then this young swain would be as good a choice as any and better than most.

Godwin had been half watching the pair with interest. They seemed to be getting along famously, and Cyneburg had been eager to discuss the formalising of the betrothal and the wedding. Gytha seemed pleased, too, at the prospect of Edith as a daughter in law. As much as she adored her sons, it would be a relief to have at least one of them become someone else's problem.

Eventually, Edith stood up, picking up the now empty jug to return it to the brew house. She excused herself, and walked slowly the length of the hall to the door, Harold's eyes following her every inch of the way. He glanced towards his father, questioningly. Godwin smiled and nodded , waving him away in amusement. He bowed quickly to his mother and Cyneburg then raced down the hall in the direction of the doorway.

"I think we can safely say that this will be a marriage with every chance of success," the Earl grinned in satisfaction, and the ladies raised their drinks in agreement.

CHAPTER 5

The night air was sharp as a knife blade and Harold felt himself shivering as he left the humid warmth of the mead hall. It took a moment or two for his eyes to adjust to the darkness and at first he could not see where Edith had gone. Eventually, he could just make out a silhouetted figure against the light from the open brew house door. He could hear soft humming, sweet and gentle and far more entrancing than any scop or gleeman in the hall could manage. He crept across the yard as silently as he could manage, sneaking up behind his prey and slipping his arms tentatively around her waist. The girl spun on her heel, finding herself facing the lad she was intended to marry. She lowered her eyes, her dark lashes veiling the sparkling blue. Harold was almost certain that she was blushing.

"I hope I didn't scare you, Edith, only I was enjoying our conversation too much to end it yet."

"As was I. You did scare me though, just a little."

"I am sorry, truly. It was not my intention."

They were staring into each other's eyes now, both hearts hammering so loud and fast that each was sure the other must hear it.

"I forgive you, just so long as you promise never to do it again."

"Never, ever. On my honour."

Their voices had become a whisper now; they were so close that it was all that was needed.

"And just to prove it , I am not going to try to steal a kiss from you. But I would like to, all the same." Edith reached up and slid her hands into Harold's mop of hair, pulling his head down towards her as she did so. Their lips brushed gently against each other, tingling with the delight of anticipation. Then he pulled her towards him, caressing her back as he opened his mouth against hers and felt the first tinglings of desire and love.

It seemed to Edith that the stars in the heavens were raining down around them as she pulled away from Harold's lips. She wiped the back of her hand across her mouth, smoothing away the traces of moisture he had left. Harold's eyes were upon her, drinking in the light reflecting on her face from through the open brew house door. She gulped, feeling so inadequate that it hurt,

"That was my first kiss, my lord. I have never done so with another. If it was not satisfactory, tell me what I should have done, that I may do better in the future."

"Yours and mine, Edith. My brother is the one who chases the girls, not me. And no, it was not satisfactory," Edith's gaze dropped, embarrassed. Harold laughed softly, "It was beyond satisfactory, so far beyond that . But I think if we were both to practise a little more ..." He gently tilted her chin upwards, and bent to cover her mouth with his. Time was standing still : he was sure of it.

The sound of a hound barking broke the moment. Footsteps could be heard ringing from the cobbled yard surface, making the couple leap apart as if stung. Godwin hove into view, whistling tunelessly as he strolled towards them. That will have given them plenty of warning, he thought to himself. They have had time enough to get better acquainted but not so much as to get into mischief. Grinning, he beckoned his son towards him,

"Your mother says it is time that you retired to bed, lad. She seems to think a growing boy needs his rest. And the lady Cyneburg was concerned as to your whereabouts mistress." Blushing, Edith lifted the hem of her gown and scampered back in the direction of the Mead Hall. The Earl was cackling to himself as he threw his arm around his second son's shoulders. Swein had been created in his image, a wilful, wild boy desperate to bed any woman that crossed his path but Harold was more diffident and that had bothered Godwin. Catching sight of him in a clinch with Edith had made him happy; the Godwin reputation for fecundity was safe.

Her feet felt as if she was running on air as Edith hurtled through the hall door and on to the private space at the far end. Her face glowed pink with excitement and her heart was pounding with happiness. Seeing the curtain raised, Cyneburg looked up with a smile towards her daughter. She could remember when she had felt the same way about Edith's father. Eadfrid had been young too, and excitingly handsome to her eyes. His touch had thrilled every inch of her being and they as time wore on she only felt complete when Eadfrid was near. Now she mourned his loss and would never again feel the gentleness of his hand on hers. She could only hope that Edith would feel half the love that Eadfrid had given her. That would be more than anyone had a right to expect.

CHAPTER 6

All that stood in the way now was the always touchy matter of money. Edith would take with her properties in Cantwareburh and lands in Norfolk around Walsingham. Should anything go awry, then at the very least she and any children would not be left penniless. Godwin was well known to be careful with his money, despite the apparent lavishness of his lifestyle. He had risen to the rank of Earl from a very unprepossessing start as a low ranked thegn. He knew the value of money, and did not part with it before he had thought long and hard on the subject. Eventually he and Cyneborg came up with an amount for the handgeld that satisfied both parties. Gytha insisted that she would provide the morgengifu that Harold would give to Edith the morning after their wedding. That just left the bride's gift to the groom to organise.

The gift was always the same. It was something

that was prized beyond wealth, beyond fame. It was a symbol of strength and protection, one that shouted manhood. It was a sword. Edith thought long and hard about it. The blacksmith could craft one for her. She could pay for one of the skilled armourers from England or across the waters to make one, but neither solution made her happy. She wanted the gift to have meaning beyond the cost of it. Eventually the solution came to her in a flash of inspiration. It was so obvious that she was surprised that she had not thought of it earlier. All she needed to do was persuade her mother to agree.

"But it has sat in the chest for goodness knows how many years!" Cyneburg sat down on the stool in surprise.

"It will clean, mother. I shall clean it myself until it shines like silver."

She was not winning this one, that was obvious, but Edith was nothing if not tenacious.

"Mother, he will not be with me when I marry," her voice dropped to a whisper, "and I do miss Father. To have his sword to give as my bride gift would mean the world to me."

Her mother shivered. Eadfrid's sword had too

many bad memories attached for her liking. It still lay in the chest where Eadfrid had lain it after his last battle, where he was wounded so terribly and their son slain. Cyneburg stood and slowly walked over to the chest, pulling the key from the chain hanging from her belt. She lifted up the lid and knelt down before it, pulling out the bags of coin and jewels to reveal a length of folded silk. Out it came, and was placed reverently on the floor between the mother and daughter. Lovingly she peeled it apart to reveal a length of steel, with a twisting inlaid pattern fire welded to the blade. She turned it over in her hand , watching it glint as if it were a living thing. She traced her fingers across the inscription: In Nomine Domine. Her fingers curled around the white bone of the grip, snugged up against the gentle curve of the guard.

"I gave this to your father, when we married. He said it was the most beautiful weapon he had ever seen. You see these hollows? That is the fullering. It makes the blade lighter and easier to wield. Your father always said that the balance was close to perfect and that it felt like a feather in the hand. I don't know though. It didn't stop him being so badly wounded, did it?"

Edith reached across , touching her mother's hand.

"If it had not been so fine then perhaps he might

not have been able to fight off his attacker and been killed outright. It is a beautiful thing, mother, and it deserves to be used."

Folding the silk covering back, Cyneburg passed the sword into Edith's hands,

"Take it with my blessing. Have it sharpened and polished. It will look like new. Gudbrandur will shine again. Harold ought to be pleased at so fine a gift."

"Gudbrandur?"

Cyneburg smiled , remembering, "That is the name your father gave to it. It means God's sword."

"It is a beautiful name. Thank you mother, and I mean thanks. I know how hard it must be for you to part with it."

Yes, it was hard, but not half so difficult as it had been to part from its owner.

It was decided that the wedding would take place in the summer at the Earl's home in Bosham. Cyneburg was relieved to have someone else plunged into the chaos of organisation , leaving her with just her daughter to concern herself over. Godwin sent over some of his thegns to accompany them on their journey and protect them from any of the bandits who skulked in the marshes. The party of travellers was only a little one. Edith had no other living relatives than her mother. The Viking raids had taken a terrible toll on her family.

Her belongings were piled on a cart driven by Osbern the groom, who spent the whole of the journey trying to ignore the constant stream of panicked chatter coming from the household steward who was seated beside him. Durwin was in many respects the perfect steward. He was particular to the point of obsession, and had been a great help mate for Cyneburg when she was widowed. However, he was also prey to a wild imagination and the idea of vagabonds lurking in the sedge waiting to pounce on him sent him into a flat spin of panic. The hand maids who were sitting in the cart, bundled up among the chests and packages were barely able to contain their laughter as each time the dogs scared a bird from under a hedge he squeaked like a mouse in a trap and ducked his head behind the driver.

"Your man seems to be a little nervous," one of the thegns had jog trotted his horse up alongside Edith's pony.

"He thinks there are murderers hiding behind every tree," Edith laughed. Her mood was as bright as the sun in the sky and she felt happy to share it with those around her.

"I can understand his nerves. After all, he is responsible for getting you and your mother to Bosham without incident. I should imagine the thought of having to explain to the Earl that you have been spirited away by some wild brigand is enough to make him vomit on his shoes."

"He is not the bravest of souls, I agree , but should it be necessary he would die to defend my mother and myself. Have no fear of that." Edith thought it necessary to put the thegn right on that point. She would not have him look down on the old man.

"Tell me, my lord Edmond, is the Earl really that terrifying in his own territory? He has always seemed most reasonable when he has visited."

Edmond paused for thought before he answered, "Well, he is not a man to cause displeasure to. He is charm itself when it suits his needs, and I am sure that he is a kind and generous man, but when he is crossed or angered then it can be a different matter."

Edith rode in silence for a while, taking in the

information and processing it, "What about his sons? Are they like him?"

That is a tricky one, Edmond mused. He glanced at Edith, taking in the stubborn set of her jaw and the gleam in her eyes. The truth would be the best course. She would expect it,

"Swein is like the Earl and he is his favourite. He is popular with the ladies at the Earl's court but he does not favour one over another, if you catch my meaning. He will make a fearsome warrior one day, if he can learn self control. Tostig is an odd one. One day he can be the most companionable lad and the next he hides himself away, not wanting to speak to anyone. Leofwine and Gyrth are just babes really, but as close as brothers can be. They are a pair of jokers, full of pranks."

"And Harold?"

Edmond coughed cautiously. This answer would have to be a diplomatic one.

"I think you will have to make that judgement for yourself, my lady. I would not colour your view but I will say that I like him very much indeed."

Edith sighed. There would be so many people to get to know and so much to learn. Life at Hintone had been so quiet in comparison to the busy Bosham. For a moment, she felt a pang of sadness and loss. Within a few days she would be a married woman, responsible for her own home and the happiness of her lord when all she still yearned for was to spend her time alone,barefoot and windswept , roaming across the empty marshes she loved to call home.

CHAPTER 7

The warm water closed over Edith's head as she leaned back in the tub. She felt hands pulling her up again, rubbing oils into her silver gold hair, then pushing her back beneath the water again to rinse it. It was usually a very pleasant experience to spend a while wallowing in the bath but this was anything but a relaxing experience. Preparing for the wedding was a serious business and this was a part of the cleansing ritual, nothing less. Edith chuckled to herself as she thought of Harold undergoing the same experience. She could not imagine that the men who were attending him would be half so gentle as her maids.

Meeting Harold again could have been a distinctly uncomfortable experience, but it was as if they had never been apart. He had grown a little and now he was taller than both his father and Swein and was growing into his frame. There was a hint of shadow on his cheeks and chin where his beard was starting to grow darker than the fair hair on his head. Still tousled and floppy, she thought, just as it was. The grin he gave her as he ran to grab the reins of her pony sent waves of relief coursing through her body. Thank goodness he had not turned into a sour faced misery who had changed his mind over her. Proudly he had introduced her to the rest of his family. Swein was just the same too, arrogant and cocky with an air of superiority. Tostig seemed shy. It seemed hard for him to make eye contact but when he did, and finally smiled, it felt as if the sun was breaking out from behind a cloud. The boys were just as Edmond had said, blonde haired jokers.

They presented Edith with a box, saying it was a gift for their new sister. Harold had looked at them warningly but they had maintained an air of perfect innocence. That was enough to alert Edith and she opened it very, very slowly. In the dark interior she could see the wide open eyes of a very large frog. She smiled, thanking them both, then slid her hand into the box to pull out the frog. Patting Leofwine on the head, she slid the frog down the back of his tunic, leaving it to wriggle its way down towards the floor. He howled and ran towards the fish ponds, pulling off his tunic as he went followed hard on his heels by Gyrth, desperate to avoid the wrath of his father. By now the whole party was laughing with delight, any air of seriousness banished by the two rogues.

Now here she was, standing dripping wet and naked on the drying cloths the maids had placed on the floor. They bundled her up in more of the cloths, then rubbed her up and down ,the friction making her skin glow pink. Her mother's handmaid, Wilone, went to the chest by the bed and pulled out a large bottle, filled with an oily substance. She pulled out the stopper and sniffed the oil approvingly. Then she walked to the girl and, pulling away the drying cloths, began to pour the oil across her shoulders. It ran down between her shoulder blades, and trickled between her breasts. The older woman encouraged the others to start to rub it into Edith's skin, down her arms and her legs, across her breasts and belly and between her thighs. The oil was scented with a hint of roses that curled comfortingly into her nostrils. It reminded her of the little petal she still had in her scrip which somehow still smelled as fresh as the day she had removed it from her father's coffin.

By now Wilone was combing through her hair, smoothing out the tangles with more of the oil. Seeing that Edith had started to shiver, she beckoned the two maids to bring her fresh shift and slip it over her head. Once that was done Wilone dismissed the maids and pulled Edith over to the stool by the window. She began to comb through her hair again, humming to herself as she did so. Edith began to feel sleepy, from the warmth of the bath and the scent of the oil. It took a moment or two for her to realise that her mother had entered the room. Wilone curtseyed and, passing the comb to her mistress, left.

Cyneburg ran the ivory comb through the hair over and over, until it shone like the scales of a fish in the river. Then she braided it into one long plait which hung down thick as a bell rope. It was a sweetly sorrowful moment, a mother preparing her child to join the world of adults.

"It still isn't too late to change your mind, if you wish. If Harold is not a suitable husband the marriage can still be cancelled."
Edith turned to face her mother, her eyes glowing in the light of the evening sun,

"He pleases me, mother. I like him. I like his family too. It will be fine." Her eyes began to shine with unspilled tears, "I shall miss you though, mother, very very much."

Cyneburg hugged her daughter so tightly that she thought her ribs would break, "I shall miss you too, my child, but I wish you well and I wish you happiness. Always remember, if things should go awry you can come home . That is allowed for with a Danish handfasting and sometimes I think it is a very wise idea. At least a woman can keep her dowry and the morgengifu. She will not be destitute, nor tied to a man she finds she cannot abide."

Shaking her head as if to shake away such unhappy thoughts she lead the girl across to her bed and pulled up the sheets around her after she climbed in. A chill went through Edith's body, despite the warmth of the evening. The next time she went to bed she would be a married woman , with all that entailed.

Neither Edith nor Harold slept well that night. They were not young to wed; indeed twelve was considered a suitable age for wedding, but the weight of expectations hung heavy from their shoulders. Harold was sharing a bed with his brother Swein, who kept up a constant stream of ribaldry. On and on he went, about what would happen on the wedding night and how Harold would be expected to behave in bed. If only he would shut up, he railed to himself, then perhaps he would be able to shut out of his mind the images that Swein had put into it. He made what should be a sacred and loving act sound like the rutting of two wild pigs. Edith was faring no better. The sound of her maid snoring from the cot at the bottom of her bed killed any chance she had of falling into sleep. For the tenth time she turned her pillow over, punching it flat before laying her head back down on it. It was a humid night and she could feel sweat trickling down her body making her damp and desperately uncomfortable. She kicked off the sheet and lay staring at the ceiling, waiting for the sunlight to creep in through the window.

Edith must have dozed off because the next thing she knew was her mother shaking her awake. It took a moment or two for her to recognise where she was and why. Cyneburg chivvied her along, placing the breakfast tray she had brought with her onto the bed beside her,

"Wash yourself quickly, then come and have some breakfast. This bread is really very good." She broke another piece off the loaf and nibbled at it, pouring out a beaker of small beer as she did so. Edith accepted the beaker gratefully, downing the contents in one swallow. She felt the warmth spreading through her body, waking every muscle and nerve ready for the day ahead.

It felt to Edith as if she was in a dream state, as if everything that was happening was not happening to her at all. She was dressed in a beautiful new gown made for the occasion, soft as a whisper and dyed as bright as the sun. Tiny pearls harvested from the mussels in the river adorned the neckline, woven into the braid of green and blue. Her hair was loosed over her shoulders, cascading past her waist in wave upon wave. In her mother's hand was a circlet of summer flowers; daisies, corncockles and blood red roses twisted through with ivy. Gently, she reached forward and placed it upon her daughter's head. She stepped back and gazed at her critically then her face broke into a smile,

"He will be a lucky man, to marry a bride as beautiful as you."

She lifted Edith's hand and clasped it between her own, squeezing it so tightly that it seemed she could never let go.

It was time, now, to descend the stairs and face her future. Lead by her mother she walked towards the orchard which lay beyond the hall. Children scattered petals before her, creating a carpet of a rainbow of colours for her bare feet to step upon. Edith could feel the damp of the morning dew between her toes as she moved into the circle of people who had gathered for the ceremony. "Keep your eyes cast down," she muttered to herself. The bride had to seem modest and virtuous to all those around her. In truth she felt too terrified to look anywhere other than down towards her feet. She could see the dampness of the grass darkening the hem of her gown as her mother lead her forward. It should have been her father's hand, or her brother's, she thought with a touch of regret. She gnawed at her lip and promised herself that she would make them proud.

Her gaze was so focused on the speckle of petals on the vivid green sward that she jolted in surprise when she saw the well- polished toes of a pair of boots directly in her way. Slowly she raised her gaze, taking in the sight of an expensive woad blue tunic wrapped with a heavy cloak trimmed in rabbit fur. Her eyes lifted, to meet the gaze of her groom staring steadily at her. He gave a smile filled with relief, almost as if he thought she would change her mind at the last moment. Seeing that Edith was shivering from the damp morning air, he unclasped his cloak and gently laid it around her shoulders. It seemed as if that was the moment he claimed her as his own, not the swearing of vows, the binding of hands, the gift of the ring or the nibbling of the sticky sweet wedding cake. He would protect her as best he could for as long as he lived, she felt certain.

A subtle cough caught her attention and she turned to see Durwin standing behind her. He was as smart as she had ever seen him, but what really caught her attention was the object he was holding out towards her. Hands trembling, she lifted the scabbard from his hands and slowly drew her father's sword from it. The sun shattered into rainbows as it danced along its finely honed surface, dipping into shadow along the fullered centre. The handle was creamy white while the pommel was crowned with a heavy amethyst , richly purple and glowing in the sun.

"This is Gudbrandur. It was my father's sword, the head of my household. I now gift it to you as my new lord. It is not new, but it is finely wrought and honed through battle. I pray it will keep you safe."

Harold took the weapon and raised it above his head, marvelling at the ease with which he could yield it. The balance was perfect in his hand.

"It is wonderful, wife, and more than I could ever deserve. I swear I will defend you with it for as long as you allow me to. Now, I do believe we are supposed to seal our union with a kiss, if I might be so bold."

He leaned forward to meet her mouth with his,

the taste of the honey and poppyseeds still strong on their breath. They were married: for as long as they loved each other.

CHAPTER 8

Loathe as Harold was to admit it, Swein had been right. As he undressed his wife, gently and shyly, he became aware of the excitement that his brother found in the arms of his women. Edith was pliant, soft skinned and willing; more than he had ever imagined a woman could be. It was as if they were born to fit together, in mind and in body, and every night filled them both with as much anticipation and desire as on their first night together.

It came as no surprise to anyone when, in the early days of Advent tide, Harold was able to declare that his young wife was indeed with child. They had travelled to Bosham from their holdings in Norfolk where much of their time was now spent, revelling in creating their own little world of happiness. Edith had watched her father and mother over the years, learning without even realising it how to keep control of the widely spread lands which were now hers. As much as Harold knew, he learned so much more from his wife. His father may have ruled his tenants by fear alongside justice: through Edith he realised that it was not necessary to terrify people into submission. It was a pleasant feeling to see his churls and thrals wave in greeting rather than cower when he rode past. It seemed that every day was bathed in a precious golden light and that every moment seemed woven through with magic. Both hung on to each second, knowing in their hearts that this time could never last when Harold was a scion of a very ambitious man.

Godwin, bitingly ambitious as ever, had long been murmuring in King Edward's ear how talented and able his second son was and how it was about time he was recognised for his abilities. Edward prevaricated, not willing to further promote the pushy Godwin family but he could not hold out for ever if he wanted to sit safe upon his throne. Finally , unable to delay any longer, he declared that Harold should from now on be known as the Earl of East Anglia. The deed sat bitter upon the king's tongue. He distrusted the Wessex earl and his sprawling clan to the point of enmity. After all, hadn't Godwin captured his own brother and killed him in such a foul way as putting his eyes out? The very memory of it made Edward feel sick to the core. But he was nothing if not a pragmatist. He was willing to bide his time and if making the young Harold the Earl of East Anglia would satisfy Godwin for a while then so be it. There would surely be an opportunity to dispose of the Godwins once and for all if he waited his chance, of that he was sure; so sure that he could almost scent the smell of success.

"So now you are Earl of East Anglia does that mean I have to curtsey to you whenever we meet?" Edith was sitting on the edge of the bed, the sunlight shining through her thin linen undergown showing the outline of her growing belly and the swell of her breasts, much to the earl's delight.

"Of course, and leave the room without turning your back. I expect you to show full respect at all times," Harold grinned as his wife knelt in mock obeisance. If nothing else, he had learned that Edith had an edge sharp as a knife and would never be the sort of wife who would bend to her lord's every whim. He reached for her hand and pulled her back towards the bed, allowing his hands to run across her body as he did so. He could barely believe that it was only her flesh that separated his hand from the form of his unborn child. It seemed like magic. Edith grabbed his wrist and moved his hand down further, pressing it close against her as she did so.

Beneath his fingers he could feel movement; stretching and pushing. Entranced, he pressed harder to feel the little one she carried for him.

"There, he knows you already, I am sure. When you are speaking he starts to kick as if he can't wait to see you."

"He? You think it may be a boy?"

Edith smiled. She had consulted with the old nurse who had nurtured the Godwin brood, and was even now suckling Wulfnoth, the youngest of the clan . The old woman had looked her up and down with a critical eye. Then, she had run her hand across he belly, sucking on her teeth as she did so. "More like to be a boy than a girl, I think. That will please your husband, and Lord Godwin too I shouldn't wonder."

"Nelda thinks it may be so and no-one knows more about the business than she does."

Harold rolled onto his back and threw his hands behind his head in thought. He was hardly grown himself and yet here he was on the verge of fatherhood. The next time I make love to her, she will be a mother, he thought as he watched Edith being dressed by her maid. Would he feel different about possessing her body when she had been racked with the agonies of childbirth? As if sensing his thoughts she turned towards him, grinning wickedly. He felt a stirring in his loins. What a fool he was. He could never tire of her, whatever happened in the future.

"I wonder why it should be that your father has demanded our presence? It can't be anything to do with you being made Earl; that is the king's business."

Harold stirred from his reverie. He was puzzled too.

"It must be something very important to him. I was told that he has even summoned my sister from Wilton Abbey. My mother is saying nothing at all, other than that we shall soon find out when Ealdyth is here."

Edith waved away the maidservant and turned around on the stool to face her husband. It seemed odd that everything hinged on the appearance of the sister in law she had never met. Harold said she was a bit of a pain, happier with her nose stuck in a book than enjoying herself with her siblings. It was his belief that she had been sent off to Wilton not to further her learning but because his father was tired of her cluttering up the family hearth with her presence. If that was the case why was it that she had been recalled to the family so suddenly.

"Perhaps your father has decided to get rid of her

once and for all and sign her off to join the abbey?" she mused. Harold rolled his eyes in despair.

"Then Heaven help them. She will be the Abbess before they have time to blink and then they can look out for trouble. My sister is nothing if not strict in her observances. They will wear holes in the floor from all the kneeling."

"Oh no!" Edith shrieked in mock horror, "What will she think of me! The wicked woman , wed out of Church and with child to boot. A heathen hussy, that's what she will say!" A thought struck them both at the same time. "Maybe that's it. She is to be married."

The thought seemed to cause Harold some amusement. He began to laugh, little giggles at first then chuckles and eventually howls of laughter, the tears pouring down his face. He clutched at his sides as they began to ache but he still couldn't stop. His wife looked at him, bemused, trying to grasp what was so funny.

"It would be like being married to a block of marble! I love my sister, truly I do, but for the life of me I cannot imagine her canoodling with some swain, lovesick or otherwise. She is far too self possessed. It would take a better man than me to romance her into warmth."

CHAPTER 9

That evening, in the mead hall, the air seemed brittle with expectancy. Servants scurried around , lighting the rushlights that adorned the walls and throwing armfuls of sweet herbs on the floor. The long tables and benches had been scrubbed clean of the grime of everyday existence. The running dogs were being chased away from the fireside where they were anxious to curl up together and sleep. As beautifully elegant as they were, they were also well skilled in tripping up the servants carrying the trays heaving with roasted meats then gorging themselves on the fallen joints.

Casting a glance around the building, Edith could see that although there were many well dressed and obviously high ranking lords lounging on the benches, none of the family were to be seen. Harold gestured towards the heavy tapestry draped across the far wall, behind which was a cosy room for the sole use of Earl Godwin and his family. So they were closeted in the solar then. That would only happen if what they had to say was so secret, so sensitive, that they could not risk eavesdroppers overhearing.

Harold lifted the tapestry and lead Edith into the room but rather than the expected cheery hail, the welcome was subdued. Swein, Tostig and Gyrth were huddled together in a group, beakers of mead in hand. They made way for Harold to join them while Leofwine poured him a drink from the jug on the sidetable. Their mother sat rocking a cradle with Wulfnoth lying red cheeked and teething within. Even Nelda had been chased away from the meeting, someone so much a part of the family from their first cry onwards. Swein wandered across the room towards her, managing to muster his usual leery grin,

"I see that my brother has been doing his duty. I hope that it has been a, shall we say, pleasant experience," he purred.

Edith looked him straight in the eye. He would not embarrass her, however hard her tried, "My husband has been a delight, in every way, dear brother. I am sure that he could give you some tips, should you require them."

Swein laughed. He knew when he had met his

match.

"I shall remember that. Now, this is a little difficult, sister. Tonight my father has asked if you would mind attending to our guests in the hall. It is not that he does not think you are a part of the family, but someone has to play the host and deflect any inquisitiveness. You do understand, don't you?"

Edith looked towards Harold. For a moment she barely recognised him. In this company she suddenly realised that he was a grown man. Tall, fair and handsome he was, and he seemed other worldly to her as the lighted candle glinted on the embroidery which traced around the hem and neck of his gown. Her eyes sought his approval. He gave her the slightest nod, no more than a lowering of his long dark lashes. Inclining her head towards Swein in acquiescence and with a swish of her gown, she swept back into the hall. Picking up a pitcher of mead, she began to pour drinks for the guests in the hall, chatting amiably and charming everyone who she turned her brilliant blue eyes upon.

As she bent forward to refill the cup of one of Earl Godwin's nephews, she felt a sudden blast of the wintry air upon her back and heard the slamming to of the great oaken hall doors. She turned her head to see a young woman walking the length of the hall towards the solar. She greeted the steward as if he was an old friend then caught Edith's gaze upon her. Taking the beaker she was offered the woman threw a cold stare back in reply. Edith could see her back stiffen as she drew herself up to her full height. Waves of disapproval flowed from her as she flicked her eyes from Edith's bare feet to the crown of her head. Turning away, she carried on down the length of the hall and disappeared behind the tapestry curtain into the privacy of the solar.

"My dear cousin Ealdyth, if you were wondering," the young man gestured towards the retreating figure. Beorn reached forward and grabbed the pitcher, filling his beaker until it was brimming. "A lovely lass, don't misunderstand me, but a little too enamoured of the rules of Rome in my opinion. Not at all like the rest of the family,"

Edith sighed. No wonder that she had been given the dismissive look. As the only person she did not know who was serving the noble guests she had to be Harold's wife ,although to her way of thinking she must seem to be a whore. Everything must seem so black and white when you had spent most of your life tucked away in the confines of an Abbey. Edith preferred to deal in shades of grey.

Moments later her ears pricked to the sound of

raised voices drifting into the hall from behind the heavy curtaining and it was apparent that every ear in the room was straining in the same direction. Swiftly, Edith beckoned to the musicians to play something loud and lively to drown out the voices. Balancing the heavy pitcher on her hip, she swayed over towards the solar just in time to see the brothers leaving the room. The shock on their faces was apparent. Even Swein was ashen. Edith grabbed Harold by the wrist and dragged him into one of the alcoves that lined the wall.

"I always knew my father was a scheming bastard , but this is just beyond the pale even by his standards." The words spat from Harold's mouth, curled in anger at what he had heard. Edith scanned his face for some clue.

"Do you remember how he bartered for our marriage? He was lucky that we were happy to go along with his plans, but if not I cannot imagine that I would have had a choice in the matter, even if you did. This time I fail to understand how there can be anything approaching happiness from this coupling."

Edith still stared at him uncomprehendingly. " You saw my sister, I presume? She is younger than you and more innocent than you can imagine, despite her learning. Imagine , if you can, what it would be like to be that girl and to be sold off in marriage to a man thirty years older than yourself."

Tears were brimming in Harold's eyes, tears of fury and frustration. "This is a man, mark you, that hates your family for the murder of his kin. A man of power you would think,who actually has so little power that he has to creep and crawl to keep the power of Wessex on his side, even to the extent of taking my sister to wife."

Edith's mind was racing. She mentally lined up all the possibilities and discarded them one by one until she came to the one which seemed so unlikely that it must be the case. "The King? Edward? But he is an old man and she just a young maid!" She shuddered at the thought of his wizened hands on her flesh and the shock that this must have given Ealdyth when she heard it. She slid towards Tostig and tapped his shoulder. The boy was muttering under his breath, clearly distraught. "Go to her, support her. She will need someone and I know you are her favourite. Say nothing to your father, just stay by her side." Tostig nodded, and withdrew to the solar again. Harold looked at her quizzically. "I know she disapproves of me. She made that perfectly clear. But I wouldn't wish that fate to anyone. The shock must have been terrible to her." Harold reached his arm around her back and pulled her as close as he could. He was a lucky man to have such a wise and understanding woman by his side.

They leapt apart as if hit by lightning as they heard the bellowing voice of Earl Godwin echo around the room. He announced the news to those assembled with all the pride of a man who had just overcome his opponent once and for all. Edith shuddered. Her face must have betrayed her feelings, as when Godwin's gaze settled on her a look of irritation flashed in his eyes. He beckoned towards her, crooking his finger in her direction. She picked up the pitcher and walked slowly towards him, then leaned forward to refill his goblet. Godwin's hand shot out, quick as an adder, and grabbed her wrist, forcing her to look him in the face.

"I know what you are thinking, that I have sold my girl for position. Sometimes sacrifices have to be made to secure safety for the rest of us. Edward's court is crawling with his Norman friends and other hangers on who cannot even speak a word of our tongue. Should he die, what chance would any of us have to keep the comfort we have become used to? They would snatch the throne before we could blink and steal every yard of land we own. If Ealdyth is his wife, and they have children, then the succession is sealed and we are safe.

He is an erudite man and and will at least be a man on her intellectual level, not a bluff soldier such as I am. She must make what she can of it"

He released her hand and she strode slowly back to her husband. The conversation had given her much food for thought. The politics of court had never before darkened her existence and she didn't like it. At least she and Harold could retreat back to Norfolk and keep clear of all this manipulation.

CHAPTER 10

"And what makes you think that I would want to go anyway? Say I'm too close to having the baby. Say what the hell you like, Harold, but don't expect me to show up to be treated like a leper!"

Harold groaned. He had been expecting this. What possessed his idiot brothers to tell Edith what his sister had said he would never know. No wonder there was no sight of marriage for Gyrth and Leofwine. No woman would be daft enough to have them.

"She didn't mean it that way, I'm sure. I expect she is just worried that someone might make a comment about our marriage arrangements that would upset you, and she wouldn't want you getting distressed in your condition." He hunted desperately for some plausible explanation he could offer to his wife. The truth of it was that Ealdyth was still making a fuss about their handfasted marriage. She had expressed the opinion that it was nothing more than an arrangement for a man to take a mistress, which in her mind was little better than being a street whore. And to bring a child into the world in that situation was just about the biggest sin that she could imagine. Therefore, in her eyes, Edith's presence in the Cathedral could well bring the whole building down on their heads. Which left Harold stuck between the pair of them. He always thought he was the Godwin boy with the most diplomatic skills. He would never have a better chance to use them than now.

"We can tag along at the back of the party well away from my sister. She will have enough to worry about in any case," he slipped his arm around his wife's waist and pulled her close, snuggling into her neck and kissing her earlobe.

"My father wants the whole family there, and there is no way that I will go without my beautiful wife on my arm. So you see," he murmured as he kissed further and further down her neck and across her shoulder, "you just have to attend. Be the better person, my love. Turn the other cheek."

The weather matched Edith's mood. Snow tumbled from the sky, wet and cold, settling on heads and shoulders and chilling everyone there to the bone. Harold edged her in next to his mother. Gytha was very fond of Edith and she respected his mother deeply. That way Edith wouldn't get up to any mischief, he hoped.

The ceremony passed without trouble. Edith had no intention of making a fuss in church anyway. Just because she had married in the old style didn't mean that she had no Christian faith. Her faith was strong and deep. She would never disrespect Holy Mother Church. The feast afterwards, though, that was a different matter.

Never in her life had she seen anything so dazzlingly magnificent as the wedding feast. And never had Edith seen a couple enjoy their special day less than the king and his new queen. Edward looked as miserable as if he had toothache. Ealdyth looked even more so, poking at the meat on her trencher as if she would rather plunge the knife into herself than the choice morsels she had been provided with. Godwin was enjoying himself though, pouring wine down his throat as if the Pope was about to declare it forbidden.

She noticed Harold whisper to the serving girl to water it down somewhat when she served his father. The girl shrugged, and wandered off to dilute the wine she carried. Edward's wine was full strength , though, and he was drinking it down even more rapidly than his new father-in-law. Sweet Gods, what a delight on your wedding night, Edith grinned to herself. She would have her revenge alright. Ealdyth might have tried to keep her from the wedding but she would make sure that the bride would be dreading the bedding if she could.

Gytha gestured to the ladies sitting at the top table that it was time to escort the bride to her chamber and Edith was the first to respond. It was tradition that the married women would prepare the bride for her husband, undressing her as far as her shift, combing through her hair, putting her into bed and terrifying her with tales of the behaviour of their menfolk on their wedding nights. "Your brother was utterly relentless!" giggled Edith. "I certainly had no sleep that night, or many nights since." she ran her hand across her belly, obviously swollen with the child she was carrying. "You will be like this before you know it!" She sniggered to herself at the thought of prim and proper Ealdyth with her head over the bowl vomiting with morning sickness then feeling her breasts ache as they became swollen and heavy with milk.

"Don't worry. Edward is a grown man, he will know what to do. You do not need to be afraid, just do what he asks of you and try to relax."

Edith rolled her eyes. From the morose look on his face the last thing that Edward wanted to do was to initiate his child bride into the ways of lovemaking. That was always supposing he even knew what to do himself. The gossip was that he spent all his time on his knees in church and none of it enjoying himself with any of the women with dubious reputations who hung around court.

"All men are the same," sniggered Edith again, making Ealdyth cringe in horror, " Once he has climbed on top of you and satisfied himself you will know all there is to know about being bedded."

Gytha threw her a sharp glance. Perhaps she had said enough. Maybe Ealdyth would be a bit less high and mighty now. In the end it didn't matter what ceremony you went through. It all finished with a man and a woman in bed, expected to satisfy each other while someone eavesdropped to make sure the marriage was consummated. There was a raucous racket now, signalling the men dragging the reluctant groom up to his bedchamber. Ealdyth looked terrified, tears brimming in her eyes at what was about to happen. Edith finally took pity and, as she leant forward to pull the coverlet straight she whispered to her, "Don't worry. The amount of drink the king has downed I don't think he will be in any state to do anything but sleep. Just get him to take his time with you and it will be fine, I promise." The bride smiled at her in thanks. They had called a truce.

CHAPTER 11

The baby lay nestled in his mother's arms, warm and tender and so beautiful. She counted each tiny finger and each tiny toe time and again, hardly able to believe that she and Harold had created something of such utter perfection. The little rosebud lips were latched onto her nipple, sucking strength into his belly from her laden breast. Edith could barely believe that everything had gone so well. She had felt pain, that was true, and it had seemed almost unbearable the closer she had come to birthing but the midwife was old and experienced and her calmness had filled Edith with confidence. And here was the baby, safe and sound. It felt like a miracle.

There was a rap on the chamber door and the midwife called to enter. There was a maid , asking if My Lord could come in to meet his child. The old woman was still cleaning bloodied cloths up and throwing them in a bucket and she threw a questioning glance across to the new mother who nodded with a smile. Within moments the door opened slowly, almost reluctantly, and Harold peered round the door. He knew, as one of nine children, how dangerous and bloody a business childbirth could be and his heart leapt to see his wife lying in bed with a live child suckling at her breast. He sat on the stool beside her and looked questioningly into her tired, sparkling eyes.

"Everything is well?"

"Fine. The child is formed perfectly, and the midwife says that I have had an easier time than most, although I must say that it did not seem so at the time. She says I should recover quickly."

"And our baby? Is it a boy, as you thought, or a daughter?"

Edith pulled back the bindings sufficient for Harold to see for himself. He grinned so wide that she thought his face might split in half, then he wrapped his arms around them both, loving and protecting.

"Might we name him for my father? I mean, I know you might have your own ideas but it just feels right to me. He is a survivor, who can change every situation to his own advantage. I pray that our boy will have that skill too. He may need it in the future. Who can say?"

Edith lowered her eyes to meet the bright blue ones of her boy,

"Then Godwin you shall be, little one." She kissed him softly on his forehead and Harold squeezed her hand in gratitude. He knew she would rather have named him after her father, not his. Perhaps the next one....

As soon as Edith had been churched and given thanks for the safe delivery, and the child was happily settled into the care of his wet nurse, she decided that it was time to take on her role as Earl's wife in earnest. It was time for the Spring Shire Courts, and the Earl was expected to preside over the meeting. He said it was often boring to the point of coma, listening to the shire reeve reading out the king's new laws in the droning legal language they were written in, for hour after hour. Then it was a case of judging matters from murder to boundary arguments and everything in between. The hours that the ealdormen could spend picking apart whether someone's great grandfather had gained the right to plough to the left or right of a tree that had died years ago defied belief, he claimed. Nevertheless, he had to attend as it was his duty. It was Edith's opinion that he protested far too vociferously, and that it was much more likely that there was much more hunting and drinking involved than he wanted to admit to. Worse than that, there would be a proliferation of buxom young women whose head could easily be turned by the sight of a bright new silver penny. She trusted Harold, truly, but she was a mother now with the body her child had given her, and knowing the way the rest of the Godwinson boys behaved with women it was better to be on hand to nip any trouble in the bud.

It was pleasant to be riding out in the Spring air. The swallows were arcing across the sky, scudding in and out of the foamy white clouds. They kept to the ancient tracks which wove in and out of the marshy landscape. Blossoms studded the trees which lined their way and the air hummed with the sound of bees. It seemed like a spot of Heaven on Earth. The thought had sprung unbidden into her mind, but on reflection it was true. Such a pretty spot. Somewhere you could be happy to spend eternity. Edith shook herself back to reality and cantered her jennet further along the track to catch up with Harold and his thegns. Seeing her approach, they reined back to allow her to join their group. Normally they would not be so chivalrous, but Edith was a rich and powerful woman in her own right and could be a useful ally to a young man looking to improve his position. She noticed that among the chattering crew was a face she recognised, the thegn who had accompanied her to her wedding. Nodding in greeting, he urged his mount closer to hers. Some female company would make a change from the masculine world he usually inhabited.

"What a pleasant surprise, my lady, to see you amongst our band, and in my own country too," Edmond bowed in the saddle, throwing his hand down below the stirrup as he did so.

"It is such a beautiful place that I wonder how you could ever leave. If this were my home I should refuse the call of any lord, even the king himself!" sighed Edith, breathing in the sweet clear air. "Tell me, what is the name of this place?"

"Walsingham, my lady. It has belonged to my family for nigh on a hundred years now and every generation has loved it just as much as the one before."

"I can understand why. Is it your home to which we are heading?"

"Indeed so. It is good to remind those of us who live on the fringes of the kingdom that we are subject to the same rules as the rest. Sometimes it can seem that London is so far away that the royal edicts are meaningless. Besides which, everyone wants to see the noble Earl and his beautiful lady."

Edith felt the flush rising in her face. She never really considered how other people thought of her, but as she looked around at the travelling group she began to see them as others did. Wealth. It was present in everything; the cut of the fine cloth, the jewels worn with such careless ease, the standard of the animals they rode, even the number and dress of the servants. To someone who existed on rough bread and pottage, sharing their homestead with their beasts, they must have seemed touched by the hands of angels. And in reality it was all just an accident of birth. Remember that, my girl, she whispered to herself. It could all disappear just as easily.

The hubbub in the hall ceased as if it had been cut off by a knife. Benches of men and women held their breath as the far door opened and the men who would give judgement strode in and took their places on the bench on the dais. Edmond was there, as the lord of the manor and shire reeve. He was in deep conversation with the Bishop of Elmham, who was draped in his finest regalia. Edith bridled. Surely the representative of Christ should show a little more humility. And then, a step behind the rest and a model of self possession, came the Earl of East Anglia. Her lord, her husband, her man. No longer the boy she had wed, he had grown into his frame. Tall and fair, his curls lay bright on the collar of his cloak. She noticed that he wore just enough of his expensive finery to impress but not so much that he flaunted his good fortune. He dominated the group who sat in judgement, by no other means than his personality. He would listen to evidence given, thoughtfully stroking his moustache and treating each person before him with respect and fairness. Then he would sit back quietly, impelling the others to ask his opinion rather than dominating the conversation. It was then that Edith realised what a remarkable man she had married. He inspired confidence in others simply by his bearing. He was sensitive to the feelings of others and respected their views. A shiver passed down her spine. A man of his talents was never going to remain in the political backwaters. Sooner or later he would find himself dragged into his father's scrabble for power whether he wanted or no. She had better enjoy these quiet days while she could, for there was no saying how soon her family life might be torn apart.

CHAPTER 12

"He did what?" The new baby Edmund squirmed in his crib, his nose wrinkling ready to burst into howls. Swiftly, his mother slipped her foot onto he rocker, desperate to hush him back to sleep. "Surely not. Even Swein would not be so utterly stupid. Good Lord above!"

"According to this he has," Harold passed the letter over to Edith. She scanned his father's spidery writing over and over, not wanting to believe what it seemed to say.

"But an Abbess! I know that once he has the scent of a woman in his nostrils he can't control himself, but an Abbess! It isn't as if she would have given any signs of welcome to him."

"His blood was up, I suppose. He has taken his role

of Earl as carte blanche to go and interfere in any situation he sees fit. He's been off campaigning in Wales, messing about with the balance of power there. Then on his way back he decides that the Abbey at Leominster is a bit too wealthy for him to ignore and...."

"And this," Edith waved the note at Harold, the distaste obvious in her face.

"We have to go. Both of us. Father has insisted and I fail to see how we can refuse. Bloody idiot as he is, Swein is still family."

Oh yes, he was part of the Godwinson family, and his complete lack of any sense was trampling over hers. The boys would have to stay here in Waltham while she and Harold hauled off to Bosham to try to make some sense of the crisis. Why in God's name could he just not find some nice forgiving maiden of rank and beggar off into the countryside somewhere like any other son would do?

The weather was as miserable as Edith's mood. Rain dripped from her hood and blew into her eyes, mingling with the tears of anger that would well up in them as she stewed on and on in her mind. She really couldn't grasp why Godwin had thought her presence necessary. After all, when the whole business of Ealdyth's betrothal unfolded she was left out in the cold, so to speak but now, suddenly, she was important. The sickness she had felt all morning rose in her throat and she bent sideways , vomiting onto the roadway. Trembling, she pulled a rag from her scrip and wiped her chin. She always suffered like this early on, and the last thing she needed was to be rocking back and forth on her jennet when all she wanted was to lie down and wait for the feeling to pass. Harold glanced at her, guilt washing over him. He knew better than to talk to her when she was in such a bitter mood. It would pass, he was sure as it always did, but for now a wise husband knew to keep his head down and his mouth firmly closed.

"Your hands are frozen child! Come inside and warm yourself. Harold, fancy letting her get so cold! Bring some rugs from the chest to wrap her in. Now, not when it suits you!" Gytha took Edith's hands between hers, rubbing the life back into them as she lead her to sit by the fire which burned brightly in the solar. Before she knew it, Leofwine and Gyrth had bounded towards her, thrusting a beaker of mead into one hand and a hunk of cheese into the other. Even at a time like this they were grinning, glad for the arrival of their favourite brother and his wife. They hugged her like a long lost friend.

"Thank God you are here at last! This place has been miserable for weeks, all hushed voices and sideways looks. You know what I mean, no fun at all." Leofwine smiled in relief. For some reason, it seemed that her arrival had taken a weight from their shoulders.

"Is Tostig here?" Gyrth shook his head.

"No chance of that. You know what a queer character he is. When all this business blew up he spent half a day ranting about the shortcomings of his eldest brother. By nightfall he had saddled up and ridden off to court."

"No doubt to put his head on our sister's knee and whine about the wickedness of men!" Leofwine sniggered. There was obviously more to that little comment than met the eye but Edith let it pass. Time enough for that later.

"And where is said brother? I thought Harold and I had been dragged here to sort out his latest little transgression."

"Mother has banished him to the stables. She says no woman is safe in his company and is making him sleep among the nagsmen. Even father agreed! It has caused him a terrific amount of trouble, both with the Archbishop and the King himself. It will take more than a sweet tongue and a sharp sword to sort this one out."

Gytha re-entered the room and chased the boys out , leaving just the two of them. The older woman eased herself wearily onto a stool and took a long draught from the beaker in her hand. Edith saw the pain etched across her face. Swein would always be special to her as her eldest son but this was behaviour that for once she could not ignore.

"I am so worried, child. I suppose you know the whole of it?"

Edith shook her head, "Only what was written in the letter. Earl Godwin did not say much, only that Swein was involved with the Abbess of Leominster in some way."
Gytha nodded, taking another sip from her beaker as she worked out in her mind how to frame the tale,

"You know Swein had been in Wales, fighting alongside the King of Gwynnedd. It was to preserve the peace in his Earldom, at least so I believe. In any case they were successful, and according to his thegn, Tursten, Swein was in a distinctly jovial mood as they rode towards Leominster. They had decided to ask for shelter at the Abbey to break their journey. Anyway, they all partook far too much in the hospitality and Swein, as is his way, became roaringly drunk. I'm sure you remember what he is like when in his cups. The Abbess tried to calm him down but..... well, he is lead by his loins at times like that and he took the poor girl by force. Which would be bad enough, but then he threw her over his horse and rode off with her. When Godwin heard the news he was livid. I have never seen him as angry as that, not only for what Swein had done but for all of us. He went to where Swein had hidden himself and the girl and dragged them both back here. "

"But why should you send for Harold and myself? I would have thought the less people were involved the safer for all concerned."

Gytha leant forward, the firelight glinting in eyes that were large and terrified,

"The girl, Edith. She is fading before our eyes. She drinks little and eats less, just kneeling at prayer for hour after hour. She won't speak to me , or anyone else no matter how we try. I just hoped that maybe she might confide in someone young who is less tied to the family than I am. Would you try, Edith? Things are bad enough for Swein but if she should die..."

So that was it. Harold had been pulled in to provide as much of a united front as possible and she had to try to convince the poor violated girl that life was still worth living. Not now though. She was hopelessly tired, the child inside her sucking up her energy as it grew. Her eyelids felt heavy. All she wanted was sleep. She was vaguely aware of the presence of Harold in the room, of his arms lifting her from the floor and carrying her off to her bed in the guest block. It could all wait until tomorrow.

The door groaned as Edith slowly slid it open, letting the daylight flood into the little chamber. A brazier stood in the centre of the room, the charcoal glowing warmly and casting shadows against the wall behind it. There was a little bed, topped by a feather mattress and soft rugs and furs, standing amidst the sweet smelling bedstraw that was strewn across the floor. No effort spared, she thought, to keep the occupant comfortably safe. And there was the occupant herself, crouched low on her knees, clutching a crucifix in her hand and fervently whispering the offices of the day. Edith waited in the doorway until she saw the girl cross herself. Stepping forward, she cleared her throat. The girl turned, her eyes wide like a hunted animal.

Edith could see the tears on her gown that had been hastily repaired. Swein's handiwork. It was hard to imagine how awful it must have been for her, to feel his drunken weight on top of her, tearing at her clothing and invading her body with his. Then, to be left lying there, bleeding and sobbing and with no-one to comfort her. No wonder that she had withdrawn into herself. Maybe she hoped if she prayed enough then everything would turn out just to be a bad dream. No such fortune, my dear.

Edith perched on the edge of the bed and beckoned the girl to join her. She seemed about her own age, but the flush of youth had left her face. Her skin was pale as snowflakes and her eyes were circled with deep black smudges.

"Your name is Eadgifu? I am Edith. My husband is one of Earl Godwin's sons. The thoughtful and sensible one , that is." The shadow of a smile flitted briefly across Eadgifu's face. "You don't have to talk to me, or anyone else. It is just nice for me to have someone to talk to who isn't part of the family. They do tend to stick together. Much as I care for Harold I sometimes want to shake him and remind him that he isn't his father's lap dog."

Edith talked about anything that crossed her mind

to fill the silence. She told Eadgifu about her family, her home, her children, anything at all. She told her about the fuss at Ealdyth's wedding to the king because she and Harold were not churched . She made light of it all, making mock scandal to try to make a bond with the young nun. She could see that Eadgifu was relaxing a little. Bracing herself, Edith laid her hand across the pale slender one that still clutched at the crucifix.

"Swein is a fool. He acts without thought, especially when he is drunk, then he regrets it afterwards when it is too late. The first time I met him I ended up drawing his own knife against him, and the only person who was hurt was poor Harold who was trying to act as peacemaker. We were children then, but he is still the same. He sees what he wants and grabs for it, then thinks about the consequences later. His parents might try to protect him but I see him for what he is; a spoilt brat who still behaves like a child. Maybe this time he will have to answer himself for his actions, rather than his father sorting things for him."

She lowered her voice so it was barely a whisper, "It must have been terrible for you. A wedding night is bad enough but what he did was beyond the pale. You don't have to tell me anything, not a thing, but please don't blame yourself for any of it. You did nothing wrong, but you are punishing yourself by not eating and locking yourself away in here. I beg you, eat a little something for me. I would hate to see you suffer more harm than you have already." She felt the little hand squeeze her fingers gently and Eadgifu looked at her ,smiling uncertainly. Edith threw her arms around the thin frame, hugging her close. She could feel every bone in her spine and ribs, she had grown so thin. From behind her, Edith pulled out a plate of bread, cheese and fish. "Come, share this with me."

The young woman began to pick at the little morsels, placing them between the pale lips and swallowing hard,

"When they arrived at the Abbey, we thought nothing of it. We fed them, cared for their beasts, looked after them as we are bidden. One of them found our wine store, though, and before we knew it so many of them were drunk. It was awful! They were grabbing at the novices and even the older sisters. They barred the door to the dormitory to keep themselves safe. Only I was outside and when I tried to reason with their leader then her cornered me so I could not run and then…"

Eadgifu's face was wet with the tears she had tried to hold back all those weeks, but now they poured freely down her face. Edith raised her hand, she had heard enough but Eadgifu shook her head. She was ready now to tell her tale and it had to be done this moment.

"He kissed me. He forced his mouth against mine and it was awful. he stank of sweat and liquor. Then he grabbed my wrists and pushed me to the floor. I tried to struggle, to get away, but here was no escape from his strength. He ripped my gown across my breast then pulled up my skirts. His knee was between my thighs, I couldn't stop him and then he.... Well, then he satisfied himself and left me there. I covered my body as best I could. One of the nuns had come looking for me, and she managed to drag me back to the dormitory and get me inside. I couldn't believe what had happened. My head was full of the sight and the smell of him. He had hurt me so much. I had bit my tongue when I tried to keep his out of my mouth and all I could taste was blood. When the others lay me down to salve my bruises and they realised I had been defiled it was even worse than the act itself. Some expressed pity, but I could hear some of them whisper that I must have wanted it, that I was lustful and unfit to lead them, that I should be sent out as a whore! I was given some poppy juice to try to give me some rest and the next thing I knew Swein was hammering on the door, begging to be given entrance. He claimed he wanted to apologise, to beg forgiveness. I agreed to see him. What else could I do? How can I believe Our Lord will forgive me if I cannot forgive him? So I let him in. He fell to his knees, crying like a child and begging me to forgive. I did and I do. I had to for my own sake. I think perhaps he saw how some of the Sisters were thinking and when he and his men left I was thrown across a horse and took me away. In his mind he was saving me ,but without his heinous act I wouldn't have needed it. He treated me well enough, and made no more attempt to force himself on me after that first time. Anyway, eventually Earl Godwin must have found out and he insisted that I was brought beneath his roof. My fate is within other's hands now. The only thing I can do is pray."

She pulled on the sleeve of her undergown and wiped it across her face. She looked calm now, is if telling someone everything had released her body from the burden. But there was still something that puzzled Edith, something that was forming into a thought.

"But why are you not eating? The Lady Gytha is worried beyond belief about it. She fears you intend to starve yourself into the grave over this."

Eadgifu shook her head in surprise, "Oh no! I would never commit such a sin. It is just that I have been feeling ill, and anything I eat seems to taste awful . Not that I would dream .." Her face went green and she began to retch. Edith picked up the night bowl from the floor and held it while the girl brought back the little food that she had eaten. She helped her lie down on the bed, pulling up a rug to keep her warm. The thought in Edith's head suddenly sprang to the forefront of her mind. "Forgive me," she muttered, and she lay a gentle hand upon the young nun's belly. She was so thin that it was obvious. Much more so than it was in her case, where her well rounded form hid the evidence from public notice for months. She told the girl to sleep, that she would take care of her and not to worry about anything, then slipped from the room and strode angrily towards the great hall. Swein had really done it this time. Try as she might she could see no way to solve this problem. Eadgifu was in fine health, even though she seemed ill. It was just that she was carrying Swein's child .

CHAPTER 13

The news that Edith brought to her mother-in-law fell into the conversation like a stone. Her face became ashen, and the spindle she had been using clattered to the floor. She had never even dreamed in her worse nightmare that this might be the case. She sent for her husband and stammeringly reported to him what Edith had discovered. He picked up the wine pitcher which stood on the side table and threw it angrily against the far wall. It shattered into a thousand pieces, cascading to the floor in a shower of sticky mead. The page boy who waited in the corner cringed as the flying object just missed his head. As he bent to clean up the mess Godwin stalked towards him. He grabbed the boy by the shoulder and pinned him up against the wall. "Whisper one word of what you have heard and I will rip out your heart and ram it down your throat. Do you understand me?" The boy nodded, his whole body shaking with terror. The Earl threw him towards the door and the boy ran without a backward glance. He bellowed after the youth to find Earl Swein and tell him to get into his presence at once.

Swein was leaning against the stable wall trying to explain to Harold what had happened. In his mind, Eadgifu must have been sent by God to save him from his sinful path. Harold held his council. He had learned that it was best to let people state their case before you began to poke holes in their logic. When the page scampered across the yard towards them, both men turned in surprise. To see the boy in this state of distress could only mean trouble was in store for someone. Glumly, Swein began to walk towards the hall, head down and cowed. This took Harold aback. Never before had he seen his bullish braggart brother look this sheepish. Somewhere inside, he felt a little sorry for him. They way Swein had been talking about Eadgifu sounded just like the way he thought about Edith. He clapped his arm over his brother's hunched shoulders. Whatever was going to happen, they would face it together.

Swein picked himself up from the floor, his eyebrow split in two from his father's fist slamming across his face. Godwin was towering over him, daring him to retaliate . For once, he just stood, seething, refusing to snap at the bait.

"You just couldn't control yourself, could you? Time and again I've turned a blind eye to your behaviour. I've stood by and let you lie with every woman between here and the coast, married or not, and thought you were just being a lad. No harm done, I thought. Little bastards of yours running round every corner and I let you do it. Well now you have pushed your luck far too far. I might have been able to square things with the king, pay the fine for what you did and send the girl back where she came from with no more said, but not now. You and your bloody rampant cock! Well I hope you are ready to be a father!"

Swein looked at his father, uncomprehendingly.

"She is with child , you idiot , and unless there has been some divine intervention I assume it is yours!"

Harold cast a quick glance to Ealdyth, who nodded in return. She was holding his mother's hands, supporting her as she trembled under her husband's rage. There was a moment of deafening silence while everyone waited for Swein's reaction. Slowly, so slowly, he dropped to his knees. His hands were clasped together, as if in prayer. It was not the reaction that anyone expected.

"A child! God has gifted us with a child!" Tears of happiness were streaming down his face. I doubt that God had anything to do with it, Harold muttered cynically to himself. Still, there seemed to have been some sort of divine intervention to make Swein behave like this. "Now no-one can prevent our marriage!"

Marriage? Where had that come from? Swein had hardly seemed the type to settle down with any one woman any time soon. Perhaps the wealth of Leominster that Eadgifu would bring with her may have tipped the balance. That would be the cynical view, Edith pondered to herself. Still, such a pretty and gentle girl as Eadgifu may just have changed him and his ways but it remained to be seen.

CHAPTER 14

In Swein's head it all seemed so simple. He liked Eadgifu enough to spend the rest of his life tied to her, she was not as wealthy as Edith but rich enough and she was carrying his offspring. Therefore, he would marry her. Certainly he would have to do a bit of bowing and scraping and perhaps some sort of penance, but he was a scion of the strongest family in England and who would argue against them?

The family sat huddled together, no one daring to utter a word for fear of saying the wrong thing. Swein had been marched back to the stables, his head full of marriage and children while Edith had gone to talk to Eadgifu. Nothing could ever have prepared her for that conversation, having to explain to the girl who had spent most of her life cloistered away from men that the changes in her body were due to pregnancy. For a second or two Eadgifu had stared confusedly into Edith's face, her brain unable to process the words she was hearing. Then she broke down, sobbing uncontrollably, and no amount of words could ever have consoled her. Edith hugged her tight, rocking her back and forth as she did with her own little ones when they cried. Eventually, she sobbed herself into a fitful sleep and Edith sought out Harold .

He was leaning over the edge of the well, staring down at the reflection of the moon in the water when he felt his wife's hand gentle on his shoulder. He spun round and held her tight in his arms, his head buried against her shoulder,

"What a bloody mess, Edith, what an awful bloody mess! Swein thinks he can just play happy families with her and nothing said. As if the Archbishops would let that happen without a fuss, not to mention the King! He dislikes our family enough without giving him such cause. Bad enough that he has ruined that poor girl's life with his stupidity but now a child is being dragged into all this." He slumped back against the well wall, hands thrown up in despair, "My father is saddling his horse as we speak and is riding to Winchester to see Edward and try to save something from the situation. He says there is some law about anyone who abducts a nun paying a fine and returning her to her order but Swein has made things a thousand times more complicated than that. Father hopes that if he talks sweetly to the King he can save Swein from himself. It isn't as if Eadgifu and the baby are the worst of it."

Edith looked at him, a puzzled expression wrinkling her brow. Harold reached up to her face, sweeping away loose strands of silver blonde hair that had escaped from beneath her veil.

"It's like everything, my love. It all comes down to money and power. Eadgifu is wealthy and has large estates in the Midlands, which would suit Swein down to the ground because it would strengthen his position as Earl to have a bigger powerbase. Edward fears the strength we have as a family already. I cannot see any way he will permit it to increase. In fact, I can imagine he might see this as a good way to clip our wings. He would like nothing better than to see Swein disappear from this country and to give his lands away to someone else. Someone else, that is, who is not part of our family; Leofric of Mercia or Siward of Northumbria probably. The balance of power is a curious thing. Tip it too far one way and you ended up with trouble. We can't afford that here, especially as there are those overseas who would walk in and take the lot while we fight each other."

He pulled up the well bucket and dipped the ladle in the water, sipping from its bowl to cool his throat. All the talking and shouting had left it raw.

"So what do you think will happen?"

Harold wiped his mouth across the back of his hand, the water droplets silver in the moonlight while he considered his answer, "I honestly don't know. The fine should be 120 shillings, and that is no mean sum, but that is if the girl is returned. Swein has messed that up royally though. My father will try to do what he can, but I think he will abandon Swein to keep all he has worked for safe."

Godwin to cast aside his favourite son! He must be really worried if he would even consider that outcome. Edith slipped her hand into Harold's and pulled him reluctantly to his feet. There were still practicalities to consider. Eadgifu would need such gentle handling over the coming months and Edith wanted to make sure she would be safe.

By the time Godwin returned from Winchester, Harold and Edith had made their way back home to

Waltham. The king had sent notice for Harold to make a tour of his holdings to collect the heregeld. Maybe it was a little early in the year, muttered Edith to herself, but it was a very convenient way of scattering the Godwinson boys around the country. Still, it would be lovely to see the children again and to see to her own affairs. Earl Godwin had a way of sucking every ounce of energy out of you for his own use. The word of King Edward's decision came by messenger a few weeks later. Harold ripped off the seal and scanned the letter quickly. The king had been livid at the abduction and wanted the immediate return of the Abbess to her abbey. In his usual manipulative way Godwin had not told the king of the pregnancy, but had his daughter approach Edward with the news. Edith was disgusted. Poor Ealdyth had yet to show any sign of being with child. To have her beg forgiveness for her stupid brother and clemency for the mother he had sired a child on must have been bitter in her mouth. At least she had persuaded him to delay Eadgifu's return until after the birth of the child, who could remain with the Godwins, but under no circumstances would he sanction marriage. That was hardly to be expected but he had not finished yet. Swein was to be banished from the land as soon as the child was safely born and all his lands were to be relinquished to the Crown. It was just as Harold had suspected.

"It seems that Swein has barely raised a complaint! It would appear that impending fatherhood has caused him to grow up at last. If he behaves himself , father is certain the King will call him home before the child can walk." The surprise was evident in Harold's voice. He tipped back his chair and placed his boots firmly on the table top that Edith had just swept clear of crumbs. She swatted at him with the cloth she was carrying, and he reached out and grabbed her, pulling her onto his knee and kissing her firmly on the mouth. Perhaps now things would settle down a bit and he could turn his attention towards his beautiful, comely and most delicious wife.

CHAPTER 15

Baby Magnus arrived; red faced, strong bodied and bawling fit to burst the ear drum. Another boy had been born to fill the family cradle. In Bosham, around the same time, Eadgifu had been delivered of her child, a little lad she called Hakon. He was slight like his mother, but had the mop of gold brown hair and piercing blue eyes that were the stamp of his sire. Such little time she had with him, until she was churched and declared clean. Then she was escorted back to Leominster, head bowed and tears in her eyes, clutching in her hand a tiny bag holding a snippet of silk soft fair curls she could hold to her heart for the rest of her life, and remember.

Swein went; not willingly. Hakon was his, a tiny bundle of life that he had created and leaving him behind hurt so much more than he dared admit. But now was not the time to create more trouble. He would behave himself and soon he would be back home, he was certain.

Harold sighed. His wife had made enough fuss about his constant absences on the king's business before, but now that he had been gifted a portion of Swein's lands he would be away even more. She liked home. Never was she happier than when sitting on the floor, feet tucked beneath her, playing with their sons. Motherhood was her calling, and she hated it when he insisted she travel with him. He sneaked up behind where she sat, sewing a new tunic for the baby in the light from the window, and planted a kiss on the top of her head."Whatever it is, the answer my lord is no."

It was almost as if she could read his thoughts before he had even thought them.

"It will only be a short trip. We can be there and back within the fortnight."

Edith stood and turned to face him, hands on hips, "It may have escaped your notice, my lord, busy as you are but yet again you have permitted me the honour of bearing your child. That being the case, I would beg your lordship's leave to stay exactly where I am." She sat down with exaggerated weariness. Harold sat beside her on the floor and rested his head against her knee. She began to twist her fingers through his blond curls, winding them absent mindedly around her fingers. She could feel that he had slid a hand beneath the hem of her skirt and was gently stroking her calf. His fingers traced around the dimple in her knee and began to toy with the garter which held up her stocking. He lifted his head and gazed at her with such a plaintive expression that she dissolved into a fit of the giggles.

"Very well, you win. But only a fortnight, do you hear? This little one is tiring me terribly, perhaps because it follows so soon on the last."

She had thrown the words out flippantly, but in truth Edith was worried. Barely had she been churched before Harold had given her another babe. She had been much more sick than usual, all through the day, and somehow she did not feel the same as she had before. Perhaps a trip might do her good. She always felt better for feeling the sun against her face and the wind ruffling through her silver gold hair. Let Harold think she was doing him an enormous favour, though. It never did any harm to have a grateful husband.

The fortnight flew by, then another and another. By now Edith was in despair. She was unbearably tired from the sickness she was suffering and from the continual show she had to put on in public. Everyone wanted to meet the wealthy and beautiful wife of their Earl so she had no alternative to the continual round of greetings. Every time Harold promised that they could return home, it seemed that a herald would arrive from the king sending Harold on more of his business. Perhaps she could have returned home alone, but she needed him by her side and she didn't know why.

He hadn't noticed. The little changes every day had added up so slowly and it had been so easy to hide beneath the heavy folds of her gown. He had been so tired that he had fallen into bed and landed in sleep before his head hit the pillow. This was the first time in weeks he had actually looked at her properly. He had neglected her, and now, as he saw the extent of the problem, he hated himself. Edith had always carried a comforting amount of flesh across her body; not fat, but healthy and strong, but standing before him now, Harold could see that she had become horribly thin. Her hip bones jutted, her collarbones rose high above her flesh, echoed by the line of ribs below them. Pulling her towards him, he could feel each and every bone of her spine against his hands. There was a problem, and the problem was the child she was carrying.

"I can't help it. I can't keep down a morsel of food.

Even water makes me ill. I ache the whole time, as if the child would be born soon, but I cannot understand why. There is something wrong, Harold, I just know there is," Edith lowered her eyes to hide the tears . She had kept it all to herself for so long, and to let the words out made it all real and frightening. Harold held her close, cradling her in his arms, " The king can go hang. I will not have you tramping round the countryside in this state just to suit his ends. We are going home; now. Come on, dry your eyes my love, everything will be alright."

The wagons were loaded, the horses saddled and the Earl's retinue were ready to depart. Harold insisted that Edith lay in a carriage, on a bed of feather and covered with furs. Her maid stayed by her side, holding her hand and chastising the cart driver every time the carriage lurched on the pot hole riven tracks. Wilone had known her from a child, gifted to Edith by her mother when she left for the nunnery. She had been by her side for the birth of each of the boys. Edith's mother had told Wilone to be another mother to her daughter and she took the role seriously. The sight of her mistress' grey pale face worried her deeply. So too did the moans of pain she could hear from her lady, even in her sleep. The further they went, the more apparent it became that the baby was on it's way. Fast as light,

Wilone scrambled out of the coach, and screaming at the top of her voice to halt she grabbed the reins of Harold's mount and dragged it to a standstill. The look on her face told him more than any words could. He threw himself to the ground and ran back to where Edith lay whimpering to herself. Sweat was pouring from her, but she was shivering as if packed in ice.

He looked around him, desperate for any sign of settlement. On the horizon, thank God, was a small huddle of cottages that might be called a village. He bellowed to the driver to follow and leaping back to his mount he galloped headlong towards the buildings. Heart beating like a hammer, he kicked open the door of the nearest hovel. The ceorl leapt to his feet, spilling his supper on the floor. His wife cowered behind him in terror, and indeed Harold must have been a terrifying sight. His blond hair flew wildly about his head, eyes darting about furiously. Leaping forward , he grabbed the arm of the woman and pulled her outside to where the carriage was just arriving, "My wife, the baby is coming.. and it's too soon! She needs help! Please!" She looked into his face and saw not a proud Earl, or a vicious intruder, but a young man fearful for the life of his wife and child. Turning on her heel she barked to her husband to run and rouse Goodwife Mildrythe. "She has saved many a situation, young my lord. Often she will save one at least, when others would lose both." Harold felt his knees buckle. Never had it occurred to him that either of them would die. His mother had nine children with no sign of trouble, and his boys had been quick and simple to birth but now.....

Scuttling up the hill towards them came the ceorl, hustling along before him a tiny old woman, bent almost double with age , and carrying a sack under her arm. She hurried up to Harold and thrust the sack into his hand, "Here, make yourself useful. Brew up some of the raspberry leaves in water. The drink will help. And chop up some of the mint leaves while you are at it. Come on, move yourself." Almost in a trance, Harold went into the cottage to do as he was told. The ceorl's wife and Mildrythe climbed into the carriage, "Keeps them busy and out of the way," chuckled the old woman, "T'aint to say I won't need them things but better off if the men are doing something I think." Quickly Wilone told the midwife what had been happening and how worried her lady had been. The old woman frowned, then pulled away the rugs that covered Edith's frame. Her gown was soaked, and she was curled up, whimpering in pain. "Bring the raspberry leaf, and the watermint. Things are going badly here. The sooner it is all over the better and the herbs will help." She turned her attention back to

Edith. Hopefully she could save her.

The door opened slowly. Harold looked up expectantly, feeling the hand of Caflice, the old ceorl, tighten on his shoulder. They had sat together, Harold pouring out his woes to the old man, as he would to a father less self obsessed than his own. Now they both waited in dread to hear the midwife's news. "She will be alright, in time. It was hard on her though. The child was laid the wrong way, poor little soul. By the time her body came into this world her soul had departed. I'm sorry lad. I did all I could."

"I doubt another could have saved her. Without Mildrythe and her attentions she would like have bled to death." Caflice's wife had followed the midwife in, and she too had laid a hand in solace on Harold's shoulders.

He sat; dumbstruck, unable to move. His head was buried in his hands as he bit his lip, desperate not to shed the tears that were brimming in his eyes in front of strangers, however kind. He tried to control his breathing, stifling the sobs. He needed time to sort his thoughts before he could face Edith. She would blame him, he knew she would. If he had not been so insistent in her bed she would not have been pregnant so soon. If he had not allowed himself to be dragged all over by the king's orders and insisted that she accompany him, she could at least have taken some ease and been with her own midwife rather than strangers. He wanted to give her back her father's sword, to run him through with it. How could he have let this happen?

The midwife tapped his knee, and beckoned him with a gnarled and twisted finger. He rose unsteadily and followed her into a dark corner of the building. She grabbed him by the tunic, pulling him down so that she could whisper into his ear,

"There was nothing that could have made a difference. Sometimes a child just doesn't grow properly, and coming out feet first didn't help. There will be more after this one. Your wife is good breeding stock, she has the body for it and this little soul's done no lasting damage. Take time to grieve and then when she is ready she will let you know." She smiled, a toothless kindly smile, and lead him towards the door. He walked slowly toward the carriage where they lay, casting back a worried glance. Mildrythe waved him forward. He was what she needed now.

Edith was curled up on the carriage floor, her head

resting on Wilone's knee. Seeing Harold, the maid slipped a cushion beneath her lady's head and stepped out into the night air. Looking down, Harold felt his heart almost burst. Cradled in Edith's arms was a tiny bundle. The tiny head had a shock of dark hair and a perfect rosebud mouth. A minute hand was tucked into her mother's as she kissed it over and over again, whispering love and sorrow. So tiny and so perfect. Only one thing was wrong. The little chest had no rise and fall; the heart had no beat. Harold knelt down and swept them both into his arms. His first beautiful daughter. He thought of all the things he would never have chance to tell her; how he would never be able to warn off all the swains wanting her hand; how he would finally relent and give her to the best. She would have been so special but now he would have to take her little body and lay it in the cold earth before she ever had chance to tread it. Oh God! He had never even thought of it! She had been born dead, unchristened, and had no place beneath the protective wing of The Lord. He felt the blood rush through his body, full of fire and anger. He would not let it happen. For Edith, for the baby and for himself.

She was crooning now, crooning a little tune she had sung to the boys after they had been born. It was impossible to fool herself. She knew how hard this would be. Her breasts would leak and there would be no child to joyously suckle. Every cell of her body would cry out for the baby, in the dark hours of the night when nothing could distract her. But for a few hours she could cuddle the little mite, and commit to memory every little bit of her.

"I want to call her Eadgifu, "she whispered, "She knows what it is like to be torn from her child as I will be from this one."

Harold kissed her head, anointing her hair with his tears, "That is a fine name, It means a precious gift you know, and she has been precious indeed."

CHAPTER 16

They were not far now from Cantwareburh. Every inch
of the journey Edith clutched the baby to her breast, as
if she was keeping her from harm. The carriage
trundled along the road up to the cathedral and came to
a halt by the west door. It was time now, she knew.
Slowly, she gently wrapped the swaddling bands tight
around the little form then kissed her, before covering
her face as if to protect it from the harsh light of day.
She handed the pathetic little bundle and stepped
down from the carriage, leaning on Wilone's arm and
making her way towards the cathedral steps. What
Harold planned, she had no idea. The baby was not
baptised. She could not be buried on hallowed ground
however terrible that might be . Edith ached to know
she would never see the baby again, even in heaven, but
what could she do? The Church pointedly refused to
listen to bereaved mothers in particular nor women in

general on this point. But here was Harold, marching up the stairs with the baby in his arms and heading straight for the cathedral itself.

The door had slammed back against its hinges as Harold swung it wide. Monks tugging at his sleeves he strode purposefully up the aisle towards the elaborate tomb of St Dunstan. He knelt on the floor, and began to pick at the floor tiles with his fingers until the blood dripped from their ends, then pulling out his seaxe he started to chip at the mortar, levering the tiles out one by one as the monks rushed to fetch the Archbishop. By now Edith had made her way up the aisle and was on her knees beside her husband, begging him to stop.

"To Hell with your laws and to Hell with your rules. I am Earl here and Church or no I will rip this building apart stone by stone with my bare hands if I should have to. This is my daughter, my precious daughter, and my heart breaks to have to bury her at all. She will not go into some hole in a field to be forgotten. She will lie here, by this good saint. Our Lord called for the children to come to Him and He can start with this one!"

The Archbishop stood, unsure of what to do. He was used to being lord in this domain but Harold had no time for such niceties. He decided the best plan would be to fall back on the church's teachings.

"Baptisms? You talk to me of Baptisms? This child is baptised! Not in your Church, with Holy water and prayer books and censers furling smoke about the place but with a name given in love, her mother's tears and the stink of blood about the place. Her mother's tears! Aye, and mine too! I am not such a man as is afraid to admit to it. Now you will open a hole here, by the tomb of this saint, and she will be buried here in this Holy place. But should any word reach me that you have moved these little bones, and it will, then I shall call up every thegn owed me and we will destroy this place and everyone in it. Do you hear me?"

They heard and they feared. Harold was a Godwinson and they were known to be fearsome enemies. Perhaps it was possible that this unusual baptism might be permissible after all. And did Our Lord not say "Suffer the little children to come unto Me and forbid them not"? The bag of gold dangling from Harold's belt would go a long way in doing good, would it not. So little Eadgifu was laid to rest beside St Dunstan under the care of Holy Mother Church and safe with God.

CHAPTER 17

The old woman had been right. Before Swein had even tried to worm his way back into the country a new baby was occupying the cradle at Waltham. Gytha was chubby, fair and noisy just like her brothers and the relief felt within the family was huge. Her father doted on her, insisting in tucking her up safe in her crib each night when he was home and sitting by her until her blue eyes closed and she fell into little snores.

Word reached home that Swein had taken refuge at the court of Baldwin of Flanders. It was something of a relief to know that he safe. With Swein anything might have happened. Even now he might have been planning an invasion with their Norwegian relatives, who were still annoyed that Cnut's throne had not passed to one of them. At least he couldn't cause too much trouble in Flanders.

Earl Godwin had been steering clear of court since the king had banished Swein. He wasn't used to losing, especially as the king had never before showed such strength of character as to carry through his threats. It unnerved him, particularly as the drip of Norman knights residing at court had become a steady trickle. He had taken to roaming around his holdings, making certain that his ceorls and thegns held true to him, so it came as no surprise when Harold announced that his father was coming to visit. He wanted to see his grandchildren, he declared. Edith was not so sure. She could not believe that he had no other purpose. Still, she was a good hostess and threw a feast that the king himself would have been proud to serve. Godwin was the perfect guest, praising her housekeeping skills and the quality of the food. He insisted she sit beside him, sharing the finest of each platterful with her. As the food was finished, and the entertainment from the musicians and poets concluded, he pushed back his chair with a contented smile on his face. Getting to her feet, Edith begged leave to go and attend to the guest chamber herself. It was unnecessary, of course, and they all knew it, but it allowed Harold and his father some time alone together. Harold lead his father off to the solar. Sitting on a stool, allowing his father the one closest by the charcoal brazier, he sat back and waited for Godwin to reveal the real reason for his visit.

"Now, are you going to enlighten me as to the real

reason you have honoured us with your presence? I know that is was not really to see how your grandsons are growing, nor the baby."

Godwin held up his hands, laughing hoarsely,

"You have seen through my disguise! Of course, it is nice to see how your boys are growing up. Like weeds! They will soon be taller than you, Harold ,and then you will have to watch yourself. And your daughter is as beautiful as a newly opened rosebud,No, there is a reason, and I did not want to commit it to parchment. Our conversation is strictly between us. Not even that pretty and intelligent wife of yours can hear it. Have you noticed, when you are at court, just how many Normans seem to be appearing?"

Harold nodded. Every time he had attended court of late there seemed to be more and more of them. Not that he had really seen it to be a problem. It made the king happy and that meant a happy court , and ultimately a happy country. Peace was too precious to give away so easily.

" Think about this, then. How soon after your marriage did Edith fall pregnant?"
Harold grinned , blushing a little. It felt strange to discuss this with his father,"Immediately upon our

wedding night."

"Quite so. Now, think about how long your sister has been married to Edward."

Harold wrinkled his brow in thought and nodded slowly. He could see now what his father was driving at. No child meant no direct heir. No heir meant war, as all the possible contenders to the crown battled to reach the top of the pile.

"We have to prepare ourselves for the possibility that he won't have an heir from his own flesh. We need to see to it that we are in position to take advantage . The last thing we need is any of the king's relatives from Normandy stealing the throne. The first people to be ousted would be the biggest danger to them and that means us."

Harold could see the logic in what Godwin was saying. He himself had no desire to be king, anything but. He enjoyed being the king's lieutenant, making things happen, seeing that laws were kept but he did not want the pressure of being the ruler. There was always someone else wanting to take your seat, and more than likely your head from your shoulders. Even so, he would not stand by and let his sons be robbed of their rightful inheritance .

"I am not saying that we need to do anything now. Just keep watch and make certain that nothing happens without our knowledge." Harold nodded in tacit agreement. His father could do the plotting though; Harold had enough to keep him busy.

Later that evening, as Edith curled up in their bed next to Harold, she asked him about what he and his father had discussed. Harold stroked her hair as she laid her head softly onto his chest. "Nothing really, he is just fussing. He wants to make sure the family are well and that we are all sticking together. He thinks Swein may be home soon and wants us all to be prepared for any trouble that brings." Edith nodded and closed her eyes, satisfied for now with the answer. Harold , though could not sleep. He had never lied to Edith, even sins of omission, from the first moment he had met her and it sat heavily on his shoulders. One day his father would ask too much of him. He hoped this was not the day.

Their peaceful existence did not last for long, but for once not one of the Godwin clan had instigated it. The south of England was a very wealthy place, the sort of wealth that invited envy . It was hardly a surprise when Viking raiders sailed down from their homes among the celts of Germany with a force of twenty-five ships. The two leaders,Lothen and Yrling, had ransacked churches, razed villages and abducted many of the people whose homes they had torched. By now they would have been sold into slavery, or worse. They had slunk across the channel to sell their captives in Flanders. Which was, unfortunately, exactly where Swein had decided to wait out his banishment. Somehow the queen had got word to him and he had scampered off to Denmark, out of the way of any repercussions. still, something had to be done. If the Godwins failed to retaliate for the assault on their lands then it would do nothing more than invite wave after wave of raiders to try their luck.

Even the king, who would prefer peace at any cost, knew that his bluff was being called. He gathered together the navies he was owed by each of his earldoms off the coast at Sandwich; a show of force to anyone who dared test his strength. A fine sight it was too: ship upon ship crowded into the harbour, filled with sailors from one end of the country to the other. The only conspicuous absence in this whole melee was Earl Godwin. He claimed illness, that such an old man as he was not fit to take part in such an enterprise, and the king accepted the excuses with grace and not a little relief. Harold was there, though. He had kissed goodbye to his children and held his wife close in his arms before he left Waltham for the coast.

In an odd sort of way, Edith was amused. The thought of war of any kind left a nasty feeling gnawing in the pit of her stomach, but somehow the thought of Harold as a naval commander was just too ridiculous.

"Supposing you are seasick," she had giggled to him, "It would hardly inspire your men to see you losing your dinner over the side of the boat!"

Harold scooped her up in his arms, sweeping her off her feet and spinning her round, "Perhaps I ought to take you and tie you to the mast, madam. Such a dragon as you have become would make my ship the most feared in the fleet."

"You will come home safely, my lord." Edith bent to gently kiss his hand .

"I hope so too. I am not yet ready to depart this life. Particularly over the side of a ship." He moved his hand under her chin and tilted her head up wards. Then he kissed her, full on the mouth and with as much desire as he had done their first night together. "I will come home. It is my promise."

He did as he had promised. Not only was he safe

but he had acquitted himself well. The king was pleased, apparently, and was starting to think that Harold had the ability to make an excellent lieutenant in the future, notwithstanding his troublesome family. Proudly he told his wife about the impression he had made, but rather than smiling he saw a familiar scowl flit across her features. He cocked his head to one side in puzzlement.

"Because, my lord, if the king starts to think of you as his closest ally and right hand man you will get dragged more and more off to court and I will be left here, on my own, trying to bring up your extremely energetic offspring!" Magnus and Edmond had just hurtled past the open door to the solar, with Gytha using Godwin as a horse to chase after them, waving a stick and growling like a hound. Harold laughed, dragged her on to his knee and nuzzled into her neck. The smell of the sea was still on his clothes and his hair was sticky with salt spray.

"There is no man on this earth can keep me from spending time with you. The king is not master in this house. He will have to wait his turn." He carried her off to their room to remind her of just how much he loved her.

CHAPTER 18

Anyone else would have crept back into the country with their head hung low and barefoot in penance, but Swein Godwinson was not just anyone. It seemed that his new leaf of good behaviour had not lasted long and having taken up residence in Denmark he had annoyed enough people, mostly women, to be asked to leave and not take his time about it. Godwin had welcomed him back like the prodigal son that he was. Harold was livid. So was Edith. It was as if he had learned nothing from the fiasco with poor, innocent Eadgifu. He was back, and he expected everything to go back to the way it was before he left.

What he didn't realise was that Harold had blossomed into an efficient and effective Earl, backed by his loving and patient wife. Harold was enjoying his new position and he was not going to give back the land that he had been given by the king from Swein's holdings. Nor was their cousin Beorn.

Edith had met Beorn once before, on the day when Ealdyth's engagement had been announced. In her memory he was a sweet boy. When he came to Waltham to discuss tactics with Harold he showed nothing to her that would change her opinion. Like the rest of his family he had the fair hair of the north, and the bright blue eyes, but his face bore a softness that the Godwin boys did not possess. Somehow, he reminded Edith of one of the hound puppies that snuffled around the hall, tripping up the servants and wagging their tales in apology. She put her ear to the solar door, straining to listen to the conversation the two men were holding. As the door swung back she almost fell inside. She scrambled to her feet to the sound of Harold and Beorn howling with laughter.

"You may as well come in. Better you hear the tale straight than concoct your own version!" She stalked over towards the window and picked up a piece of embroidery she had left there, furiously digging in the needle and glaring at her husband in annoyance. Then, shaking her head and smiling, she pulled up a stool and sat with them. Harold knew she was the smartest advisor he could ever have. Why exclude her just because she was a woman?

"I am sick of having to dance to Swein's tune. Time and again he has caused trouble and it's usually me that ends up having to placate everybody. I won't do it this time, and my father can just keep out of it. The king gave us these lands, to me and Beorn and we have done well with them. I see no reason why should hand it all back just for Swein to mess it up again." Edith was surprised. It was so unlike Harold to question his father's judgement, let alone to butt heads with him like this.

Beorn swilled the wine round and round the glass goblet, watching the light dance across the surface of the ruby red liquid. He needed a moment to think about his reply. The problem was that he could see both sides. If Swein was back, then how could he be expected to be Earl of nowhere? He was furious, of course he was, at having to lose part of his holdings, but family was family and he was sure that Swein would do the same for him if the position was reversed.

"I honestly don't know what to do. Maybe if I had the chance to talk with him, if he really was contrite, then perhaps I would feel better about returning his holdings to him. After all, he does have the little boy now and perhaps that will teach him a sense of responsibility."

Harold scoffed, "The only person Swein ever felt responsibility for his himself. He can gild his nature but he can never change it." He threw his wine down his throat, pouring another goblet full. Edith raised an eyebrow to him in warning and he grinned back at her, sipping his next mouthful like an elderly dowager. "In any case, I have written to my sister, the queen, and informed her of my feelings on the matter. She has the ear of the king and I doubt he is so foolish as to want to create trouble at home, especially as he has just been so successful with the fleet."

Beorn tipped his head sideways in thought. Although Gytha was his aunt, he always felt a little on the outside of the political twists and turns the Godwins seemed so fond of. And hadn't Swein been causing such trouble in Denmark that he had been asked to leave at the point of a knife? Perhaps it was best to keep on Harold's side in this. After all, they were the ones with such a lot to lose.

The king had listened to Ealdyth's entreaties, but Godwin was also begging him to let Swein come home. Perhaps it would not be a bad thing to have Godwin beholden to him, but he was not so foolish as to let Swein be seen to get away with his behaviour. The middle way seemed the wisest course. Swein could return, yes indeed, but he was not getting his earldom or lands back yet, with or without the agreement of the others concerned.

Harold swept his hand back through his thicket of hair, trying to keep a lid on the anger that was bubbling up inside him. Now was no time to act in haste. That poor boy, who so recently had sat at this very table, had eaten his food, had drunk his wine, spitted like a boar by that bastard brother of his. It was almost more than thought could bear, that they should have been brought from the same womb. His hand trembled as he lay the letter down on the table. Stalking out to the stables, he shouted for his horse to be saddled, and those of five of his trusted thegns. If he was going to go toe to toe with Swein he was not going alone.

"My lord Harold has told me nothing. I have no fear of standing by his side, my lady, but I would rather die knowing the cause." Edmond was leaning against his horse, pulling tight the straps which held his pack in place. The order to move had been so quick, and spoken so tersely, that no-one had dared ask the Earl the reason. Edith had come down from the hall to see them leave, and the look on her face filled the thegn with dread.

"He is riding to the coast, and then if he finds what he fears he might it will be on to Bosham," she grabbed at the thegn's arm, dropping her voice to a whisper, "He thinks, knows, that his brother Swein has committed an even greater outrage than ever before. You recall the young Earl who visited us so recently, Beorn? Well Swein has slaughtered both him and his men and has cast his body free into the tide without burial. It is only by God's chance that one of his men escaped and told the tale. The body was found by fishermen . They knew it must have been a man of wealth by the richness of the apparel but the body was in such a state that no one could recognise it."

Edmond's eyes grew blacker as the story was told. The young Earl had seemed a personable man. They had even had a discussion about the breeding of the hounds which lay about the place. He had been impressed by the depth of chest and length of leg, he said, and he had fancied asking Harold for a pup or two to strengthen his own dogs' line. Not now though.

All the way towards the coast, the men rode in silence. Whispered words had informed everyone in the group why they were heading towards the Godwin stronghold. Harold had been to the village where the folk who had tended to the body lived. Beorn's thegn was there, sitting by the body of his lord in the chill of the church sanctuary. Harold knelt and swore to him that Beorn's death would not pass unnoticed. He would be buried beside his uncle Cnut, in the great cathedral at Winchester. Harold fumbled in his scrip, cold fingers blighting his efforts as he pulled out a bag heavy with coin. He asked the thegn to arrange for the coffining of the body and the transport to Winchester, and then for the payment here for masses in Beorn's name. Anything left the thegn could keep, for his trouble and to repay the damage that Swein and his men had done to him. He looked at Harold and smiled gratefully. His sword arm had been so damaged that he would be useless as a bodyguard to any lord in the future. Now that had been attended to they rode on towards the real reckoning.

CHAPTER 19

Harold felt his fist thud into the side of Swein's face with a satisfying crunch. He had marched straight into the great hall at Bosham, where Swein had scuttled like the rat that he was, to hide under the power of his father. Before his brother had the chance to rise from the table, Harold had leapt across it and grabbed him around the throat, lifting him from the bench and slamming his head backwards into the wall. Swein was fighting for his breath, scrabbling at his throat with terrified fingers. Their mother was screaming at them , pulling at Harold's hair to try to stop his assault. He felt nothing though, only anger and injustice. Ramming his knee up hard between Swein's legs he dropped him to the floor, howling in pain.

"Beorn was only a boy, you bastard. It was me who persuaded him not to give back your land straight away. If it had been left to him you would have had the lot!"

He kicked him, hard, in the kidneys and Swein yelped again. "I will bury him. He will lie in the cathedral with his kin and it will be bitter to do it. It is before his time!" Again Harold's boot buried itself into Swein's flesh. He bent forward over the cowering form, his anger spent into misery, hauling him up so he lay, vomiting in pain, across the bench. "I am going now to bury our flesh; the boy who ate and drank with me before you murdered him. If any other of my brothers wish to accompany me, that is for them to choose. The rest of you will not be welcome."

He turned on his heel, striding out before anyone could see the tears falling down his face. Swein was his big brother, his annoying big brother, who he had looked up to when he was young; who he had wanted to grow up to be like. Now it was as if some thread that joined them together had been severed. It was as if a portion of him had died.

It had been a miserable winter , and the day that Beorn was buried was one of the worst. A howling gale was blowing in off the channel, bringing with it driving rods of rain. Edith had insisted on joining Harold, bringing with her Godwin and Edmund. They were old enough to understand the realities of existence. They stood shivering by their mother's side, waiting for the coffin to be carried into the cathedral. Harold stood behind it, making a point to anyone who saw him. He was bareheaded, rain running down across his face. He was ashen, eyes dark hollows, as he walked slowly in front of the other mourners. Gyrth and Leofwine were there, solemn for once, but Tostig was nowhere to be seen. The king had been so distraught that he had sent Ealdyth to attend in his stead, vowing not to meet any one of the Godwins until he could be assured of their loyalty. She understood that well; they couldn't even manage to be loyal to one another.

The service began, with swirling censers and Latin words. Edith found that she was stroking her son's hair, twisting her fingers in and out of their silver gold locks, as if to bind them to her. They had liked Beorn when they met him. He had chased them around the compound, pretending to be a wolf, and they had all squealed in mock terror. When they found out what had happened at first they refused to believe it. It was almost as if they couldn't grasp how a life could be snuffed out so quickly. The hairs on the back of Edith's neck began to prickle. She could feel someone's eyes on her and glancing round she made eye contact with the queen. To her surprise, Ealdyth smiled at her. A small act of peacemaking. Edith lowered her lashes a little and smiled back, throwing the briefest curtsey. They knelt, and prayers were said, before the coffin was lowered into the grave. Beorn might be at rest, but the business was not finished, not by a long mark. Edith hung back, allowing Harold time to talk with the queen. She could see that the discussion was a difficult one. Leofwine and Gyrth were standing to one side, as if unsure what to do. They must be torn, she thought, between their loyalty to their king, their brother and their father. It seemed that the conversation was concluded, and Harold went to talk to his brothers while the queen headed towards Edith and her boys.

"What? These cannot be Godwin and Edmund surely? These boys must be at least ten years old, they are so tall and handsome!"
Edith laughed as the boys blushed to the roots of their hair,

"I think your aunt, the queen, is surprised at how grown up you seem." Edith looked at the other woman and smiled inwardly. She had such riches and rank and yet Edith suspected , from the way she bent down to talk to her sons, that she would give it all up in a moment for a child of her own.

Harold took his wife's hand and tucked it on his arm, walking close together so that they could talk unheard.

" I am going to escort Ealdyth back to London. That way I will have the chance to try to convince the king that I at least am loyal to him and his cause. Perhaps that pair too," he gestured towards Gyrth and Leofwine. "I get the feeling that the king is none too happy with our family at the moment and would quite happily kick us all into the sea. From the way Ealdyth couched her words I believe it to be so."

Edith nodded. It was hardly surprising. No king wants to feel he is a minor citizen in his own land, and Godwin had ways of making sure that he always got his own way.

"As for you, my love, I have asked my rascal brothers to see to it that you and the boys are safely deposited back in Waltham. It will give you a chance to find out what they know about my father's plans. They will likely say much more to you than they ever would to me."

Leofwine and Gyrth were more than ready to chat. The atmosphere in the Godwin compound was overwhelmingly cloying. Nobody dared say anything that might contradict Godwin, so they had learned to close their mouths but keep their ears wide open.

" And we could hardly believe it when we heard. That was why Tostig wasn't at the funeral. He couldn't be, you see. He is in Flanders, being wedded to Duke Baldwin's sister Judith as we speak!" Gyrth leaned across his horse, smiling conspiratorially.

"Trust Father to make an alliance with the only man in Europe more inclined to cause mischief than he is," whispered Leofwine, for fear the boys may overhear. "Not to mention finding a nice little bolthole for himself should anything go awry."

"And will it come to that?" Edith was worried for her own little flock.

"Who knows? All we can say is that he wants Swein back in his former position and he will start wheedling at the king anytime soon."

Yes, thought Edith bitterly, and how could any king worth his salt keep letting Godwin have his own way like that. No wonder Ealdyth was being so cautious. It would not be easy to be torn between husband and family.

"Does your father still have friends at Court? I should have thought that the Earls would love the chance to push him down."

"One or two," Gyrth pondered, "perhaps not the great Earls, but the family have plenty of thegns in our call. And there are still bishops who would rally to our cause; those who fear the rise of the Normans in our midst, so to speak."

They rode on in silence for a while, until the brothers turned their horses to ride alongside the children, daring them to race to the next village. Edith watched them go, uncles and nephews enjoying themselves together. She said a little prayer to herself that they may do so for a long time yet.

Edith had not been many days back in Waltham before Harold arrived home. He looked weary, not just from the ride but weary in the soul. He had eaten a huge portion of humble pie, he said, when he had finally been allowed into the king's presence. There was an undercurrent of change at Court. Open any door and you would find a Norman behind it. They were quietly accruing power , an earldom here, a bishopric there and it made Harold nervous. Edith went to the kitchens and brought him some bread and meat herself. She placed it on the table in the solar, then bent down to pull off his wet riding boots with her own hands. He stroked her head as she did so, absently, as if she were some loyal hound. She decided against making an issue of it. Obviously he was worried by what he had seen and heard in Westminster. She decided to try to lighten his mood a little. When she told him about Tostig's marriage , his eyes widened in surprise then he let out a huge hoot of laughter, slapping his thigh over and over,

"But I thought... well it has been said that....he and the king that.... that they.. oh the poor girl! What a disappointment!" Edith grinned and perched next to him on the bench,

"I've no idea about that, nor should I! All I know is that Swein organised it all when he was in Flanders the last time. That is why he has been welcomed back now. And of course it means your father has another ally on the continent. Maybe Tostig was only so close a friend to the king on his father's orders. And I only mean a friend, Harold, nothing else!"

Harold wiped the laughter tears from his eyes,

"Do you know, as big a conniving, duplicitous, devious bastard as my father is you really have to admire him sometimes!"

CHAPTER 20

Edith thought that it might not be a bad idea to accompany Harold to the next Royal council. If anything was going to happen that would upset the happiness of her household she wanted to hear about it sooner rather than later. Aside from which, she was looking for an occasion to show off some of the beautiful jewellery that her goldsmiths had crafted for her and Harold. Not that she wanted to outshine anyone; it was just that a mother of four sometimes needs to remember that she is a beautiful woman too.

The feast was, as ever at Court, a magnificent event. There were jugglers and acrobats, musicians and scops, taletellers and dancers to entertain the guests and food and liquor of the finest standard. Even so, when Edith entered the hall on Harold's arm there was a sudden hush. Her hair shimmered beneath the fine silk of her veil like spun silver and gold. New wrist clasps shone in the rushlight, the gold studded with garnets. The brooch holding her cloak matched them, broad and heavy and shouting good taste. Her gown was of soft blue, Harold's tunic of a gentle green. He wore the wrist clasps his mother gave him but the immense brooch holding his cloak was a gift from his wife. It was in the form of a dragon, biting its own tail. Garnets sparkled there too, but the true beauty was in the workmanship. The beast looked alive, sinuous and muscled, almost as if it were about to leap from the background and fly around the hall. The statement was made. This was an independent couple, capable of making up their own minds and following the path that best suited themselves.

They were sitting just along from where Earl Godwin, Gytha and the boys were seated. They nodded welcome then studiously turned their attention to the spread before them. Then it began. It was quite amusing at first, the loud refusal of food, the moaning, the sighing, the bleating about having no appetite because of a lost son. He may well have apologised to Edward for his behaviour, but it did not mean that he would not drop non too subtle hints about what he wanted. Edith could see Harold grinding his teeth as he tore his bread in two, so she kicked him under the table and threw him a warning glance. She had noticed the king glaring in their general direction, itching for a reason to send the whole family away. Harold turned, got to his feet, and gave both king and queen a deep, deep bow and a dazzling smile. Then he sat, turning to his wife with a scowl,

"Will that suit you, mistress? I would not wish to offend your sense of proprieties."

"Shut up you idiot! Your father is driving the king to anger and I would not wish us to get involved if we can avoid it," Edith smiled at him through gritted teeth.

"And how, pray tell, do you think we shall be able to avoid it? Sooner or later the trouble will land at our door. We are all tied by blood whether we like it or not." He turned again to nod to the royal party as he snapped a chicken leg from the bird in front of him.

Edith sighed to herself. It was difficult to argue with Harold's logic. She lifted her goblet to her lips, and stared across the rim at those seated around the hall. Harold had been right about the number of Normans who had wheedled their way into the king's court. Poor Ealdyth must be starting to feel like a stranger in her own land. No wonder she looked so pale. She was so deep in her own thoughts that she jumped when she felt a nudge in her ribs.

"See there, that bishop is Ealdred, Bishop of Worcester. Look how he has the king's ear and is looking in my father's direction."

"So he is. But I fail to see why that should prevent me from filling my trencher."

"He is one of my father's friends, and more than that he is a supporter of Swein. He is having terrible problems with Welsh raiders on his lands, stealing, destroying and murdering. He wants a strong Earl, and rightly so. The problem being the Earl he wants is Swein."

Politics, always politics. Edith flicked a glance at Godwin, who was comforting Gytha as she told anyone who would listen who wronged her boy was and how he was needed at home. Much as she adored them, if any of her boys decided to use Uncle Swein as a role model she would chase him out of the country herself.

"I've noticed something else, Harold. I assume your father has pressured your sister into pleading with him on Swein's behalf?"

Harold nodded tersely, "So I am lead to believe. Why do you ask?"

Edith nodded towards the couple seated on the dais, "Look at how they are sitting. The king may as well have his back to your sister. He has barely shared a word with her all night. And look how she pokes at her food but does not eat. It seems to me that he cannot bear even to look at her."

Harold watched for a moment or two. He knew how happy couples behaved and this was not a happy couple in any way. But Edith was not the only one to have noticed this. A tow haired thegn, seated opposite, could barely wrest his eyes from the queen, and the look in them was one of worry. Well, well, well. His little sister had an admirer. But it was not the man she was married to.

The homecoming of the renegade Swein was treated by his mother like the return of a saint. It mattered not to her that he had been declared a nithing when he had fled from retribution after his murder of Beorn. Edward had drawn the business out for as long as he dared, that was apparent. He had sent Ealdred, the bishop, to discuss personally with the Pope how to overcome the somewhat tricky fact that Swein was a murderer and a murderer of kin at that. The upshot was that the Pope granted forgiveness on the understanding that Swein undertook, at some time in the future, a barefoot pilgrimage to Jerusalem. Edith didn't think it was half enough punishment. Harold agreed, although he was a little mollified to be given some of Swein's land permanently. There was just a small gnawing in the back of his mind though:Edward had caved in far too easily. Harold had never thought of Edward as a cunning man but perhaps he was doing him a disservice.

At least it meant that there could be time spent in peace at Waltham. The children were growing fast, like weeds in summer, and they were delighted to spend a little time with their father. So was their mother. Edith wanted nothing more than a quiet life; children round her feet, a husband content to spend his days hawking and hunting and his nights loving ,and the happiness of being in their own little private world. A whole year they had, and Edith clutched every second of it to herself, like a bunch of summer flowers. True, Harold had to spend time with the king's retinue, and more time yet visiting their holdings and presiding over shire courts but she could be certain he was coming home to her in safety. The child she was carrying was born in her own bed, for which she was surely grateful ,and there was no need for her to leave the little one to her wet nurse immediately. Who knew how many more opportunities she would have to enjoy such a special time?

She knew it could never last. It was impossible that the enmity between Godwin and Edward could be kept lidded for ever. The king had bided his time. He had not retained his throne without cunning and patience, but the beginning of the endgame started with something that could have seemed so innocuous. The dear old Archbishop Eadsige of Canterbury had died. He had been trusted by the king; indeed he had been his own personal priest and he had been the one wise enough a priest and subtle enough a politician to bring a conclusion to the whole business with Swein. The monks mourned him deeply, then in chapter they decided that their next leader should be Ethelric, one of their number and unfortunately for him a kinsman to Earl Godwin. Edward would not let this happen, even if Ethelric was next in line to Jesus himself. Now was the time to clip the wings of the Godwins. He would have his own man as Archbishop, and that man was Robert de Jumieges.

Robert de Jumieges was a Norman and not an especially likeable one at that. He made it plain that his fielty was to Edward and , after that, the king's relatives on his mother's side, each of which were Norman. As the news was passed around by the Royal Heralds, the members of Godwin's family stood by and awaited the explosion.

But it did not come. Not one word came from Godwin's lips on the subject. There was no summoning of the family to Bosham, no letters flying back and forth; nothing. Edith was surprised. When she had heard that the king was overriding Godwin's choices she had begun to repair Harold's gambeson, ready for war. Her needle flew back and forth , stitching threw the thick layers of wadding, patching holes, replacing fabric too torn to be of use. Then she waited for the word that never came.

Bemused, she discussed the situation with Harold one early summer evening. The sun was hanging low in the sky, turning the clouds from pink to peach to purple. A soft breeze blew through the air, whispering around the servants as they went about their business. In the solar, Harold had kicked off his boots and was resting his bare feet in Edith's lap as she sat beside him.

"The thing is, I expected your father to storm straight up to the king and offer to take him on in single combat. After all, the king may as well have thrown down his gauntlet at your father's feet by pushing that Norman bishop in where he wasn't wanted." She tickled Harold's toes with a feather from the cushion she was seated on. He twitched, reaching down to take it from her hand for the price of a kiss.

"I've been thinking about this, I have to confess," Of course he had. His life could be turned upside down at any moment, "and the conclusion I have reached is that my father won't react to the provocation from Edward. That is, until Edward puts him into such an untenable position that he has to jump." That made sense. Godwin had not become as powerful as he had, for as long as he had, without being as cunning as an old fox.

"It won't stop at this, will it? The king is going to keep on pushing until your father can take no more, won't he?" Harold nodded, biting at his lip. It was like waiting to be executed. Everyone knew that it was going to happen. it was just a question of when.

"I will make sure you are safe, my love, you and the children. I would never let anything my father does affect all this," he waved his arm, taking in the whole of the vista before him, "Besides, as far as our new Archbishop is concerned you, sweet one, are no better than a common whore, living as my mistress all these years. You are far below his attention!"

Edith feigned mock horror and smacked Harold on the hand in fake disgust. She knew how handfasting was viewed by the Church and couldn't care less. At least they were happy and blessed with children which was more than the king could say. On either score.

CHAPTER 21

Warm Summer had ended with a storm so ferocious that it seemed like the ending of time. Lightning flashed in great forks, illuminating the landscape in an eerie blue-white light. Raindrops hammered down from the sky, bouncing high from the ground, flooding the watermeadows and washing away roads as if they had never existed. Edith pulled closed the shutters on the chamber windows, trying to exclude the feeling of impending doom the weather had brought with it. Harold, too, was edgy. He paced the floor, bellowing at his hounds as they followed at his heel, snapping at the servants and causing the children to run off and hide. Something other than thunder was in the air; he was sure of it.

"Oh, dear God, not this," Harold was shaking as he laid down the message from his father, "I never realised how bloody devious that Norman crowd could be.

Why do they think they can drag innocent people into this? Christ Jesus, what a mess!"

Edith had run into the room when she heard the howl of anguish. She swiftly scanned the message, sitting down on a stool in shock.

"Those poor souls! They were only protecting their wives and daughters! I can hardly believe that Edward would create such a wicked plan." She read the note again. Count Eustace of Boulogne had been passing through Dover with his men and when they decided to assault the wives of the burghers and steal from their businesses, the locals retaliated. That gave Edward just the opportunity he had been waiting for. Godwin was their lord, and as such the king demanded that he punish them for their deeds. "How could he ask such a thing! If your father harried Dover then who of his men would ever trust him again? He should be defending them, not destroying them."

Harold was staring into the flames curling from the brazier, " My father has seen enough destruction in his life . It would take a great deal of persuasion for him to do something so terrible. He has summoned me to Bosham to hear the words of the merchants who were involved in this fracas. Only then will he know whether he must agree to the king's demand or whether he has to stand strong against him." Edith could feel a sickness in her stomach. All the grumbling, all the dislike and mistrust , had finally come to a head. The boys would gather around Godwin, the king would have his Normans, and Hell would break loose. The only sparkle of hope lay in the other great Earls, Leofric of Mercia and Siward of Northumbria. It was not in their interests to see the country crumble into a squabbling mess, as it had done so often before.

CHAPTER 22

Earl Godwin was an old fashioned lord. He ruled with strength, with violence when it was necessary and was a shifty as a snake with those from his own social group. But if anyone in Wessex was asked they would swear hand on heart that as fearsome as he was he was completely fair to all. Which was why he had no qualms in summoning a group of the townsmen of Dover to Bosham as soon as he had received the king's order. They would tell him the absolute truth, he knew, otherwise death would be preferable to his wrath.

When they had arrived, and were ushered into Godwin's presence, he was sitting patiently in his chair in the Great Hall, his chin resting on his hand , fingers stroking his moustache in thought. "My lord, the first thing that we knew was when the door was beaten open and some French thug fell through the door. He grabbed at my daughter and tried to make her kiss him.

When my son tried to stop him, the bastard ran him through with a dagger. It was lucky the boy was not killed but he is maimed, my lord, and badly so. I could hear the chaos in the streets; screaming, shouting, crying! My neighbour. Iden the wool merchant, had his house ransacked and his wife raped by these foreign devils. They were ready for trouble , my lord! They were armed and were dressed for battle, with chain mail and helms. We did what we could, but how much damage could we inflict? We are not soldiers: we are merchants and sailors and we were not ready to fight with anyone. You must believe us , my lord, for we swear that this is the truth." The group nodded their agreement. Godwin looked at them intently. Usually anyone embellishing the truth or outright lying would quail underneath his stare. These men, the bruises of their encounter still vivid on their faces, looked back at him steadily.

Godwin stood up abruptly, dismissing them. He summoned his steward and told him to make sure that the guests were fed and watered before they left and to take a handful of coins from his treasury for them to use as restoration to those who had suffered in the attack. It would never be said that he was not a fair and generous lord. He walked across to the table where Swein and Harold had been sitting, pretending to play chess but all the time listening. It was the first time the two had met since the murder of Beorn. Harold had a deep urge to slice out his brother's evil lying heart but this was not a time for vengeance. Now they needed to act as one.

"Well, my boys, it would seem that our king is being poked into action , like a pig in a passage. He has put us in a very nasty position and I doubt he would be cunning enough to come up with this on his own."

"It will be the Norman rabble that he likes to fill our Church with, I would wager," Swein drained his beer mug as he spoke. He might have an unreliable temperament but he was a shrewd judge of character . Harold nodded in agreement, filling Swein's mug back to the brim. He picked up the white king from the chessboard, turning it backwards and forwards in his hand. "He's just like this, isn't he? Pushed and pulled in all directions and barely able to move on his own." Godwin reached out his hand, taking the piece from Harold and tucking it into his scrip. "I would rather he was there, for all our good."

To Harold, it felt as if he was a pawn in his father's game. What they all needed was a plan that would outwit the king. The first move they made was to prepare themselves an escape plan. It would be pointless to call the king's bluff without a backup plan ,should things go wrong. Swein had already sent a boat to Bristol when he had returned from exile. After being banished twice he knew that a third time may well mean execution so he had kept the boat prepared just in case it should be needed. Godwin had already ordered the boats he kept at Bosham to be made ready.

"Should the worse happen, we shall go to Flanders with your mother and the little ones. Tostig is already there and we should have a warm welcome now that he is married to the Count's sister. From there we shall be able to probe the king's defences. Sooner or later we shall return. Siward and Leofric may be backing Edward now, but if there is the slightest chance of a civil war they will vanish from his side. We three have fought far too many battles on our own soil to let it happen again."

"But Ealdyth, what about her?"

"She will have to do the best she can. My concerns are for our futures. I cannot help that she will be left behind."

And what about his family? What about Edith and their brood? He shuddered to think how easily his father had abandoned his daughter to her fate. He would not do the same. He would protect his own. Neither would he share expulsion with Swein. To find himself rubbing shoulders with him in such a situation was more than he could face.

"Father, if I may suggest, I will head to Ireland to try to gather support from the Irish king. His men are rightly feared as fighters."

Godwin thought for a moment, tapping his fingers on the tabletop,

"I find merit in your plan, boy. Take Leofwine with you, should it come to it. You will be safer together. And what about your lady? She will join with us?"

Harold stared at Swein, their eyes locked. "I think not. She will be much safer at home with the children. After all, she can declare that we are no longer wed if needs be. And she can at least keep her holdings in her own care." And she is particular who she shares her time with, he snarled at Swein under his breath.

Godwin clapped his hands together, and stood. He was, it seemed, happy with the arrangements that had been made. Now he turned his attention to how he would deal with the king. The first move had been made.

CHAPTER 23

Edith had learned that time alone was one of the penalties of being married to a great Earl, but it was also a pleasure to be able to relax in bed without having to share it with someone who seemed to want all the bedspace to themselves. She was lounging, enjoying the luxury, when Wilone came scampering into the bedchamber. She could barely spit out the words, so desperate was she to tell her lady that her lord had been sighted just a few fields away. She sat up sharply, then changed her mind and sprawled back across the pillows. It was more than likely where he would want her anyway, having been apart for a while.

Indeed, it was not long before he burst through the dooR, soaked to the skin and exhausted. He had ridden all night, through the foulest of weather, to spend a little time at home before he had to be about on his father's business. He stripped, and pulled back the coverlet to reveal his wife's naked body. She was still as wonderful to his sight as she had been as a bride; yet more so for the scars of love the children had left on her skin. He ran his hand across her body, sliding it beneath her back and lifting her up for his kisses before lying her back down on the bed and enjoying her with such fierce love as if it was the first time.

"Can't you stay a while longer?" Harold was tugging up his leather boots, still soaked from the night's ride. He bent, kissing Edith deliciously hard on her open mouth.

"I'm sorry. Honestly. I have to send out for the men I am owed, then I have to get back to Bosham with them. My father wants to present a united front to the king. He seems to think that a show of force will make him back down."

"And you think that will work? That the king will be willing to lose face to that degree?"

"Of course he won't. Maybe once but not now, especially with that De Jumieges pushing him forward . It seems that there will always be someone telling him what to do. Anyway, at least it will give us some breathing time, chance to get things sorted. You know, just in case the worst should happen."

Edith frowned, "Which leaves me where exactly?"

Harold laughed, but the smile did not reach his eyes. He picked up Edith's hand, kissing her fingers one by one, "You, sweet pet, will be exactly where you are now. Which is to say, here at Waltham. If the worst should happen, and we are expelled from the country, I want you to swear that we have dissolved our marriage and that you are free from ties to me and my family. Please, no, listen to me. That way you will keep your lands, and their income, and neither you nor the children will be tainted by what has happened. I shall be headed to Dublin, with Leofwine, to try to garner some assistance, and I don't want you to go to Flanders with the rest of the family. Not with Swein."

It made sense. Perfect sense. And she was so glad to be spared the thought of being with Swein. She would not trust him, ever. He was the type who would take his brother's woman just to put him in his place. At least, looking deep into Harold's azure bright eyes, that was what he feared. He would have enough to worry about, should the worst happen.

It seemed weeks since Harold had ridden with his men to join his father. There had been no word from him, nothing to give the slightest clue as to what was happening. Whether that was a good or bad thing it was difficult to gauge. If there had been some awful battle and Harold had been on the losing side then there would surely have been news of it from one or other source. She clung to that hope like a drowning man clings to a branch. During the day she glided about her home with a cool and calm demeanour, like a swan serenely sailing across a mirror calm lake. Night, though,was a different matter. She would lie in bed, turning over and over, until she could no longer bear the sleeplessness when she would commence hour after hour of pacing the floor. Back and forth she prowled, chewing her nails and aching for the sun to rise, when she would resume the role she had decided she should play.

She had almost given up hope when, one afternoon, she was in the buttery talking to the steward and heard a strange and yet familiar sound. There , hanging in the air, was a tune being whistled cheerily. She turned and ran out into the yard, just in time to see the compound gates thrown back and a gaggle of horsemen trotting through. And, oh thanks be to God, riding at the head was Harold. He grinned, raising his hand to call a halt. Throwing his reins to Edmond who rode beside him, he slid from his mount and ran to

Edith, picking her up and spinning her around until they were both giddy. A huge wave of relief swept across everyone as they appeared from each building, eager to see the return of their lord. Surely everything would go back to normal now.

The steward, with a keen sense of what was required, came around the corner bearing a tray filled with beakers and followed by some of the kitchen boys carrying a beer keg between them. Seizing the opportunity, Harold grasped Edith's hand and escaped the hubbub, slipping inside the hall. He walked across to the dais where the table bore a jug of wine and the best goblets. Slaking his thirst took some time, the road dust clogging his throat. Then he sat down on the edge of the platform but rather than smiling, he threw his head into his hands as if the effort of seeming confident had cost him all the energy he had.

"It's a joke, Edith, just a bloody sick joke. All nicely nice on the surface, oh yes. Edward walked towards us with his hand outstretched, offering friendship and being so bloody reasonable about everything. I know who is behind all this! It's De Jumieges, I swear!"

Edith waited for the torrent of bitterness to subside. She knew that eventually he would calm down enough to tell her the full tale. Pouring herself a glass, she sat down beside him, placing a calming hand on his knee. She could feel the gritty dust on his tunic and automatically began to dust it off onto the floor. Harold laid his hand over hers, squeezing so hard that she bit her lip in pain.

"Apparently, it will all be discussed at the Michaelmas Witan. They are going to hear both sides of the argument and then pass judgement." He downed his drink and threw the goblet to the floor, where it shattered into shards sharper than knives. "Thing is, my father had to show a sign of his willingness to co-operate. The king asked for two hostages."

Edith's hand flew to her mouth, her eyes widening in terror. "No, love, no child of ours by some grace of God, but my brother Wulfnoth and little Hakon." Relief filled her heart followed swift on its heels by guilt. How would Gytha feel, who had birthed one and was grandmother to the other? What sort of wicked world was this, where children were so easily caught up in grown men's problems?

"But they will be released, won't they? When the Witan has ruled in your father's favour?"

"I would say yes, my love, but for the fact that the king has sent them into the care of that snail eating slime trailer De Jumieges."

Him again! Before he poked his big Norman nose into the business of England everything had been peaceful and quiet but now..... Edith stood up to kneel behind her husband. She laid her hands on his shoulders and began to ease the knots out of his muscles with her fingers. Something else was worrying Harold, that was plain. He was just about to speak when his servants came into the hall to set up the tables for the evening meal. It would have to wait for later.

The moonlight shone through the splintered edge of the window shutters. Edith was curled up against Harold, her head on his chest listening to the regular thud of his heart beating. She lazily traced a finger across his ribcage. He stirred, stretching the arm that was curled around her then hugging her back as close as he could. It did not matter that they had not made love. Holding each other was enough.

"I'm sorry, sweet. I just have too much on my mind to concentrate on you as I should."

Edith lifted her head, her silvery hair falling across her shoulder like cloth of gold. "Tell me. Now. I would not have you bear your worries alone." He tried to turn his face away, but she would not allow it.

"It's my father," he sighed heavily. "It is not like him to be outmanoeuvred like this."

"It happens. He will come back like the lion he is, tearing off heads and out thinking everyone around him."

Harold shook his head in sorrow. It was hard to admit to what he was thinking, even to his wife. "No. Oh, I don't know. The thing is, for the first time, I mean he has always seemed so strong and powerful and in command of every situation. But this time, well, I realised that he is getting older. He looked weary . Nobody else noticed it, I don't think, but I saw it. If he should fail, Edith, if he should die, then I dread what might happen to us all."

CHAPTER 24

Harold pulled tight the girth on his saddle, looping has arm through the reins and bending down to hug his daughters. Godwin, Edmund and Magnus stood by with expressions on their faces they thought of as grown up. Their father grinned and ruffled their hair,

"I want you to look after your mother and your sisters while I am away now that you are such fine young men. They will need your care. Also, I want you to make sure that the kitchen and stables run smoothly. They are your responsibility." The boys nodded, faces grave and eyes wide, "Have no fear , father, it shall be done just as you would do it yourself," uttered Godwin seriously, who as the eldest saw himself as the leader of the little gang.

Edith turned away, biting her lip to stifle the laughter. She felt Harold's lips against her ear, "I've spoken to the grooms and the cook. They will make an allowance for them," he whispered softly, making the hair stand up on the back of her neck. "And as for you, my lady, I have instructions for you too, but they are not for public hearing." He threw the reins to Godwin, and took Edith's hand, pulling her off towards their chamber, she half resistant in jest. He closed the door, leaning his wife against it and placing tender kisses down her milk white neck, from ear to shoulder. He pulled away slowly, obviously wanting to continue down her body but time would not permit,

"My task for you, little love, is vital and I don't want you to be frightened by what I say." Edith tipped her head to one side and wrinkled her forehead, but she did not dare speak.

"Things will go badly for us. I know it. I've been thinking it round and round in my head. I think the Witan will agree with father that the people of Dover were well within their rights to act as they did, and that Eustace and his men went in to provoke trouble. That isn't the problem. We raised our men, do you see, me and father and all my brothers and we stood against the king; we were ready to fight and that was our mistake. To raise arms against the king can only mean one thing; we will be exiled and I have no idea for how long.

Remember though, father has a plan. He is not done for yet and neither am I. You and the children will be fine here, you have enough properties of your own to be safe. Play the innocent if you can, a woman who has been my plaything and been abandoned. Use the Church if necessary; we still have friends in the clergy. Now, I will ask one more thing before I must go. Take my strongest chest and pack it with clothes and a bed roll. Underneath I want gold; in small sacks, as much as you dare. I will need it when I reach Dublin. I do not think that the king will have our baggage checked , but hide it well just in case someone decides to remove it for their own use. I doubt we will have much time to leave the country and it is something I don't want done in haste. And now, sweetheart, I must go. It never looks good to keep the Witan waiting. Or my father for that matter, grown as I am." He laughed and chucked her under the chin, trying to lighten the mood as best he could.

The boys were still solemnly holding the reins between the three of them as they stepped back out into the Autumn sunlight. The girls came skipping up with a handful of fallen leaves each and presented them to Harold, red cheeked and beaming with pride, "There! They are for our Aunt Ealdyth and Uncle King. You will make sure to give them won't you dadda?" He made a great show of tucking them into the scrip which hung from his belt and threw himself up into the saddle. "They will fall out of it, I'm afraid , before I reach the road," he mouthed to his wife as she smiled at him. Then he turned his horse and was gone.

Practically before he had vanished from their sight, Edith strode off towards one of the little workshops which littered the compound. There was a little tapping sound coming from within, and she pushed back the door to reveal a groups of men and boys engrossed in their work. Some were hammering metal on leather pads. Others were smelting small pots of liquid then pouring it into moulds. Sparks flew through the air like a rainbow of stars as the molten metal hit the moulds, landing safely on the leather aprons and armguards they were all wearing. The room was as hot as Hell.

"Grimwald! I fear that you are busy."

"Never too busy to speak to you, my lady," the man seated at the bench had turned and stood, wiping his hands down his tunic, conscious of the sweat and grime on them. "Would you like to sit?" He cringed as he realised the only stool in the room was the one he had left and it was just as filthy as his hands had been. Eagdyth smiled in thanks and perched herself elegantly on the stool without a flinch. That, thought Grimwald, is the sign of a true lady. He waved at the others to show some respect and remove their hoods, and he stood clutching his in both hands, afraid that he had committed some terrible mistake.

"Please, relax yourself. I have only come to you to ask if some little favour can be done for me. I have some old jewellery that I wear no longer, and some things that belonged to my mother that she was never too fond of. I want to know, could you possible melt it down and form it into something that could be used, for instance, for a traveller to pay his way. Or somesuch. Can it be done?"

Grimwald scratched his head in thought. He had no interest in why his mistress might need to do this, just what could be done. "We could make some little moulds, and pour the melted gold into them. That would work. If we made them small enough then they might serve as well as coinage, at least in foreign parts. Yes, my lady, it can be done."

Edith breathed a sigh of relief. In her hand, hidden among her skirts, she held a bag which she emptied out onto the workbench. There was as clatter as chains, bangles, torcs and rings fell onto the table in a glittering , sinuous mass. "Get on with it, Grimwald, quick as you can but," she stepped closer and whispered in the goldsmith's ear, "Make sure no word of it goes beyond these walls. For my sake." For her, he would have poured the molten gold straight into his hand, had she asked him to.

The man was as good as his word. A half-week had not gone by before he stood smartly in the doorway to the great hall, a large sack in hand. The steward looked at him in disdain, then lead him through to the solar, where Edith was just finishing stitching the braid onto a new tunic for her husband. She smiled, inviting Grimwald to sit at the table beside her and dismissing the steward. Leaning forward, she lifted the heavy sack from the goldsmith's hand and pouring the contents onto the table. There were bags, lots of them, and in each one were ten small pieces of bright gold. He had fashioned them into blocks, longer than they were wide. When he saw the puzzled expression on Edith's face he smiled. He had done that for a very good reason and he was just going to have to show her what it was.

CHAPTER 25

If Harold had been an elderly woman, people would have decried him as a witch. As it was, all he could do was to be thankful that he had foreseen the outcome of the meeting and prepared for the worst. Five days. That was all the time the family had to attend to their business before they had to leave the country. As soon as the verdict was announced, the family had scattered to the winds. Their mounts had been readied and no time had been wasted in retribution. Whatever had gone before, now *was* the time for action. Harold reached Waltham as the moon scudded out from behind a cloud and illuminated the smoke rising through the thatch. Reining back, he stared at the peaceful scene before him. He was about to destroy it.

Sleeping bodies cluttered the floor and benches. Steadying himself, Harold picked his way between the figures, avoiding hands, heads and feet for fear of waking the whole room. His hounds were lying by the cooling hearth and idly lifted their heads to stare at him. Happy that they recognised the intruder they stretched and yawned, sprawling on top of each other as they went back to their dreams. He slipped through the door to the bedchamber, bread and cheese clutched in one hand, a flagon of mead in the other. Their steward might be haughty sometimes and pernickety at others but he took his job seriously and when the guard alerted him that the Earl was home he had a snack in Harold's hand before he could sneeze.

Harold perched himself in the window recess, hungrily swallowing the bread and cheese and washing it down with the amber liquid. He edged the shutters open a crack, and for a moment or two he watched the moonglow light up the sleeping figure of his wife. A perfect image to keep in his mind for however long they would be parted.

"Are you coming to bed or not, only there is a terrible draught through that window and I shall end up with a stiff neck in the morning." Harold pushed the shutter closed again and knelt beside the bed, inhaling the scent of Edith's hair as he softly kissed her neck,

"I thought you were asleep, love."

"It would have taken a draught of poppy juice to enable me to sleep through your racket. You sound like one of your hounds when you eat, you know. In any case, I was only dozing. I had a feeling you might be back tonight." Edith yawned, turning over to look her husband in the eye,

"So it went as you feared?" Harold nodded sorrowfully. "How long?"

"Five days, my darling, and I have to be gone from these shores."

"Well, stop wasting time, then," she murmured, throwing back the coverlet and inviting him to bed.

Throwing wide the shutters, Edith felt the sun warm against her bare skin. Padding back to bed she burrowed her way under the bedding, kissing every inch of flesh that she came across until her head popped out into daylight and she found herself eye to eye with Harold. He was stroking his moustache, trying to hide the grin on his face. Well, she thought to herself, if I have to be thought of as a wicked mistress, steeped in the sins of the flesh ,then I might as well enjoy it. She let him push her onto her back, encouraged his kisses across her breasts and her stomach and didn't complain at all when he lay on her and satisfied his lust, and hers. Perhaps the mistress thing had a lot to recommend it after all, she giggled as she covered his body with hers and, to his surprise, made love to him.

Reality soon pushed its way into their cocoon, though, and Harold dragged himself from the bed with the reluctance of a bridegroom. He dressed in silence, leaving the room to allow the maid in to assist his wife to do the same. Wilone brushed her hair out quietly, teasing out the tangles Harold's searching fingers had caused. She had known her mistress since she was a tot and could read her moods like a well worn book. There was trouble in the air. She could almost taste it. Without asking, she held up the gown she knew the Earl loved to see Edith in best and slipped it over her mistress' head. Before she could leave, Edith grasped Wilone's wrist,

"Promise me, whatever should happen, you will do and say exactly as I ask you. I will need someone I trust to talk to, and you are the person I trust above all." She reached out for the older woman, hugging her hard. Wilone stroked her hair, like a mother would a child. For Edith to behave like this she must be terrified,

Edmond clattered into the compound that
morning, hair blown about by the wild ride to his Earl's
call. As soon as he had received Harold's message he had
set off to reach Waltham as quickly as he could. Harold
took him straight into the solar and shut the door
firmly. Whatever he wanted to discuss, he did not want
Edith to hear, but in truth she had enough trouble
keeping the children under control. The boys were
lined up before her, lead by an indignant Godwin, who
wanted to know why he had not been warned of his
father's return. They were desperate for him to know
what an excellent job they had done of keeping the
stables and kitchen in perfect order. The girls were
struggling to drag a huge basket of apples between
them, up the step into the hall. They wanted dadda to
eat them, they said, because they had saved him all the
bestest ones. Edith threw her hands up in mock despair.
They would have to learn patience. Father was talking
to Lord Edmond and had not to be disturbed. Then
Magnus and Edmund flopped to the floor in a huff
while Godwin tapped his foot in a show of annoyance
while Gunnhild and Gytha burst promptly into tears.
At just that moment the solar door flew open and there
stood Harold, hands on hips and asking what the noise
was all about. The children ran at him, all babbling at

once what they wanted their father to hear. The great Earl laughed, sitting down cross legged on the floor, to be swamped by his loving family.

Eventually the children were satisfied. The boys had grown at least an inch in stature with their father's heartfelt thanks for their work and Harold munched away on an apple, telling his girls that it was undoubtedly the sweetest that he had ever tasted. Pulling his daughters on to his lap, he gestured to the boys to sit down beside him.

"I am proud of you all, for the way in which you have done as I asked you, and I have to ask even more of you now. I have to go away, to Dublin with your uncle Leofric, and I cannot say when we will be back. As that is so I want you to keep on with the duties I have given you. Godwin, you are coming to an age where you need to know what it is to be a man with the responsibilities that brings. I have asked the lord Edmond here to take you under his wing, to begin to teach you what you need to know to take up your place in the world." Edmond smiled at the boy, then glanced up at his mother, catching the flash of worry that crossed her otherwise impassive face.

"But father, I am doing well in my lessons, Brother Oswin says so. I can read and I can write a little and I can reckon my numbers! I try hard with my sword training and I can ride as well as any boy I have met. " He jutted his jaw with pride and not a little worry, "What else would you have me learn that Grandfather could not teach me, if you are not here?"

Harold felt a gnawing at his heart, "Grandfather is going away too. He is going with Grandmother and Uncle Gyrth to see your Uncle Tostig and new Aunt Julia in Flanders. And before you make protest , boy, Uncle Swein is going on pilgrimage to Jerusalem. Lord Edmond is a good man and a loyal thegn. He will help you to understand the responsibilities a lord must undertake. Hopefully I shall be home before he has the chance to teach you anything that you will be able to correct me on! He has offered to remain here for a while and I have agreed. I trust that he will make sure that you keep up with your lessons and with any chores he sees fit." Edmond made an exaggerated bow, causing the boys to dissolve in a fit of giggles. They dragged him off to show him around the compound leaving the girls trailing in their wake, still tugging their apple basket along with them.

The room seemed to echo with words that could not be said. Neither Edith nor Harold wanted to move, for to do so would mean his leaving. The pain became too much. Harold stepped quietly to Edith's side and took her hands in his.

"I promise I shall be back. My father is not a spent force yet, and I have a feeling that the King is not quite so in the thrall of De Jumieges as that prattling prelate would hope. Swein has no hope of return, the king declared him a nithing and this time he truly means it, but as for the rest of us.... Oh God, sometimes I wish that I was a scion of some other branch."

"But then would we have met? I am not a fool. I know how your father likes to be in charge of everything and everyone around him, but your strength is from him, and you learned from him how important family is. I am stronger than you think, my love. I will keep everything safe until you return to me, have no fear." Edith placed her head on his shoulder, inhaling his scent and filling her mind with him. Deep inside, and she did not understand why, she knew without doubt he would be safe."

Harold picked through the objects in the chest,

mentally ticking off the list of his needs. Clothes were there, and blankets, a heavy leather cloak for bad weather, and chainmail. Here was his helm and here his coif and gambeson, and a few bags of coins but nothing like enough for his needs. He turned in irritation to see a smug look on Edith's face. How could she even think he would be able to hire troops on such meagre rations? And now she was clapping her hands in glee!

Edith felt pleased. The trick that Grimwald had taught her had fooled even as sophisticated a man as her husband. Deftly, she picked out one of the blankets and began to fiddle with the edge, unpicking the hemming with her teeth. Then she held it up, shaking it , then giggling with glee as the shower of golden bars fell into Harold's cupped hands.

"If all the gold had been in bags, how easy would it be for anyone to take them from the chest? They would not have to search for it; it could be done within a moment. This way it is hidden. I suppose you have not noticed it sewn into the quilting of your gambeson, or in the lining at the bottom of the chest?" Harold threw up his hands in surrender. He should have trusted that his clever and cunning wife would have followed out his instructions to the letter. To hide the gold this way was just what he should have expected from her. But now it was time to load the chest onto the cart which waited outside. It was nearly time to part.

"I am meeting Leofwine at Bosham, then we shall sail over to Dublin together. The king will welcome us, I am sure. Particularly with the wealth I am bringing to him. I am sorry about that, though, that you had to melt your own jewellery to help me. That is not how it should be. Anyway, at least I can get enough support to return to you." Harold murmured, voice kept low to avoid eavesdroppers.

"I am not worried about gold. I would give everything I have for you. You will be safe, I know it. But do look after Leofwine, won't you? He is liable to get himself into trouble, even without Gyrth's help." They both laughed. The thought of Leofwine involved in such a serious situation was just too incongruous. Harold pecked Edith fleetingly on the cheek, then climbed up into his saddle. With a wave of his hand he was gone.

CHAPTER 26

Christmas seemed strange without the Earl there to lead the revelries. Edmond had offered to take the family back to his home at Walsingham, but Edith refused. She had no intention of acting like the kind of woman who would weep over the breaking of a nail. Aside from which, she had a home to run, children to raise and tenants to feed.

She leaned back against the high table, nodding in approval. The hall servants were heaving great armfuls of holly and ivy in through the doors and hanging it all around the walls. The smell of fresh greenery filled the air, triggering memories of past years in all who smelled it. The first swirls of snow were blowing through the door, melting in the warmth. The wall hangings had been dusted and the thread of gold glittered in the glow from the rushlights on the walls and the candles that festooned the tables. The high table was furnished with bright pewter plate and goblets of glass, heavy stemmed and casting rainbows where the light hit them. From outside came the squealing and laughter of the party who were hauling in the Yule log. Edmond had decided to stay over the Yule season, and had taken charge of the selecting of the log from the surrounding woods and the transport back to the hall for burning. Godwin was following him round like a puppy dog, watching his every move and marking his every word. He was taking his father's orders very seriously indeed.

Gunnhild and Gytha came hurtling into the hall and ran to their mother, cheeks bright from the cold winter air. Grabbing her hands, they pulled her towards the door to see the log and to give her approval. Godwin walked up to her and offered his arm, like a gentleman, and escorted her around the great piece of oak lying on the frozen ground. It was indeed a very fine piece of timber and it would certainly burn for the full length of Yule, so she nodded to the assembled crew, peasant and lord alike, and with a cheer they dragged it into the hearth to be burned.

The feast was, even by royal standards, extraordinary. Mead and wine flowed like a ceaseless river of warmth. There were geese, venison, eels, beef piled high on every plate; spiced and herb strewn, tender and delicious. If the diner still had room they could gorge on curd cheese pastries and honey shortbreads, sweet and sticky. Edith had truly decided to celebrate in style. She wore a deep blue gown with a silken veil, bounded by a twisted band of gold. Her belt held a buckle and tongue decorated with tiny enamelled forget me nots, matched by the clasped cuffs around her wrists. Neck and hem were bounded with embroidered braid threaded through with strands of gold. She could have passed for a queen in any land. The children, too, were dressed in their finest ware and thrilled at being allowed to stay for the whole feast. Musicians sang and played, jugglers amazed, scops told tales old and new, ladies danced with their suitors. All in all, it was a magnificent affair.

"You seem to have made your point, my lady." Edmond was licking the crumbs from his shortcake from his fingers. Edith demurred,

"I really don't know what you mean, Edmond. If you are saying that I put on a delightful spread for our Yule celebrations then I thank you for the compliment."

"Indeed, my lady. In fact, I doubt the king himself has sat down to a better table. If I did not know better I should think you were showing that it was, as you might say, business as usual within the Godwin family."

Edith sniffed, "And yet it is not, Edmond, nor will it be until my husband is seated at his own table. However," she grinned conspiratorially, "if that is how this is perceived, then it might just remind our King that out of sight is not necessarily out of mind. But of course, I am not part of that family, am I? Just the mistress of a noble lord who has been cruelly set aside."

Edith slipped closed the door behind her and threw herself face down onto her bed. The strain of seeming to be without a care had given her a headache. She called to her maid to pull out the long pins which held her veil in place, then shook loose her hair, teasing through it with her fingers until it lay across her shoulders. Wilone helped her out of the heavy gown and hung it up to air, placing the fine gold objects back into the chest for safe keeping. Eagdyth motioned the maid to leave her and she lay back on the bed to allow her thoughts time to settle. Then she slipped her hand beneath her pillow and drew out a thin cylinder of parchment. Lives had been risked to get this letter to her; it deserved to be treated with care.

"My dearest heart. I have sent this to let you know

that I am safe here in Dublin. The crossing was awful and Leofwine was sick as could be. He is no sailor. King Diarmid is an excellent host and his court is as grand as its reputation says. He tells me that he will certainly furnish us with ships and men when we are ready to return home, but only if he is secure in his own seat. Very subtle, I thought. He wants our help to dispose of his enemies before he will reciprocate. I cannot get word to father. It would be too much to expect word to reach him without being intercepted. I expect he has a plan of his own by now in any case. Leofwine has been surprisingly useful so far; he has a gift for picking up languages quickly, it seems. He has even found himself some female admirers, buxom and bonny to a woman! Be sure that I miss you and the children, and I will return to you as soon as ever I can. Your lord and love, Harold Godwinson."

Edith carefully curled the letter back up and hugged it to her breast. To hear from Harold was a greater gift than she could have asked. Not only that, he was working on his return. It was only a question of staying patient.

"Wake up, my lady, wake up!" Edith was sitting bolt upright in bed, eyes staring unseeing at the far wall.

She was dripping in sweat, despite the cold, and her heart was pounding so hard Wilone could see it against her sweat soaked shift. The maid shook her mistress' shoulders as hard as she dared as she tried to bring her back from wherever her dreams had taken her. Nothing was working; it seemed that time had stopped, but she suddenly turned to face the maid: eyes wide, not with fear but surprise.

"Did you see her?" Edith's breath came panting with each word. Wilone looked around the room, afraid she might have missed some intruder,

"See who, my lady? No-one has entered the room since I went to bed. Perhaps it was a nightmare; they can seem so real sometimes."

Edith slipped quietly back under the covers and placed her head gently on her sweat soaked pillow. It was no dream, of that she was certain. She recognised the face as quickly as if she had seen it yesterday. The sweet face, the dark hair, the gentle hand reaching towards her; it was her lady, that was certain. Edith could still hear her words circling in her brain, though her mouth did not open once. She would care for Harold; she swore it and Edith knew that she would. But the lady wanted something in return , as she had said so long ago, and Edith had been shown exactly what it was.

CHAPTER 27

For the next few days, although she went about her business with her usual efficiency and grace, Edith seemed to be elsewhere. She barely spoke, answering questions with one syllable answers when she spoke at all. Wilone was concerned. If her mistress was ill then someone of importance needed to know. The only person around who fitted that bill was Edmond.

In truth, he too had noticed the change in Edith's demeanour after that night and he had delayed his return home for a few weeks in case there was a problem. When the maid had spoken to him, all curtseys and red faced embarrassment at what she felt was a betrayal to her lady, he drew in a deep sigh. It wasn't his imagination running wild ,then. Something was definitely on her mind, and it fell to him, Edmond to broach the subject as carefully as he could.

As it transpired, Edith herself approached him. He had taken the older boys out to hunt boar, their first ever ride after the dangerous prey, and they had all clattered into the hall with their laughter ringing to the rafters. Edith was seated near the fire, spinning wool, with her feet perched neatly on a footstool and a rug thrown over her knees for warmth. She had been humming to herself, stopping when the rowdy children rushed up to her, hugging her with cold hands and ruddy cheeks. She sent them off at once to change out of their wet clothing, but as Edmond bowed to leave she held up a hand to detain him. He pulled up a three legged stool and sat opposite her, trying to get some warmth into his frozen hands. He looked up at Edith inquiringly.

"Remind me, Edmond. Your home is called Walsingham, is it not? I seem to remember passing through there once, with my lord. If I recall correctly, it was a beautiful place."

Edmond smiled, "Indeed it is , my lady. I would hazard to say it is the most wonderful stretch of land in this country or any other. True, there are no rolling hills or towering peaks. The land is gentle, soft to the eye. It is good for the growing too. For crops, yes, but for woodlands too! The trees grow so tall, like great spires reaching up to the heavens. As lovely as it is here, my lady, I miss it awfully."

Laughing, Edith placed her spindle firmly onto her lap, "In which case, dear Edmond, I insist that you return to your own hall at once. On one condition, however. I have a mind to accompany you; and the children too if you will have us. They must be starting to feel a little trapped here, as do I. That aside, I have a fancy to find somewhere that might serve as a place to build a shrine in thanks for my husband's safety. Only, of course if he should return safe to us. Call it superstition, or even a woman's whim, but it will make me feel that I am doing something useful."

Edmond nodded. Worry. That must have been why Edith had been acting oddly. Thank goodness that it was nothing serious.

Wilone grumbled to herself as she packed the clothes chests and tied them closed. Her mistress must have lost her senses, to want to travel anywhere at this time of year. It was not necessary; therefore, from Wilone's point of view ,they ought to stay where they were safe and warm rather than go through all the hassle that moving Edith and her entourage brought with it. Her mistress could hardly fail to notice the maid's irritation so, after a great deal of thought, she summoned Wilone to her bedchamber.

Edith was seated by the window, hands folded neatly on her lap. The maid curtseyed low. Her stomach was churning. Had she pushed her luck a little too far this time? After all, it was not for servants to judge the decisions of their masters. Tremblingly, she seated herself next to Edith when beckoned. She could feel a soft, gentle hard being placed on her rough ,red one and looked up to see Edith smiling in her direction. On her lap was a small and battered scrip, the leather stiffened with age. Edith was stroking it , gently, as if it contained something deeply precious.

"I know you are annoyed at me Wilone, but I am going to tell you why I am acting as I am. You might think me a liar when I explain, or deluded, but I believe what I am going to tell you is a Holy truth." Edith took in a deep breath. Never had she told anyone about the lady, but it was time now to share her secret,

"When I was little, out on the marshes, I saw a lady who I knew somehow to be very, very special. She was dressed in deepest blue and gold, and she told me to remember her. That was the day that Earl Godwin brought Harold to our home, if you recall it. I saw her again when my father died. She promised that she would care for him, and left rose petals by his body in the coffin. I took one, and put it in this scrip. Now think, Wilone, how many years ago that was. Look."

Edith slid her hand into the pouch and slowly withdrew it. She turned her hand over and slowly opened her slender fingers. There, nestled in her palm was a petal. A blood red rose petal, soft and fresh as if it had just fallen from the bud. The maid's eyes opened wide in shock. She reached forward to touch the precious object and as she did so felt a tingle of warmth spreading throughout her being.

"She came to me again, Wilone. She came in a dream. She said she would take care of the Earl, that he would be safe. But she wants me to do something in return. The lady is the Holy Mother, Wilone, I am certain of it and she wants me to build a shrine to her, to praise the birth of her Son. It will be fashioned to look like the home of the Holy Family, when our Lord was a child. The thing is, I want to build it in the most beautiful place, as it deserves, and the most wonderful place I have ever been is Lord Edmond's holding of Walsingham. She wants me to do this now and I will not deny her. You understand now, don't you?" Edith was staring deep into the eyes of her oldest and closest companion. It was obvious that she wanted someone to believe in this as much as she did.

The maid stood, slowly removing her fingers from the petal. The heady scent was still strong in her nostrils, more beautiful and unearthly than any incense could ever be. Then she fell to her knees in prayer. It was all the reassurance that Edith needed.

CHAPTER 28

Edmond stood with his hands on hips, whip dangling by his side and brushing against his riding boots. He was trying to resist the urge to brag about how beautiful his land was. Already he had been regaling Edith with tales of the fertility of the soil and the fullness of the granaries. They had been following a narrow road through a little wood, shafts of watery sunshine spearing between the naked branches. The boys were bouncing along on their little ponies, Godwin insisting on riding without being lead by a groom . Gytha and Gunnhild were sitting on the bench next to the driver of the carriage, driving him to distraction with their endless questions. Suddenly, without warning, they found themselves on the edge of a great clearing. A river lazed its way across the landscape, weaving back and forward in easy loops. Edmond tugged on the rein of his horse, turning it to follow the bank . He realised, with a start, that he had ridden on ahead of the rest of the party. Edith was cantering towards him, gesturing to him to dismount.

"Over there, Edmond, alongside the river, can I see a road?"

Edmond nodded. It was one of the pack horse roads that wove between the villages and the market towns, linking the little centres of humanity with one another. Just hiving into view, on the horizon's edge, was the compound of Walsingham. It was home, and feeling the chill in the air Edmond would be glad to reach there.

By the time he had chance to remount, Edith had ridden on ahead, to where the road crossed the river by a sturdy stone bridge. She threw herself to the ground and was surveying the land with a huge grin on her face. Edmond galloped up to her, face filled with concern,

"Be careful, my lady! This land is waterlogged at this time of year. You will get wet!"

Edith threw her reins to Edmond, and began to hitch her skirts up, tucking them into the belt around her waist. She pulled off her shoes and stockings, throwing them towards the astonished thegn to hold, before stepping carefully onto the marshy soil,

"I was born on land like this, Edmond! I spent my entire childhood exploring on the marshes at home," she laughed with genuine delight. She felt like a child again, stepping lightly from tussock to tussock with the mud squirming between her toes. Curlews spun around her in the air shrieking noisily as they spiralled upwards; bright clouds scudded above them across the wintry sky. The air felt sharp as a knife and smelled of the salt of the sea. Somehow, this place felt right. It was where the Holy Mother wanted her to build.

Thankfully, Edmond had managed to provide Edith with a bath tub, lined with cloths and filled with deliciously warm water. She wiped the streaks of mud from her shins, then slipped deeper into the water up to her shoulders. Wilone was standing beside her, dabbing the drips of water from her hair, "I take it that you found the place you were looking for? It is good that the Earl was not here to see you prancing around like an eelcatcher's wife emptying the traps!"

Edith laughed and threw a cloth at her maid. Harold, of all people, would understand. He understood that beneath the veneer of sophistication beat the heart of the scruffy little mud skipper he had first met so long past.

The thegn bowed in delight. For Edith to decide to build a shrine and a priory here, in his manor, was a great honour. Aside from which, it would create work for the masons and bring in wealth from the pilgrims who visited and it was always wise to keep the ceorls happy. Of course, as she pointed out, she would need to speak to someone from the Church before she could begin the process and as far as she was concerned there was the rub. The thought of being in the same room as De Jumieges made her want to spit. He was a spiteful, power grabbing devil as far as she was concerned. And yet worse, he was a Norman to boot. There was no way on earth that she would make obeisance to the slimy toad who, she was certain, had twisted the king's thoughts against her lord and his family. She needed a plan.

Harold sat, elbows on knees, blowing warmth into his hands as he stared out across the sea towards home. He was by nature a patient man, but it was difficult to think of his wife and family being so far away. At least Edward was fair minded. He would not make them suffer just because of their ties of kinship. After all, he had not even divorced Ealdyth, although his lack of an heir would have given him just cause. De Jumieges had not had everything his way. Hearing a giggle, he turned round to catch sight of Leofwine disappearing beneath an upturned boat hull, hand in hand with one of the serving wenches from Diarmid's court. He seemed to have grown up so much away from the heavy hand of their father. Before this, he would never have thought Leofwine would make a good lieutenant, but he had watched and listened and learned from those around him here in Ireland. The giggles soon turned to the moans of lovemaking so Harold stood up, stretched his limbs, and headed back towards the King's enclosure. He needed no reminder of what he was missing.

Gytha was also thinking of home. It was pleasant enough in Flanders. Duke Baldwin had been most welcoming to the whole family, and even seemed to have taken Tostig under his wing which was just as well for everyone. He had ever been a moody child and ever since their expulsion he seemed more bitter than ever. It was almost as if he took it all as a personal slight rather than just politics. Swein had set off on his pilgrimage and seemed, finally, to have come to terms with himself. He had sworn that he would return a better human being ready to be the father that Hakon deserved. Even Gyrth seemed happy. He had struck up a friendship with the Duke's eldest son, young Baldwin, and the pair revelled at the hunting and hawking that life in Bruges offered them. Even so, Gytha felt nervous. As delightful as the hospitality was, she knew that they would soon outstay their welcome and Godwin was getting fidgety. He wanted to be back in England putting the Norman upstarts in their places and this could not sit well with Baldwin for ever, especially as his daughter was wed to the Norman Duke William himself. Hopefully, now he had acquired the mercenaries he needed and the boats to carry them he would be able to expend some of that pent up energy finding them all a way back home.

Edith smiled graciously at the prelate seated at her table. She proffered another goblet of wine, which he accepted without pause. As he sipped at the ruby liquid Edith too k the opportunity to weigh up her guest. Bishop Ealdred was small in stature and grey haired, but full of energy and brightness of spirit. He had found reason to meander his way across country and found himself at Edmond's manor at the same time as

Harold's family. Of course, it was in no way related to the missive he had received from Edith outlining her plans for Walsingham. Such a happy coincidence, he purred. Now they were alone together and it was time to find out exactly what it was that she wanted of him.

"I will come straight to the point, my Lord Bishop." Ealdred smiled to himself. She had read him well. Although he was well versed in the veiled language of Court, he disliked and distrusted it. "Since I was a child I have had meetings with Our Holy Mother. I suppose you might call them visions. It is her desire that a shrine is built to Her, in the form of the house that the Holy Family shared in Nazareth. She wants it to be built here at Walsingham, my Lord and I have promised that I shall do this. Of course, it would make the path much simpler if I have the blessing of Mother Church." She paused to drain her goblet to the dregs, then stared the Bishop in the eye, "Whether I do or not, the shrine and its priory will be built. I always fulfil my promises."

There was a heavy silence as the two held each other's gaze that seemed to last an aeon. Finally, the Bishop's face cracked into a smile and he proffered his hand towards Edith. "Well, then, I suppose that we ought to go and survey the site of this new edifice."

The sun broke through the cloud, like a spear from Heaven. The riders pulled their mounts to a halt and sat in silence, staring as if entranced at the scene before them. The beam of light was illuminating something that should not be there, not in the cold edge of Winter's end. But there it was. A field of the most beautiful flowers bloomed before them; lilies and myrtle, marigolds and violets, and rising above them all in sweet profusion grew roses, white and red. The scent was almost overpowering in its sweetness. Then, almost before they had chance to take breath, the cloud scudded back across the sun's face and the land before them was bare. Edmond was trembling in shock, almost unable to believe what he had seen. He looked across to Bishop Ealdred and Edith. She was smiling at the priest as if they were sharing some secret knowledge.

"The Church will be glad to sanction your building, my dear. I see now exactly why you want to put it in this place. Truly, it is blessed by hands more sacred than these." He looked down at his own, as if trying to be sure that he was not dreaming. It was not for him to question why the Virgin had chosen to appear to a mother unwed in the eyes of the Church. The miracle he had seen proved it to him beyond any earthly measure.

CHAPTER 29

Springtime came to Waltham in a rush. Flowers and leaves leapt into life on every hedgerow; lambs gambolled in the meadows and birds darted hither and yon garnering sticks to construct their nests. Edith too was busy. Now she had something to occupy her mind, and she set about the preparations with all her energy and verve. She needed to employ a master builder who could understand her vision and help to bring it to life. Bishop Ealdred had suggested a man who had been involved in work on the cathedral at Worcester and he could not have been more perfect, in Edith's view. He had arrived on foot, with a raggle taggle group of workmen and their families, much to the amusement of the children. They had never been in contact with quite such a colourful band before and in no time at all they were chasing around playing catch and hide and seek, much to the horror of their tutor. He ran around like a shepherd's dog, trying to round them up for their lessons, before throwing his hands up in defeat. His appeal to Edith fell on deaf ears. Lessons would wait, she admonished. Learning to deal with people was just as important as the most complex mathematical concept and , to her mind, would be much a much more useful skill.

As the women set about organising the little camp, Edith invited the master builder, Alfred of Malmesbury, into the great hall. Summoning one of the servants, she ordered bread and cheese to be sent to those outside and meat for her guest. The steward brought a flagon of wine with two cups, leaving it on the table for the lady Edith to pour. Once the builder had eaten his fill, it was time to get down to business.

"So, my lady, the priory will be built using the flint that is local to the site. That will make it easier to get the materials . I can build it to the same design as those I have built before if that is your wish. The shrine, on the other hand, well I have to say I am still not completely certain what you want. Maybe you can use these to show me." He reached down into a sack by his side and pulled out a handful of wooden blocks, pushing them towards Edith and sitting back patiently. Slowly, uncertainly at first, she began to move the blocks around,standing them one atop the other, trying to create the picture she had in her mind. She stuck out her tongue in concentration as the little walls grew slowly higher, topped by a roof that was flat.

Alfred looked at the model with a critical eye.

" I can see what you are aiming at, my lady. It is a simple enough design, and can be made from stone blocks. The roof could be a problem, though. It will need to have a slight pitch on it to shed the rain. It cannot be completely flat."

Edith nodded in agreement. She was happy now that he understood exactly what was required. All that needed to be done now was to discuss the fine details,

"Edmond, the thegn whose manor the building is to take place, will oversee this project on my behalf. He is the one you will speak to if you need anything that we have not already agreed to. I have given him what should be enough money to finance the building, but if more is needed then he will inform me and I will either agree or not. If you concur, then I see no reason why you cannot begin as soon as possible."

Alfred laughed, then stood with his hand outstretched,

"The good Bishop told me that you were not a

woman to be trifled with! I am happy to agree, my lady, and I thank you. I pray that my work will be exactly what you desire,"

A wave of satisfaction flooded over Edith. She had fulfilled her promise to the Holy Mother and she felt sure now that her husband would soon be safely speeding across the sea to her side.

If she had known how close he was at that moment, she would have leapt to her feet to run to him. Since the beginning of March, the Godwins had begun to launch raids all along the south coast. Little ones at first, probing and prodding to see if the king had set up stronger defences than they expected. Edward had committed a fatal move, in Godwin's eyes, that left the whole country in danger. Money was at the root of every decision and in order to keep down the tax burden Edward had dismissed the navy from his service. Now he, Godwin, would show the king just what a bad decision that was.

There were rumours that his father had been a pirate, and if that was so then the son was like the father. Beginning with those of his thegns who had refused to come to his side, he pillaged and destroyed then fled as fast as he had appeared. Again and again he sallied forth, teasing and taunting. It was then that he sent word to Harold and Leofwine.

The brothers had waited anxiously for word from their father, but for different reasons. Harold could hardly wait to leap into action, desperate to get under way before Diarmaid had chance to change his mind about offering men and ships. But Leofwine was terrified. He had hated sailing through the storm , when he had been so sick he thought he would die and he dreaded the same thing happening again. Harold mocked him gently but he understood. They had lost men overboard that night, never to be found. Aside from that, for the first time in his life, Leofwine thought himself in love. The thought of leaving his little servant girl made him depressed, so much so that the thought occurred to him that he might just stay in Ireland. Harold rolled his eyes in despair. He could imagine the scene if he had to tell his father that Leofwine had run off with a servant girl. The prospect was far too awful. When he had pointed out to his brother exactly how furious Godwin would be the flames of love were somewhat dampened. Leofwine might be lovelorn, but he was no fool.

As soon as word came they set sail, Leofwine's girl

blubbing on the quay and waving until they were out of sight. "You didn't tell her you weren't going back did you?" Harold raised an eyebrow and fixed his brother firmly with his gaze. Leofwine stared at the floor, shifting from foot to foot uncomfortably. "Well, so long as you haven't left her with something to remember you by." Leofwine blushed crimson. " Oh, no! She is with child?" Leofwine nodded miserably. Harold threw an arm around his shoulder, "Perhaps as well to make a quick escape then!" The last thing he needed now was his brother's attention to be elsewhere. They would need their wits about them for Godwin's plan to succeed.

CHAPTER 30

It had been inevitable, really. Edward had scrabbled together a pitiful fleet to face the battle honed ships of Earl Godwin and his sons. Casting round for willing captains, he had bid his nephew Ralph de Mantes and the Earl Odda to take command. An inexperienced lad and an old man sent against experienced admirals could only end one way, and that was in shambolic defeat. Edward was furious; not at Ralph and Odda but at himself for allowing his Norman allies to talk him into the whole sorry plot. Where were they now, he raged to himself. Gone, disappeared like frost on a sunny morning, leaving him to taste the bitterness of defeat and the pain of the return of that irritating Earl.

Godwin clambered up onto the gunwales of his dragon ship and stepped onto English land again. It felt good to have had one last battle but he was feeling the weight of his years. Perhaps it was time to let the next generation step forward whilst he gave Gytha some of the attention that he had deprived her of through their marriage. He had visions of sitting in the Great Hall at Bosham, a fire roaring on the hearth as his grandchildren chattered around him and his wife rested her head on his shoulder. Eventually every old war horse needed turning out to grass and, he thought, this was his time. Harold had done well in Dublin, and despite his misgivings so had Leofwine. They had not needed his hand hovering over their shoulders. Let the young fight the battles now.

The king waited at Westminster, pacing up and down nervously. He could hear cheers from the crowds which lined the route up from the docks. It had not taken long for word of the Earls' return and everyone wanted to say that they had been there; they had seen the moment. Finally, the brigand lords marched into view. They strode up towards the hastily assembled platform where the king stood alone. Behind him stood his nephew Ralph and Bishop Stigand, along with a rank of loyal housecarls. The king had been left with no choice other than to rescind his order of expulsion after the debacle at the mouth of the Thames . Edward's fleet had scattered at the first sight of the enemy like chaff in the wind and even though Edward had refused at first to allow them to land ultimately he had no choice. There was strength in numbers it seemed. The Godwin family were stronger than he was and that was an end to it.

It seemed as if time had slowed to a standstill. The Earl stared Edward in the eye, locking his stare for a split second longer than was necessary. Then, he fell to his knees before the king, head bowed. Edward had to step from the platform to lay hand on head in forgiveness. The whole assembly heaved a great sigh of relief. The sons of Godwin stepped forward and knelt behind their father, four great Earls, promising obedience to their liege lord from then onwards. Mentally, Edward counted the cost; the cost of placating the lords who had been given the Godwin's lands and had now lost them; the cost of looking weak and foolish to every avaricious duke and prince in Europe but worst of all the cost of knowing that Godwin might as well be wearing his crown.

As soon as word had reached her, Edith had gathered together her boys and ridden hard to reach London before her husband. It was almost impossible to believe that he was back so soon. She had expected it to be another year at least before the king would capitulate and let the family return. If he had thought he would be teaching the Godwins a lesson in humility then it had backfired in spectacular style. She had no thought of what to do once her party reached London, only that she wanted the proof of her own eyes that Harold was safe.

She had brought enough men of the household with her to be able to jostle their way almost to the front of the waiting crowds at Westminster. The noise, and chatter, and smell of the crowd was overwhelming and Edith was finding it difficult to concentrate. On tiptoe, she tried to stare across the heads of the people in front of her, searching for sight of the face she knew so well. Magnus had convinced one of the men to let him sit on his shoulders and was laughing with excitement, shouting down to his brothers and pointing at the king and his retinue. Then a great roar erupted, echoing round and round and filling the air with noise you could practically touch.

And she saw him. There, walking towards the king she saw the crown of a tousled blond head, taller than those around him. Closer he came, striding into view, blue eyes bright in a weather tanned face. The salt of the sea was clinging to his leather cloak and glittered like diamonds under the summer sun. He was alive. He was safe. And he was kneeling before the king for forgiveness, surrounded by his brothers and next to his father. She began to elbow her way through the row in front of her, stamping on toes and poking in ribs to get through the crush with the boys trailing in her wake. Finally she was there, with no-one between her and the dais where the family knelt. She stood frozen to the spot, her silvery hair working loose from her veil and blowing across her face, clutching Magnus' hand and warning Edmund and Godwin to wait where they were.

It seemed an age until Harold saw them. Over his father's head he could see, blowing in the wind, that familiar hair he had smelled so often in his dreams. Without a moment's thought, he leapt to his feet and raced across the ground between them , his great strides eating up the ground. Then she was in his arms, almost crushing her with his desire to hold her safe. Edith could feel Harold's heart beating against her chest, powerful and strong. He kissed her and his kiss tasted of the sea and happiness. She wanted to remember that moment for ever and she concentrated hard on every single nerve, each little feeling. Then slowly he released her, just holding gently onto her hand as he hugged his boys, telling them how much they had grown and how grateful he was that they had looked after their mother and sisters for him.

Before they even had chance to speak to each other they were swamped by family, hugging and laughing and crying all at once. Edith felt utterly overwhelmed and was grateful when Harold tugged her hand and lead her towards the guest quarters which belonged to the Palace.

"The king has graciously offered us his hospitality this evening. I expect that he will not want to stretch that any further." Harold held Edith's hands between his, like young lovers.

"It must have been like swallowing broken glass, welcoming you back like that. Whatever else might be said about him, the man has dignity."

Harold nodded, "It is just that he has been badly advised, nothing else. I only hope that he and my father can find peace with each other. We need stability now, not arguments." He looked down at his clothes, crusty with salt and grime. "Dear God I must smell! I haven't had a proper wash in weeks. I hope the King's hospitality will stretch to a bath."

Edith began to drag him over towards the open doorway, "The children seem to be busy with their grandparents. Perhaps you would like some help in removing those clothes and getting clean?"

"Not before I've got more dirty first," growled Harold into her ear as he followed her into the darkness.

CHAPTER 31

They shuffled late into the meal that night, both pink
cheeked and a little embarrassed. Why had she let him
pull her into the bathtub with him? Why had she let
him take her to bed, wrapping the sheets around their
damp bodies as they poured out all the feelings they had
kept close for so long and why had she let him love her
again, slowly and gently, making sure she was satisfied?
They had fallen asleep in a tangle of bare limbs and
damp linen and it was only when Gytha had thought to
knock on their door that they leapt out of bed, giggling
as they tumbled into their clothes and ran across the
courtyard.

Edward was watching from the window in his
solar. He sighed, seeing the two lovers scampering hand
in hand, stopping only for yet another lingering kiss.
The sooner Ealdyth returned to him the better. He was
tired of being surrounded by advisors who were really

only concerned for themselves. True, they had not the lust that was apparent between Edith and Harold, but in his aesthetic way he adored his wife and he knew in his soul that she would never do anything that would cause him harm. He strode across to the table and hastily scratched a note onto the parchment that lay there. Sprinkling sand and warming the sealing wax, he summoned the young thegn who was standing in the doorway, waiting to accompany him to the hall. "Aldin, take this to Wherwell at once. Tell the queen, my wife, that she is required here. No , tell her that I would like her to return to my side, if she so wishes." Aldin nodded, tucking the letter into his belt and striding down the stairs and off to the stables.

Harold sat snug alongside his wife, a smile of satisfaction on his face. He tucked into the food with an appetite born of the sea air and exercise. Edith, meanwhile, took a moment or two to take in the scene. She had to admit that the queen had done a remarkable job in decorating the palace, but the Great Hall was beyond belief. Heavy tapestries hung on every wall, bright with reds, blues and golds. There were silver candlesticks not only on the high table but everywhere. Crystal goblets were filled with wines from across the continent. All in all it reeked of good taste and wealth mixed together in perfect proportions. Very much like home, she thought smugly. Suddenly a movement caught her eye. It was Gytha, and she was heading for the king with an expression of fury written large on her face. She stood before him, hammering the table in fury. The king was holding his hands up, as if in apology, then as the woman burst into tears he consoled her, gesturing to Godwin to come and tend to her. Edith poked Harold with her elbow, then pointed to the tableau. Sighing, he got to his feet and made his way through the throng towards his parents. Just for once could he not enjoy a meal without his family causing him indigestion.

"It's the boys, my love, Wulfnoth and Hakon. It seems that prick de Jumieges has snatched them from the king and run back to Normandy with them. My mother is distraught. So is Edward. It makes him look like a fool who can't control his priests. He seems to think he will have taken them to Duke William , a little gift for his Norman master."

"At least they should be safe there. He is married to Baldwin's daughter, isn't he, and through Tostig that makes him family ."

Harold shrugged. He had learned that life was never

that straightforward.

"For as long as it suits his purpose I am sure they will be fine. Anyway I have other things to worry about, like how soon we can get out of here and back home to Waltham. There are little ones of my own that I haven't seen in far too long."

It seemed that Gytha had other ideas. She insisted that the whole family accompany them back to Bosham, to show to all and sundry that the family was back in force. Harold tutted and sulked like a schoolboy which made Edith collapse in fits of laughter. She could see his point; he was, after all, a grown man and one of the great Earls ,but as far as Gytha was concerned he was her little boy and he would damned well do as he was told. Edith opted to travel in the carriage with the other women. It gave her a chance to get to know Tostig's wife and to chat to her mother-in-law. Judith seemed a pleasant enough girl, quiet and demure, but being amongst the whole of the Godwin clan when they were together was overwhelming to anyone. At least, mused Edith, she was spared the attentions of Swein.

As the carriage rattled along the conversation turned, as ever, towards their menfolk. Gytha pretended to be outraged at the state Edith and Harold had turned up in the previous night. Edith merely said that it had been like trying to fight off a wolf that hadn't eaten in weeks so in the end she had let him have his way or they would never have got beyond the door of their room. Judith blushed scarlet to the roots of her hair , then began to chortle. It seemed Tostig was not quite so busy in the bedroom as his lusty older brother, but what he lacked in quantity he made up for in quality. "Godwin was like that, as rampant as a wild boar. I had to try to tire him out in other ways otherwise I would not have been on my feet before noon and in bed before sundown! In fact, he was still insisting on satisfying his urges every day until very recently." A look of worry passed across the older woman's face, "Between us, it is as if something has changed inside him. He keeps talking about staying at home more, sitting by his own fireside with his children and their children around him, when usually he can't wait to get out with his hounds chasing down the deer." She sighed as Edith patted her lightly on the shoulder, "I wouldn't worry. I expect that he has been turning all his energy towards getting you home safely and he wants to enjoy what he has achieved. At least for a while. Before you know it he will be calling for his hounds again." Judith giggled, "Or chasing you around the bed!"

The raucous laughter caught the attention of Harold, who rode alongside, peering in through the slatted window. Edith sent him away with a flea in his ear, explaining that no good came to Earls and thegns who eavesdropped on the conversations of married women. It warmed his soul to hear the happiness emanating from the carriage. Perhaps life might just get back to normal now.

CHAPTER 32

They stayed for as short a time as they could at Bosham, without upsetting their hosts. All Harold wanted to do was get to his own manor, greet his daughters, ride to his hounds and sleep in his own bed. He had everything he had ever yearned for here at Waltham and had no desire to be anywhere else. Even so, there was a tiny nugget of worry in the back of his mind and it threw a little cloud over the sunshine of his days.

One morning he had ridden out to visit one of the manors on his land and decided, on impulse, to ask his wife to accompany him. The man who had held the land for as long as either of them could remember had died, and his son had taken over from him. It seemed to spark an odd mood in Harold,

"Do you remember old Turstan? He always seemed as strong as an ox and as cussed as a mule. I thought he would outlive me by a long straight. It will be difficult for his lad to follow him. How can he command the same loyalty from his serfs and ceorls? They will forever be comparing the two and the son will doubtless be seen as a lesser man."

Edith studied her husband closely for a moment. It was unlike him to be so philosophical,

"It is always so. The young always have to step into their forebears' shoes, however high a step that is to make. But... I do not think that it is Turstan's boy you are thinking of, are you? Are you thinking of a father closer to home?"

Harold reined his horse in, turning it in until he was sitting knee to knee with his wife but turning his face away. He did not wish her to see the worry in his eyes,

"My father is like Turstan, strong and virile, always quick to act. He is a lion of a man and he has needed to be to hold his Earldom together, let alone keeping the balance of power with Siward of Northumbria and Leofric of Mercia. His whole life has been a fight, and not just to further his own cause. Without his strength, God alone knows what would happen with a king such as ours. But he can't go on forever. Sooner or later he too will die and then......"

"Then one of his sons will have to take up the burden? Is that what you mean?"

"Can you imagine what would happen if it were Swein? The whole bloody country would have taken to arms within a week! I love my brother, but he has never excelled in tact and that is what will be needed in the years to come. Tact and guile."

They rode on in silence for a while, each lost in their own thoughts. Eventually, Edith spoke, her voice low and quiet ,

"Your mother is worried. Godwin has begun to lose interest in the things he used to love, like hunting and hawking or even riding out at all. He has been saying that he wants to retire to Bosham and take up a simpler life. He is getting old, Harold, and he has lived a life that would have worn out a dozen lesser souls. I think that Gytha fears he won't be with us much longer."

It was like opening the bottle and letting the genie out. The words had been said and hung in the air like Damocles' sword. In the distance they could just make out the outline of the manor complex. Things would be hard for Turstan's son, learning how to run the manor and gaining the respect of those around him. How much harder would it be for the son of Godwin to do the same.

They did not speak of it again. Summer was spent enjoying life as a family. The boys were desperate to show their father the skills they had learned at Edmond's manor. They heaved their wooden swords at each other, swinging their weapons until they poured with sweat. Harold beamed with pride at his boys' antics. As the leaves of Autumn began to flutter to the ground they would join him when he went hawking, watching and learning the skills needed to work the beautiful birds which would sit on their father's hand, talons clawing into the heavy leather. He would take his daughters walking with the hound pups, tugging on their leads as they snuffled along the ground, following each and every scent they found. Sometimes Harold and Edith would just sit together by the river, watching the children, tunics and gowns hoisted high and knee deep in the water, trying to catch fish. It was an almost unbearably wonderful time, which could never hope to last but the memory of which Edith would cling to for the rest of her life.

The year wore on, and the air began to feel crisp

with the icy winds of winter. Harold and the boys were out each day on their horses, hounds racing alongside as they chased down deer to fill the table. It was one such day in November when Harold threw open the door, shoulders white with a powdering of the first of the winter snows. Godwin and Edmund were elbowing their way past him and Magnus pulling at his cloak, each trying to be first into the hall. They were all giggling and tussling, but as they barrelled in they caught the eye of their mother. Her expression was stony, and they needed no more warning, running back out to gather snowballs and throw them at one another.

"There was no need to rebuke them, my love," Harold had removed his cloak and was tugging his sodden gauntlets from his fingers. Edith did not reply, but passed him the letter which had been clutched in her hand. Harold sucked in a deep breath, dreading what might be written, He scanned the note, eyes widening in surprise as he read on. He leant against the table to support himself as he felt his legs trembling. Edith pushed an empty seat towards him and he sat, head in hands, unable to speak. Softly, Edith laid her hand against his shoulder, feeling the sobs he was trying to smother as they racked his frame,

"How could it be? I always thought he would die

in bed serving some young wench at the age of ninety, not in a shriven state in some foreign land. Swein? I just cannot believe it. I know he could be a fool but he was still my brother. Swein! Oh God, Edith, he was father's favourite of all his sons. I never thought, he was so strong... how could he die of some sickness? I can hardly believe it."

It was true. Swein was gone. As the news began to sink in the full misery of it began to dawn on Edith and Harold both. He was Godwin's heir now and the responsibility for the whole family would one day fall on his shoulders.

Christmas was spent at Winchester at the invitation of the king. All the great Earls were there, enjoying the chance to feast at the king's expense. Edith watched, fascinated, as the little alliances were made between lords by handshakes and glances. She could see the lords of Mercia and Northumberland, the great men of Harold's father's generation, patting him on the shoulder and bringing him into their confidence, It was all too obvious that he was being drawn into the spider's web that held the king at its centre and it made Edith shudder. On Christmas morning, after church, she sought out the company of Gytha, who she found closeted in the solar with her daughter the queen. She curtseyed low, eyes to the floor, still uncertain as to how Ealdyth thought of her. Feeling a hand on hers she raised her head to see the queen smiling and pulling her up to sit by the brazier with her mother. She was being pulled in too.

They sat together, sipping wine and discussing family matters, as if they were just three country wives and not the mates of the most powerful men in the kingdom. From what was said, and even more what was unsaid, it was plain that it was assumed that Harold would eventually just slide into his father's seat. Edith felt it was all beyond her comprehension. Seeing the confusion on her face, Ealdyth moved her chair closer and looked straight at her sister in law,

"In our position, we haven't got the luxury of thinking of our finer feelings. We have to think of the future of the whole country."

Indeed, thought Edith with a hint of bitterness, even if that means pulling apart everything closest to the heart. At least she had her children to support her; Ealdyth would seem to have no-one. What a strong woman she must be to weather that. With a start, she realised Ealdyth was staring at her, almost as if she could read her thoughts.

"Believe me, this was not the path I would have chosen for myself. I wanted to stay at Wilton Abbey, to take the veil, and if God had willed to become Abbess one day. But here I am, because my father willed it should be so, and if it helps to keep the peace throughout the land then my sacrifice is a small price to pay."

The words struck deep inside Edith and wedged themselves in her heart. Harold was her lover, her husband, her lord, but he was also bound by birth to be part of the ruling class. One day, God forbid, she might have to make sacrifices too.

CHAPTER 33

That year, Winter refused to release his grip on the land. The rivers and streams around Waltham stayed frozen well into March, and the children enjoyed every second, skating from bank to bank and dragging the girls around on a home made sledge. The squeals of laughter filled the air as they hurled snowballs back and forth with the grooms and the kitchen boys, before they were hauled back to work by their harassed masters. Harold had gone to one of his hunting lodges for a few days and returned laden with meat and a ruddy glow of health in his cheeks. Edith had remained at Waltham, feet tucked up on a stool and rugs cast about her, sipping mulled wine while she waited for the sickness to subside. She ran a hand across her belly, feeling the swelling that was starting to form with a feeling of self satisfaction. Harold had not been so entranced by the ladies of Dublin to have turned his sight away from her.

She was no fool; he was as likely to have dallied with the wenches at Diarmid's court as Leofwine had been but it was just an itch he needed to scratch. His heart and happiness was here, with her and the family and they both knew that.

Cold hands landed on her shoulders, followed by icy lips nuzzling into her neck. Edith batted Harold away, and he pulled up a stool to sit by her side, clicking his fingers at one of the pages to bring him a cup of warmed wine too. He down it in one draught then gestured for another. He was in a good mood. The hunting had been good, the ride back had been invigorating, and he had been smitten with an idea. He rolled the liquor round in his goblet, watching the light refract in rosy shades,

"The thegn Edmond of Walsingham joined me, while I was away. He informed me that your priory building was progressing well, and that the building of the shrine will start soon, at least when the weather lets up a little. The mortar will not set properly in this cold, it seems, but Master Alfred is convinced that there will be quick progress as soon as possible."

Edith smiled, turning to face her husband. He had shown little interest before now in her project,

"Indeed so, my lord. I thank you for relaying the message so succinctly. I did wonder how the workers would manage in this chill. At least the masons will be able to work I think."

"So I was told. Do you know, I did not realise quite how fascinating the idea is; the thought of those stones, one atop another, still being there centuries after those who laid them have vanished into dust made me think, my sweet."

Edith sighed, gently stroking Harold's head. Although he would never say so, thoughts of the brevity of human life had been in his thoughts, ever since Swein had died, and with his father was seeming to age before his eyes. The certainties in his life were shifting before him.

" The abbey here, in Waltham, it is a pretty enough place is it not?"

Edith nodded but said nothing, waiting to see where Harold's thoughts were leading him.

"Even so, I think that the Abbot would like to improve the monk's quarters. The roof is leaking, I hear. The church would benefit from some expansion as well; lengthen the aisle, raise the roof, glass windows, that sort of thing."

"And how, pray, did you come to this conclusion?" Edith was grinning, her eyebrows arched in mock surprise.

"I had been there many years ago, even before we met. I stopped by there on my way home. It is indeed a lovely place and the Abbott a gentle soul but I could see that he was most gratified and relieved by my suggestion."

"Which was?..."

Harold took in a deep breath. "That I should gift them some land, and an amount in money. They would then be able to make the improvements straight away and have an income from the land holding to pay for the upkeep. Life is so short, my love, and memory only lasts for a few generations. Aside from which, I would rather be certain someone is praying for my eternal soul long after I have died."

Edith bent to meet his kiss, the taste of the wine still warm on his lips. He was a devout man, who tried his best to live a good life. It did no harm to make his peace with God, whatever reasons he kept inside himself.

Edith and Harold agreed that Alfred of Malmesbury would take his travelling companions to Waltham Abbey when they had finished their work at

Walsingham. The plasterers and painters would follow when the buildings were finally ready for use. Everything had to be arranged before Harold and Edith had to leave for Winchester. It was coming up to Easter, the most important celebration in the year, and all the nobility were expected to attend the court that was being held at the seat of English kingship. Aside from the religious ceremony, the Witan would be convening to discuss issues, make laws and pass judgements. Failure to attend was not an option, whatever the circumstances.

The weather had turned, from bright and cold to bitterly miserable. The winds had turned to blow in from the east, bearing sleet in their grasp. Snowdrops and crocuses struggled to flower in the teeth of the gale. Nobody with any sense would have set out in such foul circumstances, but there was no choice. Edith grumbled as Wilone bundled her up in furs in the back of the carriage. The ruts in what passed for a road made the journey impossibly uncomfortable , but Harold for some reason, would not hear of her remaining at home. There had been quite an argument about it. Never before had Harold shouted her down so strongly, spitting in fury that he was master in his own house and that she would just have to learn to deal with that. The anger and unhappiness in his face had unnerved her, so despite a great show of defiance she acquiesced to his demand. Now here she was, stuck in the back of this rickety vehicle when she would much rather be putting her feet up at home with the children.

The carriage was slowing to a halt, but Edith resisted the urge to peer out of the window. Harold might think he could order her about but she wouldn't make things easy for him. She sat back on her cushion pile, arms folded in a huff. After a few moments, the leather curtain which hung down across the back lifted, and a hand held up in a sign of peace was poked through followed by a face bearing a very sheepish expression. Edith glowered, but made no move to resist when Harold climbed up and settled himself down beside her.

"I'm sorry, honestly I am. I know that you didn't want to come but I couldn't tell you why before now. I didn't dare speak where anyone could hear what I needed to say. It could have made danger for all of us."

Edith sat unmoved. It would take more than a half hearted apology to soften her mood. Harold ploughed on, his voice barely audible,

"On may way home from the lodge, I visited Bosham. Don't ask me why, I just had a feeling that I needed to. When I got there, well, I couldn't believe what I saw. My father was hunkered down by the fire in the great hall, smothered in furs and coughing fit to burst. His skin was as grey as his hair and, oh love, he looked so weary of this world. Leofwine and Gyrth have been holding things together as far as the landholdings are concerned, and mother has tried to keep his spirits up, but just the way he looked frightened me. And he was speaking as if he was scared, wanting to make repentance for his deeds."

Softening a little, Edith spokc, "He has much to answer for. His life has been one soaked in blood. He has treated people like chessmen, pieces to be moved in a game of his own invention. There will be a great price to pay come the day of reckoning. Is that why you went to see the Abbot? To ask him about your own immortal soul?"

Harold made no answer, but her words struck home. To support his father he had committed more sins than he cared to think on.

"I needed you by my side in Winchester. I am terrified that the journey there will take what little strength my father has left. If anything should happen....." The words remained unsaid but the air was heavy with the meaning. He would have to take charge, when Godwin died, and if it was amongst the nobles and thegns who would descend on the corpse like carrion crows in the hope of grasping some of the wealth of Wessex he would need to be strong to protect the family. Only with Edith would he be able to mourn as he needed. Edith finally relented with a small twitch of a smile. She would always be there for Harold when he needed her, in life or death.

CHAPTER 34

Thankfully, the storm blew itself out and a hint of warmth began to spread across the landscape as Edith's carriage rattled to a halt in the courtyard of the Palace of Winchester. She eased her aching back as she stepped down , her hand resting lightly on her husband's. Flitting down the steps to the great hall she caught site of Ealdyth hurrying to greet them. The queen was smiling happily as she lead them to the guest house to settle in. It had to be said that she was an excellent hostess, ensuring each and every guest felt that they were vitally important to the success of the whole affair. Ordering the servants to fetch more throws and a charcoal brazier to warm the room she perched on the edge of the bed, beckoning Edith to sit beside her. Edith studied the queen's expression and got the distinct feeling that she wanted to say something important. Harold had got the hint, and withdrew mumbling something about seeing to the horses.

"I really don't know how to start this. Father has been behaving oddly, sister. He has been more affectionate to me than I have ever known. He has never shown concern about my welfare before. Ever! I don't want to pile unnecessary troubles upon my brothers' shoulders but if you know why this should be, then tell me. Please, I beg you."

Edith stroked her swollen stomach pensively,

"I fear this little one may never meet its grandsire." There was a sharp intake of breath from the queen and Edith could feel her trembling from head to foot. "Harold saw him recently. Godwin seemed to have shrunk into himself, he said. He is ill, it would seem, and he has been thinking about setting things to rights before he is called before the Lord to answer for his deeds. I think being expelled and fighting to return took a lot of strength from him and Swein's death shook him to the core. Swein was a mirror of Godwin, his heir, and to lose him must have killed a part of Godwin too."

The queen nodded, biting her bottom lip in thought. It all reinforced her own worries. Sighing, she headed towards the door,

"Say nothing of this to my brother, will you? It may be that our worries are misplaced and he will improve when the warmer weather comes."

Edith held up her hand in agreement as she felt her unborn child kick and stretch inside her. Our secret, little one, she whispered to herself.

Never could it be said that the Royal household stinted on its hospitality. The array of food the servants placed upon the tables made even the great earls take in a breath of surprise. The hall glittered with light from the wall sconces and candle stands as it reflected from the jewellery adorning the guests. Harold and Edith were already seated at one of the long tables when Earl Godwin entered, leaning heavily on the arm of his daughter. He had lost weight, his clothes hanging from his now spare frame. As he lowered himself onto his seat, the queen flashed a glance of anguish above his head in direction of Edith, who lowered her lashes in pain at the sight of the once powerful lord reduced to this by the inevitable march of time.

Edward took his seat at the table and gestured to his guests to be seated. . In an act of reconciliation he had insisted that Earl Godwin sit at his right hand side, which the Earl did with true grace. Ealdyth gestured to the minstrels to begin and the sound of harps and psalteries soon filled the building. Everywhere was hubbub and chatter, gossip sitting alongside intrigue. The king was talking to Godwin, and picking up a tender morsel on his knife turned to offer it to his guest. He stopped in mid sentence and looked at the earl intently. Something did not seem to be quite right. Godwin had a look of panic in his eyes, and the left side of his face seemed to be drooping alarmingly. His arm, which had been resting on the table, fell lifeless to his side and he started to slide from the bench, slumping unto the king's lap. Gytha jumped up in alarm and screamed, knocking her goblet skittering across the table. The whole room suddenly fell silent stared in shock towards the dais. The king's bodyguard leapt forward and gently lifted the earl from the king's arms. Harold leapt to his feet, grabbing Edith hard by the shoulder in fear. He rushed to his father's side, almost tripping over his seat in his haste to reach the ailing man. The king had gone pale with shock and was trembling, Ealdyth standing beside him statue still and ghostly white.

"Take him to my chamber at once. Send for a cinder pan to heat the bed. And you, Gyrth, find my physician and send him straight to me." Gyrth nodded and scampered to get help. Ealdyth, meanwhile, had recovered her senses and supported her mother as they followed into the chamber. The Earl was still conscious but he could neither move nor speak. Harold and Aldin , the king's man, had lain him on the bed, the king himself pulling up the covers to keep him warm. Ealdyth drew up a stool for her mother to sit beside the bed, and herself knelt on the floor with hands clasped in prayer. The king's body servant scuttled in with the cinder pan and having wrapped it in a blanket tucked it into the bed alongside Godwin's feet. They felt cold as ice. The king shooed him from the room just as Gyrth brought in the physician. He insisted that everyone save Gytha leave the room while he examined the Earl's prostrate form.

Edith had excused herself from the feast and dashed after the sad little group, wanting to help but with no idea how. By the time she had struggled past the gossiping servants who cluttered the aisles the rest of the family were huddled in the ante room, no-one daring to speak. Edward gently touched his wife's arm, then slipped quietly back to the Hall, asking those present to respect the sick man and lower their voices. The whole room was in a state of shock. Not one person present could even believe what had happened.

It was like watching the mightiest oak of the forest being felled by a stroke of lightning.

Every hour seemed to last for ever. The physician was at first full of hope. He applied leeches to the lifeless limbs, he burned herbs and filled the air with their pungent odour. Vinegar was sprinkled on the bedding to sweeten the air and Godwin's arms and legs were rubbed with fiery ointments but all to no avail. Every hour he was turned to his left side, then right, then back again by his sons, the indignity showing in his tear filled eyes. Gytha would clean and wash him, then with the boys help she would dress him in a clean undershirt. If she could help no other way she would make him comfortable. The brothers took turns to stay with him, trying to rub some life back into his cold hands and praying that he would speak again, bellowing at them and telling them to cease with their nonsense, but it did not happen.

Edith had kept to her room. She might be family but she was not blood and it was not her place to be with the Earl. Sleep was out of the question, though, and she filled the hours sewing clothes for the baby to occupy her mind. It was close to midnight on the Tuesday when she heard the door opening and lifted the candle to show Harold entering. She hardly recognised him. Great black shadows sat below his eyes and his cheeks were hollow with hunger. His hair was swept back from his forehead, as if he had spent hours running his hands through it in despair. He looked for all the world like a little lost boy, in need of love and sustenance. Edith pulled him onto the bed and took him into her arms, rocking him as silent tears flooded down his cheeks. She began to croon to him; the song she always sang to her babes, that she had sung to their little dead daughter, and now she felt she was singing it for the loss of a father. They sat there together, locked in each other's arms, Edith waiting patiently until Harold was ready to speak to her.

"We are losing him. Bit by bit. He is going and there is nothing I can do to stop it."

"The physician still holds out hope, though," Edith whispered softly.

"He might, but I am no fool. I have seen enough of death to recognise when its hand is upon a man's shoulder. Father doesn't even open his eyes to us now. It is as if his spirit is ready to depart and all that is left is the body." He laid his head against his wife's shoulder to try to ease the throbbing within. Carefully she lay down, Harold still clinging to her. He needed sleep now, more than anything and she would see to it that he got it. His arm was resting across her body and, feeling the kicking of his unborn child, he hugged them close as he sank into a restless sleep filled with dark forbidding shadows.

Edith had insisted that he had something to eat before he returned to Godwin's side, even though the bread felt like ashes in his mouth and the beer bitter as aloes. She washed him herself, wiping the cloth over his rangy body, lingering on the scar that marked his side then bending to place a kiss on it.

"That was the first time I met your father. The day when Swein got me so annoyed and I ended up scarring you instead. It seems such a long time since, but I will never forget."

Harold smiled, "Nor will I. Not everything my father arranged ended up so badly did it? Even my sister seems happy with her lot these days."

"I think that might have something to do with that young thegn who is acting as bodyguard to the king. I saw the way they looked at each other. What is odd is that Edward noticed and didn't even seem to mind."

"Well, good for her if she has found a bit of happiness. Edward never struck me as the marrying kind in any case. Far too keen on prayer to want to get involved with sins of the flesh, if you ask me. Speaking of prayer, I must get back to my father. Would you do me a favour, though? Go to the Cathedral and ask the monks if they will say a mass for him? And me? And all of us? I think we might need all the blessings God can bestow before this week is through."

That morning, the physician met with Edward and his queen. He held out his hands in a sign of failure. Whatever he had tried, and truly he had tried, had failed. The only help for Godwin now was to keep his body as comfortable as possible and his soul prepared to meet God.

Harold had just left his father when Ealdyth found him. The stress of the last few days had drained him . He looked tired from searching for the slightest sign of improvement in their father.

"Brother, I have just seen the physician," Ealdyth looked Harold full in the face. He could see where tears had run down her face, leaving her eyes swollen and red.

"He's dying, isn't he?" She nodded. Harold let out

a groan and leaned back against the wall, feeling the cold sweat running down between his shoulder blades. "I will organise what needs to be done . He can lie in the Minster until everything is ready." Ealdyth looked sick. It felt such a betrayal to speak of death while he was still alive.

"Mother will need you, Harold, and our brothers. She has suffered too much of late. She has had too much loss." Harold ran his fingers through his thick blonde mane, pushing it away from his eyes.

"I will prepare her and I will make sure that she is looked after. At least she has her dower lands. She will not lack for money." Ealdyth gave him a tender smile and hugged him close. So much would lie on his shoulders now, when he was the head of the family.

"I shall go now and speak to the king's confessor. I want father to at least die in a state of Grace if that is possible." Harold nodded at her in thanks. He heaved a huge sigh and went back into the chamber. Within seconds came the sound of her mother's uncontrollable sobbing.

Godwin had always been a fighter, and he clung to his earthly life with his usual tenacity, but even such a lion as he could not fight forever. As the sun began to creep between the shutters on the Thursday morning, with his wife and children by his side, Godwin Earl of Wessex breathed his last.

CHAPTER 35

Harold, Leofwine and Gyrth took turns to stand vigil by their father's coffin as it lay before the altar in the Cathedral. Stock still they stood, as one by one the nobility came to pay their respects. Siward and Leofric were visibly shaken. Not only had they lost an ally; Godwn's death had left a gaping hole in the balance of power; the taught thread which kept everyone in their place. Now there would be uncertainty and that always lead to trouble. They had to drip their words into the king's ear before he had the chance to be persuaded by his Norman cronies to appoint one of them to the Earldom of Wessex. Ralph de Mantes was fine, but he was not ambitious and was not one to cause problems but who could say the same for any other? They knelt by the coffin, studying Harold as he stared straight ahead, sword clutched in his hand, as he guarded the coffin. tall and strong, a man with presence. He was nobody's puppet either. Had he not stood up to his father in that business with his brother and the nun? And he had by all accounts acquitted himself well when he was at Diarmid's court. The fact that he was Godwin's son, and was well known by those who owed Wessex fielty, was just the gilding on the gingerbread. Harold was the man for the job.

Edith cried off from the funeral, using tiredness from the child as an excuse. She had said her goodbyes to Godwin, gently kissing his cheek before he was laid in his coffin. Gytha would need Harold today and he needed to concentrate on her, not be the escort to his wife. The solemn Missa di Requiem echoed out into the clear air, competing with the soaring larks for God's ear. Godwin would have liked that, she thought as she sat on a bench in the cloisters, the sweet birdsong singing him to Heaven. Suddenly she wanted to go home, to see her children, to hold them close in her arms and it struck her like a spear to the heart that the neither Wulfnoth nor Hakon would know of the great Earl's death and that when they did they would have to grieve alone.

It was decided that the family would all travel back to Bosham together. As sensible as Leofwine and Gyrth had become, Harold felt the need to make sure his mother got home safely. She had been in a trance like state since Godwin's death; unable to comprehend what had happened. Heaven alone knew how she would react when she saw the empty chair by the fireside and realised Godwin would never sit there again. Harold sent Leofwine on ahead, to make sure that the news had reached home and that the servants were prepared for Gytha's return. Edith was seated again in her carriage, mulling things over. Harold had slipped effortlessly into the role of family head and the others had accepted it as if it was his due. Where did that leave her, Edith wondered, if he was to be claimed by all and sundry? He was needed in Waltham, by his own children. She could imagine how Harold would find himself being pulled in so many directions that he would tear apart.

Edith breathed a sigh of relief as the carriage crested the road which lead away from the coast and towards home. It had been difficult to leave Gytha but she had insisted, almost shooing them out of the door. She had feared losing Godwin for so long that now it seemed almost a relief to find that her worst fear had happened,but she had survived it. As she pointed out, she had Gyrth and Leofwine with her and enough to do to keep her mind busy in managing the estate. Gytha Thorkildsdottir was nothing if not tough. They all needed to feel some kind of normality back in their lives. Harold would need to meet the manor holders to reassure them of the safety of them and their holdings. People had a habit of panicking whenever there was such a great change in the land. He would probably want to take some time to go hunting too. Riding at breakneck speed behind the dogs was the best way he knew to clear his mind of everything. And she had the children to consider. They would be upset at the loss of their grandfather, poor little souls. Godwin in particular idolised him, and the Earl always had a soft spot for his namesake. Not to mention the fact that her confinement would be fast approaching. Edith sighed, her head spinning with all that would need to be done before the little one made its appearance.

She poked her head out of the window and stared for a while at Harold as he rode at the head of the group. Even beneath the heavy cloak that was wrapped around his shoulders she could see the tension in his muscles. He had tried to hide it, laughing off her concerns as a woman's nonsense, but he was worried, and rightly so. Whoever the king chose to succeed to the Wessex earldom, it would disrupt his life and the family too. He feared the Normans getting their claws hooked into the wealthiest land in England. Surely the next step would be to take over entirely, trampling the Saxons lords into the dust. He spurred on his mount, cantering ahead a little, followed by his great grey alaunt trotting by his side. The carriage driver made to speed up the oxen but Edith shouted no. If Harold needed some time on his own then let him be. The chances were he would not have the luxury in the weeks to come.

"Well, my lord of Wessex, and how do you fare this morning?"

"The same as ever I did as lord of East Anglia. Happiest when the first face I see on waking is yours."

Edith groaned, feigning disgust at her husband's sentimentality. He was the same, it was true; an inveterate flatterer, flirt and as loving a man as any woman could ever hope for. The king must have seen his honesty and fairness too, moving as swiftly as he did to gift the Earldom to him. It meant more responsibility, not only in terms of his new holdings but also within the Witan and the King's Council. Siward and Leofric had expressed their delight at the news. If the old regime had to change then it had to be done in the least painful way.

Rubbing at her back, Edith waited for Wilone to slip her gown over her head and onto her shoulders. The fabric strained across her stomach and she sighed, staring down towards the floor,

"I wish this child would hurry along. I am beginning to forget what my feet look like, or even if I have any!"

Harold rolled over on the bed and propped himself up on his elbow. Whatever she might claim, Edith was still the most beautiful woman he had ever met and to see her carrying his child made him more proud than he could ever put into words.

"Speaking of children, my love, I want to talk to you about our little Gunnhild."

Edith gave him a half smile. Gunnhild wasn't that little any more. She was annoyingly smart, bright as her Aunt Ealdyth had been at her age. this conversation came as no surprise at all,

"I have been thinking about her future. I know she is only young, but I want to do what is best for her." He bit his lip, waiting for Edith to howl in disagreement to whatever he might propose. A wolf was a neglectful mother compared to his wife.

"You are absolutely right, my lord. In fact I have been wondering myself whether she should follow the lead of the queen and be taught by the nuns at Wilton Abbey. She is the daughter of one of the most powerful men in this land and as such must be educated to the highest level, don't you agree?"

Harold grinned in disbelief. No matter how long they might have been married he would never fully know what was in her mind. She would always surprise him.

"Not Gytha though. She is far too giddy. The nuns would despair of her! Can you imagine being asked to remove her from the premises for swinging from the church bell ropes? " Dear little Gytha. She ought to have been born a boy. She could ride as well as her brothers and climb a tree quicker than any of them. When the time came it would have to be a bold soul that took her on in wedlock; she was so much like her mother, Harold realised with amusement.

He dragged himself unwillingly from the warmth of the bed and threw on the clothes that had been laid out on the chest by the doorway. As loath as he was to leave Edith so close to her time the king had summoned him to Canterbury, not a duty he could dodge. It still felt odd to be the Wessex earl; almost like stomping round in his father's boots when he was small. The name did not fit him yet and he would need to apply himself with diligence to make sure that it would. Leofric's son at least had responsibility for East Anglia now, not that Harold was filled with confidence on that score. He had been promoted to the position while Harold had been in Dublin, but according to Edith he had not exactly covered himself in praise for his work. He had somehow managed to irritate, annoy and alienate practically every thegn in the Earldom. Even Edmond, the most affable and easygoing of men, had complained to Edith about Elfgar's heavy handed arrogance. If it happened again then every thegn, ceorl and serf from one side of East Anglia to the other would be beating a path to Harold's door to ask for his support.

Edith had her own worries. The child she was carrying seemed to suck up every ounce of her strength, leaving her nodding into her meal at the end of the day in exhaustion. She had not been this big with any of her other children, either, making her back ache furiously. Wilone seemed quite happy about it, though. According to her theory, the child would be hefty and healthy, big boned and strong and in all likelihood another boy to add to the family. Edith just wished , whether it was boy or girl, it would hurry up and make its entry. She had things to do and people to see, not least the progress at Walsingham.

"You should have known it was a boy, my lady. They are always tardy and turn up in their own time, even when they are grown! He is a fine lad though, plenty of meat on his bones."

The midwife was tidying Edith up after the birth. It had been a messy affair, and difficult, the midwife having to ease the baby along the way as his broad shoulders threatened to cause damage to himself and his mother. Edith was tucked up in her bed now, utterly exhausted and aching from head to foot. Wilone brought the little one to her, swaddled up in cloths, his tiny fist poking out from beneath the layers like some tiny warrior. His mother loosened her shift and latched him onto her breast. He sucked greedily, Edith feeling the familiar tingle as the milk let down and the overpowering sweep of love that filled her soul.

"Ulf. That shall be his name. It is a fighter's name, a strong name, and it fits him perfectly." She smiled down at the tiny face, contented now that his belly was full, rosebud lips parted and breathing softly. His father would adore him.

She was right. When Harold returned from
Canterbury he threw himself from his horse and ran
through the building, desperate to know if the child
had been born and if it was well. The misery of little
Eadgifu's birth had never left him, and even though
they never discussed it, he knew Edith worried just the
same. Thank God! He could hear women chatting and
giggling. He opened the door to the bedroom slowly,
popping his head round the door and grinning,

"Would a mere man be welcomed in your
company, ladies, or should I go back whence I have
come?" Edith patted the bed, beckoning him to sit
beside her. He could see, sitting in the corner, the wet
nurse. Gurgling noises were emanating from the bundle
tucked in her arms as the baby suckled at her breast.
Harold sat down and extended his arms towards her.
Making a clumsy curtsey, she placed the child in his
arms and he gazed for the first time on his youngest
son. Edith told him his name, and Harold nodded his
approval. What a boy! He gripped his father's finger
with such strength! Harold kissed him and Ulf
wriggled, tickled by his father's moustache. The baby
was handed back to the nurse, who Wilone then
ushered out of the room. She knew the couple would

want a little time alone together.

"Everything went well? You are alright, aren't you? He is a big lad and must have been difficult to birth." Harold was a country lad. He had seen the damage that a big calf could cause to a cow in birthing. Edith smiled and took his hand in hers,

"He was not the easiest of our brood, but worth the effort. As for me, I am recovering well, fear not. I have no intention of staying in this bed or this room for any longer than is absolutely necessary. I have far too many things to attend to." Typical Edith, unable to stay still for a second.

The baptism was to take place at Waltham Abbey, along with his mother's churching. It gave her a chance to survey the building Harold had decided to endow. Within its precept was a cross, tall and black, carved from the darkest flint. It had an aura about it, a sense of mysticism which almost hypnotised her. Edith knelt on the floor beside it, crossing herself as she stared at the forlorn figure of Christ hanging from the body of the cross. Harold knelt beside her, hands clasped in prayer. She had never realised quite how devoted Harold was to his Lord before. His lips moved silently as he prayed, eyes cast down in reverence. Then he crossed himself, helping Edith to her feet as he stood.

"When I was a child, I came here," he whispered in response to the quizzical expression on his wife's face, " I had been ill, really ill. I couldn't walk; the use of my legs had left me completely. Father was in despair. You know what he was like, he didn't know how to cope with sickness or weakness. The physicians had no idea what to do and believe me they had tried everything possible. The foul potions they poured down my throat were so disgusting it was a wonder they didn't see me off. Anyway, my mother had heard of the story of this cross. It was found at Glastonbury, the place Our Lord visited in this country and was reputed to have the power to cure. My father dismissed it as nonsense of course. She brought me here, just me and her, and she laid me at the foot of the cross. The monks poured Holy water on me, head to toe and prayed. Then they bid me to stand and kiss Our Lord's feet, here. I had to have faith to do it, you see. It was a struggle to stand. The muscles in my legs had withered through lack of use, but I did it. I stood. I walked and I got better. I owe this place a debt of gratitude and that is why I intend to endow it with land and money. I am like you, my love. I always pay my debts."

CHAPTER 36

Whatever else might have been said about Edith, the one thing she craved above everything else was peace. She had lost enough to the greed of powerful men with the death of her brother and the maiming of her father. Her children , she prayed, would never have to live in such unsettled times. Since Harold came home from Dublin , even though Godwin had died, the country had been able to relax, knowing that the Earls and King had a tacit agreement not to rock the ship of state. There was even the opportunity for Harold to spend time by his own fireside, feet up on the table, drinking ale from his own brewhouse.

He had invited his brothers to visit, much to the pleasure of Edith and the excitement of the children. They adored Leofwine and Gyrth for the simple reason that they were often as childish as they were. It would do them good to get away from the atmosphere of sorrow that still hung over the house at Bosham. The afternoon had been spent teaching the children to make rafts and rowing them up and down the river which snaked its way past the manorial complex. Everyone came back soaked and dripping, owing to Uncle Gyrth and Uncle Leofwine deliberately capsizing each other's rafts as they raced from bank to bank. The two earls disappeared to the guest lodgings to change before Edith had chance to clip their ears and Godwin, Edmund, Magnus and Gytha trooped off with their nurse and Wilone, to be dunked in a bath and dressed in dry clothes. Their mother feigned disappointment in them for being lead astray by their uncles, but as soon as they left she dissolved into giggles, clutching at the table for support as the tears rolled down her cheeks. Harold roused himself, grabbing little Ulf as he toddled towards the fire and steering him in the other direction. It was good to be able to relax, and to be able to enjoy having his family around him.

Eventually the two brothers came back into the hall, acting sheepishly and begging Edith not to hit them with the pitcher she was holding. Instead , she shoved them into their seats and poured two deep warming beakers of ale. "That should keep you two out of mischief for a while. Fancy behaving like that at your ages. You really should be ashamed. There is enough work to be done without having to wash and dry more clothes. Not to mention children!" she laughed, pushing a platter of figs and honey cakes toward them. They snatched up the treats, the crumbs tumbling onto the floor where the dogs tussled with each other to snuffle them up.

It did not take long for the conversation to turn towards political matters. There had been word of trouble along the border with Scotland, it seemed.

"Siward will have it under control," Harold espoused as he drained his tankard, gesturing to Edith to refill it, "The Scots might be troublesome but they are by no means as powerful as he is."

Gyrth shook his head, "But think about it, brother. He is old, older than our father was when he died. He can't go on forever, and where will that leave things? Northumbria needs the strongest of lords, and one who understands their peculiar ways at that." Edith sat down in surprise. To hear Gyrth show such insight was unexpected. Perhaps more went on in his and Leofwine's heads than people gave them credence for.

"I had heard that there had been a whacking great battle some where north of the border. Only rumour of course, you know how it is, but it seems that Siward's eldest lad, Osbjern, got the worst of it. You know how Swein's death affected Father. What's to say Siward won't go the same way?"

It was as if Leofwine's comments had blown an icy draught through each of them. If indeed Osbjert was gone that left no natural heir, his only other son being a mere babe. There would be chaos. Every family of note in the kingdom would be angling to get their hands on the earldom, let alone the king's ever greedy Norman friends and relatives. Harold picked up his youngest son from the floor and sat him on Gyrth's knee, placing one of the honey cakes in the baby's pudgy paw,

"Well, whatever happens there is nothing much we here can do about it. When and if a decision has to be made it will be the king's responsibility. All we can do is hope that he follows the right path."

Ulf crumbled his cake into tiny pieces then poked a fistful into his Uncle's mouth, causing him to splutter.

"Perhaps the king ought to consider Ulf for the role," sniggered Leofwine as he patted his brother between the shoulders, "I've never met anyone who can silence an Earl so quickly!"

It was only a few weeks later when a king's messenger rattled into the yard at Waltham, sweat pouring from his mount. As he entered the hall, Harold was already striding to meet him. He scanned the note, a frown settling on his brow which deepened the further down he read. Oh Hell below all Hells what had possessed Edward to make such a decision!

As Gyrth had foreseen, Siward had died, swearing to the last that he and his family had been cursed by the heathen Scots. Another link had been broken, another experienced and wise Earl had passed leaving his earldom filled with fear in every corner. The future was suddenly uncertain and the king needed to act with speed tempered with caution. He had acted with speed, that was sure, but whether he had been cautious was open to question.

"Tostig! He has chosen Tostig?" Edith could not have been more surprised if Wilone had hitched up her skirts, jumped on to the table and started to sing one of the extremely rude songs the men would bellow in the evenings. Of all the men she could think of who had the talents to rule in that northern land Tostig would be nowhere near the top of the list. He was shy, painfully so, and so close to Edward that sometimes it seemed like they were glued together. He enjoyed life at court;

he understood it. But Northumbria was not like court, or even Wessex for that matter. He would have to learn pretty quickly if he was to make a success of this.

"Who else is there?" Harold, too, was incredulous, but he could see the king's problem. Elfgar had caused so many problems in East Anglia that Harold spent half his time placating the thegns whom he had annoyed. What kind of mess he might make of Northumbria didn't bear thought. There was a lack of men of the right rank and the right experience. Only Godwin had a gaggle of sons who fitted the bill. Therefore, the king's favourite received the promotion. Be it for good or ill remained to be seen.

CHAPTER 37

It was as well that Edith had both the children and the building at Walsingham to keep her occupied. If she had only the day to day running of the home to fill her time then she might have been even more irritated by the amount of time Harold was spending with the king. It was as if no decision could be made without her husband's input. He would return to Waltham whenever he could, the signs of fatigue creasing his brow when he climbed from his mount and made his way into the hall. He would go straight to bed, without waiting for food or drink and was asleep almost before he crawled under the covers. "I cannot avoid it," Harold sighed when Edith finally broached the subject, "The king has lost all interest in anything but the cathedral he has commissioned to be built near his palace in Westminster. God knows he has reason. As long as he has reigned the Earls have always had the final say in what happens. He has just ceased trying any more, which leaves a tricky situation for all of us. Tostig will not try to cause any trouble, he has enough on his hands, but if any of the others realise the king is leaving everything to me and the queen to decide then..."

"Then there will be trouble. Somebody might try to dethrone him."

"Which will mean civil war at best and invasion at worst. So Ealdyth and I meet with him, make his decisions for him and get him to place the Great Seal on it."

So Harold made the sacrifice, keeping the king's secret and chasing up and down the country to support him, and Edith bit her lip and let it happen.

Feeling unsettled, Edith decided to take a trip to Walsingham to check on the progress of the priory. She was greeted at the manor by Edmond, who was delighted to see her arrival. He had been about to ride out to Waltham himself, to tell her the good news in person. The builders had finished their work, the plasterers had completed their task and the painters had almost done the same. The monks who had been sent from Worcester by Bishop Ealdred had settled into the priory itself and were preparing the shrine for its been sent away. He didn't even have the imagination to think of his own ideas. And poor Ralph! He was such a gentle soul, never anything other than kind to anyone but in no way a warrior Earl. Then a thought struck her,

"Tell me, is my husband there?"

Wulfstan paused, choosing his words more carefully this time,

"Not at this moment, my lady, but I believe that the king has seen fit to ask him to raise some of the men he is owed and take them to bolster Earl Ralph's forces."

In other words, he was going to try to sort out the mess that Elfgar had made. Whose idea had that been, she wondered.

CHAPTER 38

"Lady mother! Lady mother! I can see someone riding this way! Quick, come with me!" Gytha was squealing with excitement, grabbing her mother by the hand and dragging her across the yard towards the compound gate. Her spindle was tucked hastily in her belt, the woollen thread unravelling behind her as she ran along with the over excited child. In the far distance, looking like ants crawling across a meadow, she could see figures moving down the track and headed in their direction. It looked to be quite a group, judging from the number of horses she could see trotting along. She dropped Gytha's hand and marched back towards the hall. Grabbing the steward firmly by the arm she told him to run to the kitchen and tell them to prepare for an influx of, probably, extremely hungry men. There should be sufficient bread, she thought, and there was certainly enough mead and ale in the brewhouse to satisfy an army. Sending Wilone to check that the servants were preparing the guest house to her standards, she ran back outside, trying to tidy up the strands of hair that were escaping from her veil and rubbing the wool grease from her hands on the skirt of her shift. Then, taking a deep breath to calm herself, she stepped towards the gate to welcome the unknown riders.

"Well, I am surprised! I never expected quite such an enthusiastic welcome! The king himself would be proud." Gytha had thrown herself into the arms of the leading rider as soon as he had dismounted with a scream of delight, wrapping her arms around his neck and smothering him with kisses. The boys were fighting amongst themselves as to who would have the honour of leading in the horse.

"Some warning might have been nice." Edith stood by the gate, arms folded against her chest and lips pursed in annoyance. Then, with relief flooding through her, she ran to meet her husband.

The soft clouds of dusk were beginning to drift across the sky, tinted peach and crimson by the setting sun. Edith stirred, brushing her fingers across Harold's face and flicking the hair away from his eyes. It was funny, she mused, but when he was asleep his face still looked as young as the boy he was when they married. Leaning towards him, she brushed her lips across his ear, nibbling the lobe to wake him up. He opened his eyes, turning onto his side to look his woman full in the face.

"You sleep too long, my love. Our guests will expect our presence at the evening meal. Especially considering your behaviour when you arrived." Harold grinned at the memory. He had passed Gytha on to her uncle Gyrth then swept Edith off her feet and carried her straight to their chamber. He had thrown her on the bed and made love to her before she even had chance to undress. It was urgent, angry, anxious all rolled together and she could feel the fear inside him; the fear that he would never have the chance to do this again. She understood, and let him , then when he had finished and they had kissed and held each other he undressed her and loved her as she wanted; gently, slowly, lovingly. Sleep had come to them both, dreamless and sweet, but now they had to become the Earl and his lady of Wessex; at least for a little while.

They walked into the hall and seated themselves at the table on the dais. Leofwine and Gyrth were already there and when they saw Harold and Edith flushed of face and doe eyed they winked at each other, sniggering. Never, ever, would that pair grow up. Edith waited for their silliness to subside before she asked them what turn of events had brought them to Waltham. They glanced at one another, looking away from their sister in law as if uncertain what to say.

"Oh, well we hadn't seen you since the New Year and since the king had told Harold to come home we thought we would tag along."

Really, Edith shuddered, the king has sent him home? She felt her hand trembling, the wine in her goblet spilling as she lowered it to the table. Why would he do that? Surely he was the king's most trusted captain nowadays. He couldn't have expelled him. Could he?

"Thank you, brother dear. You always were the most discreet and tactful of my kin." Harold stared hard at the tapestry on the wall opposite him. He could not look Edith in the eye. "The truth of the matter is that he has asked me to travel to Hungary, to try to find his nephew Edward. It seems that the king feels the need to bring him home, to where he was born, and to name him as his heir. I can see why. If he were to die now we would all be plunged into chaos as every lord from here to God knows where would be fighting for the spoils." He paused, considering what response Edith would make to his next statement, "In any case, I had been planning to go on pilgrimage to Rome. My hands are wet with blood, love, and it is time I did something towards washing them clean."

Edith deliberately poured what was left of her drink onto the table and began to run her finger through it, back and forth, back and forth, leaving trails across the polished surface. Once, Harold would have consulted her before he agreed to anything so dangerous. Travelling across the breadth of Europe, filled with people who spoke different languages and brigands lurking on unfamiliar roads. It felt , to Edith, as if a part of him had left her and a nasty hollow feeling had settled in her heart.

"I suppose that the decision is made, and any opinion I may have is inconsequential. Do what you will. Obviously the great matters of state come before the lives of a handfasted whore and her bastard offspring. Now, I have a headache, so if you will excuse me I am going to bed. I would trouble you to sleep elsewhere, my lord. I do not wish to be disturbed."

Edith kicked back her chair and swept from the room, tears stinging her eyes.

Harold groaned and glowered in fury at his idiot brothers. He would have explained it to her in his own way, in his own time, but now they had caused such hurt to his beloved that he might never be able to mend the tear. Gyrth and Leofwine sloped off to the guest house as quickly as they feasibly could like a brace of lurchers caught with their feet on the serving table. They were bachelors. They had no concept of the delicate interplay between husband and wife. Having seen the fury with which Edith had spoken to Harold, they thought that perhaps being single was no bad thing.

The Earl of Wessex sat in his great hall, leaning on his table and slowly drinking himself into oblivion. He was no great drinker as a rule; he liked to keep his mind clear, especially when those around him were in their cups and with loose tongues. Tonight, though, he would have happily drowned himself in ale. When the steward tried to suggest that perhaps he had drunk enough, Harold grabbed him by the throat and rammed him against the wall, splitting the man's head open against one of the huge wooden posts that held up the roof, then throwing him to the floor to scrabble to his feet among the filthy straw. Clutching his wound, he brought another pitcher, which Harold drank straight from the pot. Eventually, feeling bloated and sick, he staggered to the door and out into the cold night air. As the chill hit him, his head began to spin and he was violently sick, retching until his stomach was emptied and he could give up no more. He wiped a hand across his face, staining his sleeve with the vomit that clung to his moustache. By now he was feeling sorry for himself, and self pitying tears started to flow down his face. Reeling from the drink, he staggered towards the stables, looking for somewhere warm to curl up for the night. Spotting a pile of filthy straw, he burrowed into it, wrapping his cloak around him to keep the cold away. He would teach her, he mumbled to himself. What made her think she could talk to him in that way? Could he not have his choice of women? Yes, he could, but he didn't want them. He wanted his wild girl, the mother of his children, the other half of his being. He wanted Edith and he didn't know what he would do if she no longer wanted him.

CHAPTER 39

The sun peeked above the wooden wall that surrounded the compound and its rays hit Harold squarely in the face. He moaned in dismay. His head felt as if a thousand blacksmiths had set up their anvils inside his cranium and were hammering for all they were worth. A foul odour entered his nose, and it took him a moment or two to realise that it was probably from him. Vomit, yes and manure. Piss probably, not to mention sweat and stale beer .He sat up and tried to run his hand through his hair. It was matted, and tangled with straw. What in God's name must he look like, let alone smell like. A pig keeper would not be as foul as this. He staggered to his feet and began to head towards the hall, intending to go to his chamber and strip off his stinking attire and then he remembered. That was the last place that he would be welcome. But he had to do something, even if it was only to beg for some clean clothes from his chest.

He crept through the hall, boots in hand and stepping between the sleeping forms and through to his bedchamber. No, not that. His wife's bedchamber. Sheepishly he tapped on the door, awaiting an answer.

Edith had not slept a wink. Seething, she had sat up in bed all night, ranting to her maid about the untrustworthiness of men and the wickedness of their lustful ways. Not a thought for her or the children, she railed, not one. If he was so much enamoured of the king's company then why did he not marry him? Why not lie in his bed instead of hers? She listened to the wildness of her words and cared not a jot. He had hurt her more deeply than she wanted to say and if the only way to cope was to bellow like an angry fishwife then so be it. Wilone had listened, in silence, saying nothing. She knew her mistress well. Sooner or later the fire would burn itself out, then she would be able to see her way clearly.

"I'm jealous, aren't I? A silly jealous woman who had no right to behave as I did."

Wilone considered for a moment, "Perhaps, my lady, you are jealous of the time that the Earl spends on the king's business which is understandable. But, it must be difficult for the Earl to refuse the King's orders. To do so could bring down disaster on him and his family, begging my lady's pardon for saying so."

She was right, of course she was. What choice did he have when the king demanded he fulfil a mission for him? As for travelling to Rome, she could hardly begrudge him that when she herself had built a shrine for pilgrims to visit. Even so, it would be difficult to climb down after the way in which she had flounced out of the hall. Edith lay back in her bed, fiddling with the cord which fastened her shift while she thought. She waited to see if Harold would make the first move. If not, she would have to swallow her bitter pride and hope that he would understand.

The door opened a crack and Wilone peeked warily through the opening. At the dishevelled sight before her she raised an eyebrow but said nothing. She turned towards her mistress, gesturing surprise. Make him wait a while, thought Edith as she counted slowly to one hundred, I am too long at this game to give in quite so easily. Eventually, after what seemed like an eternity, she snapped to Wilone,

"Ask him what he wants."

The maid curtseyed and bobbed her head back through the door. Edith could hear muffled talking and Wilone coughing theatrically.

"If it pleases my lady, the Earl asks if he may retrieve some fresh clothing. And if you ask me," she whispered conspiratorially, "It is not a moment too soon. He smells like a midden and looks like he has rolled in one!" She wafted her hand, her nose wrinkled in disgust. Edith straightened the bedclothes and tightened her shift until it sat tight around her neck, showing not an inch of flesh. Then, seated as primly as a Mother Superior, she gestured at the maid to open the door.

The stench entered the room well before Harold did. He stepped quietly into the doorway, head bent and boots in hand looking for all the world like an errant schoolboy waiting to be caned.

"If I may, I would ask that your maid bring me some clean clothes from my chest, so that I may change into something that will not offend those around me." How humble he sounded, for Edward's great lord. Ha! Served him right. Still, as far as Edith was concerned, there was yet a little revenge to be had.

"You stink. Even your hounds will be repulsed by that stench and they are happy to roll in cattle muck. Step forward. I would see the creature that offends my nostrils so, then I shall decide whether to accede to your request."

Harold crept forward a step or two, letting his wife see the full extent of his misery.

"Well, well, the smell of the brewhouse is all over you and , oh dear God, what is that in your hair? You do realise your tunic is beyond saving don't you? Ugh!" Edith played her part to the hilt, but as angry as she was with him a hint of pity began to creep into her thoughts.

"I know, wife, but please do not scold too loudly. My head feels like it has been trampled by the fyrd in full flight," Harold rubbed his brow and winced. "I acted like an ass last night but believe me I am truly sorry for it. If you would allow me to find something to wear that does not resemble a pigsty then I shall leave you in peace." She nodded, gesturing towards the chest. He began to rifle through his belongings; leggings, braies, undershirt, tunic, and bundled them together in his arms, bowing his head in acknowledgement before turning to leave.

"You said wife."

Harold turned to face her, "Indeed, for that is what you are. I care not how we wed, or where. Your children are mine, and I will say that freely and proudly so do not, sweet mistress, confuse me with a man who does not own to his responsibilities."

"You need a bath. I shall ask Wilone to see that one is prepared for you. I would not have you spoil any more clothes with your filth."

Harold smiled, "And may I ask if I might be welcomed back into your chamber once I am fit to be in your company? There is much that I need to explain, and I would have done so had not my fool of a brother decided to pre-empt me."

Edith considered for a moment, head cocked on one side like a little bird as she studied the forlorn figure before her. "When you are clean, and sober, then I will allow you that opportunity."

Edith seated herself at the table in the solar, next to where her errant lord was morosely poking around in a bowl of boiled oats and honey that Wilone had slapped down in front of him. She did not like men who drank themselves into a stupor and had no sympathy with their hangover the day after. As much as she respected Harold, she enjoyed the look of nausea that crossed his face at the thought of food. It was unlikely that he would get quite so drunk as that in a hurry, she thought. He was cleaner now, and was dressed in his second best tunic. Edith sniffed. At least the awful smell had gone now he was bathed. His skin glistened with tiny droplets of water and his still damp hair was curling gently at the ends.

He put down his spoon and began his tale. Yes, he had been considering going to Rome. He was feeling the weight of lives he had taken heavy on his shoulders and even his endowment of the Abbey was not enough to begin to pay the debt that he owed God. It was a thought for the future, perhaps when the boys were old enough to stand in his place, but when the king had ordered him to search for his kin it seemed that God was forcing his hand. Edward needed to know that the future of the kingdom was settled; the Witan had tacitly agreed to vote in the king's choice of successor so his nephew had to be found and trained for the role and the sooner the better. That was what he had intended to explain to her. A peaceful transition of power, when the day should come, was all that he was trying to ensure. It would be at least a month before he would be setting sail, and he had intended to spend that time here at Waltham. At least, it had been his intention until last evening. Now if Edith did not wish it, he would ride out to Bosham and spend the time at his childhood home instead.

If it was time for truths, then Edith needed to tell hers. She stepped away from the table and went to stand by the window, staring at the lightening sky.

"Last night I was furious with you. You spent the afternoon telling me how much you missed me, loved me, wanted me and by nightfall it all seemed like a great big lie. It made me feel like a brood mare, a simple minded whore, charmed by fancy words without any meaning behind them. What you tell me now makes me feel embarrassed and ashamed. I never thought that I was a jealous person before, but I was jealous; no I *am* jealous of the time you spend away from me at court, in the King's company. It is not a pretty trait and I am not proud of it, but I will not deny that every second we are apart I feel that something of my soul is missing."

"Then what would you have me do? If I refuse the king, then he will strip me of all I own and expel us from our home. If I do his bidding, then I will lose the person I love above anything else on earth. Tell me, my dearest love, what do you want of me?"

He was in earnest, that was obvious.

"Before I married you, my mother said that to be handfasted meant that if circumstances ever changed we would be free to part. What she didn't say was that to marry into such a powerful family meant that I would never be able to call you wholly my own. I cannot give up the part of you that is mine, Harold, so I leave the rest to be used for the good of the country. Just promise me that in future you will keep Gyrth under control and that you will never, ever get that drunk again. It is not seemly for so great a lord to appear in *that* dishevelled state!"

Everything was settled again. Gyrth had bent over backwards in his efforts to get back into Edith's good books. Leofwine thought the whole affair was hilarious and took every opportunity he could muster to poke fun at his brothers. Harold seemed to be invisible, he would laugh. He would disappear for hours on end, funnily enough when Edith was not to be found either, which as far as Leofwine could see was proof that Harold had been warmly welcomed back into his bed.

In truth, much of their time was spent at the Abbey. Harold wanted to share his ideas with both the Abbot and his wife. While he was away, however long that might be, she would oversee the works for him. Alfred of Malmesbury was delighted to see her. She was a woman of sense, who understood the process of construction well and who would not try to scrimp on costs where it was necessary.

Strangely, she and Harold felt closer than they ever had before. They had faced up to the realities of their lives together and knew for certain that whatever should happen in the future, they were bonded tight . The time came when Harold needed to go, dragging Gyrth and Leofwine along with him. They could get back to Bosham where their mother would keep a lid on their mischief. Either that or go to court to find work with the king. Edith would have enough to do while he was away without having to keep that pair out of trouble.

CHAPTER 40

The months rolled by, one by one, and there was still no word from the Earl. It was hardly unexpected. The only way to make contact was by messenger and the continent was a dangerous place for the lone traveller. Edith waited with patience. Sooner or later she would hear, be the news good or bad.

In the meantime, she at least had the consecration of her Priory to look forward to. Bishop Ealdred himself had promised to perform the ceremony. Edith dragged her whole family to the affair, despite the grumbling from the boys. Firstly, they had to bath which to them was a horrendous ordeal. Then they had to dress in their best attire. Their heavy woollen tunics itched, they complained, and they hated having to be stockinged and booted. Their mother listened to not one word, but she did threaten to send them to their uncle Tostig , with a note about their behaviour. That was enough to kill all complaint. Tostig terrified them. He could be as charming and kind as his brothers one moment, and a raging tyrant the next. It would not be a good idea for their mother to dispatch them to Tynecastle for punishment. Better to buckle down and do what was asked of them.

The Bishop was in good humour when he greeted the party. It was a pleasant break for him, he explained, to get away from Worcester for a while. There was constant niggling along the border with the Welsh and he would be dragged in to act as mediator, a tricky business at any time but all the more so when one wrong move could trigger fighting. Getting back to the job he had been enthroned for would do him good, spiritually and mentally. He was enrobed in a large tent which had been set up on the green within the Priory boundary wall. Then he lead the procession up to the chapel itself, sprinkling around the walls with Holy water before entering the building. The roof echoed to the Latin chants as Ealdred marked the sign of the cross again and again on every wall, with oily chrism.

The ceremony was long and complicated, and Edith could see the children becoming restless, especially Ulf. He was a fidgety soul at the best of times, but kneeling for what must seem to him like an age and listening to words he had no understanding of was like torture. When the priests moved forward to consecrate the altar she dragged him to kneel beside her, whispering in his ear that he was trying hard to be good and that if he could manage to stay still for a bit longer then she would sneak him an extra almond cake at the feast to follow. Ulf grinned in happiness. He was easily bribed.

At long last the ceremony was over, and the Priory of Walsingham was now a consecrated holy ground. The Prior offered his hand to Edith as she raised herself to her feet, and escorted his guests around the site to see the facilities for the monks and pilgrims and the shrine itself. Ealdred listened as Edith related the story of her visions to him, nodding thoughtfully. He was certain that she had been right, that the Virgin had visited her. She was going to tell him about the rose petal that still bloomed fresh as ever, but something stopped her. Such a thing might be called a Holy relic, and it would be snatched out of her care for display. It was hers to keep and to give as she wished and she could almost feel the Lady telling her this was not the time to part with it. Instead, she pulled from her scrip a tiny phial that contained what seemed to be a cloudy white liquid. It was, Edith told the others, milk from the breast of the Holy Mother herself, and it had been among the relics

Swein had been been bringing back from the Holy Land. Gytha had found it in his belongings which had been returned to Bosham after his death in Patara and she had donated it to the Priory. The Prior's eyes lit up with excitement and he promised that both Gytha and Swein would have mass said for them for as long as the Priory should stand.

The Priory could not be faulted on the quality of their food. The feast which they laid before their guests could only be described as delicious and plentiful. Thankfully, from Edith's point of view, there were plenty of almond cakes to reward Ulf with. She was seated next to the Bishop, and took the opportunity to quiz him for information. Only a year ago had he gone as the king's emissary to try to find Edward. He would be able to give her some kind of insight into the dangers that Harold would be facing.

Ealdred was more than happy to tell his tale,

"I travelled overland across to Germany, and sailed down the Rhine as far as Cologne. It was my intention to stay with Archbishop Hermann, who has his seat there. A remarkable man, you know. He came up with a plan to rebuild his cathedral to mirror that of St Peter's itself! But I digress. Whilst I was staying with him, I discovered that the King's nephew was, in fact, in

Hungary, living at the court of King Andrew. He is married, it seems, to a girl called Agatha. They have a son and a daughter. Margaret and Edgar. This is all hearsay of course as I never got to meet them. The way of diplomacy is never straightforward, as you know. The Emperor refused point blank to sanction my crossing into Hungary, despite my pleas. To attempt to do so without the Emperor's support would have been suicidal, and as such a sin in itself, so home I came. Of course, the Emperor has died since then. I should imagine that it would be much easier to negotiate with the Empress. The child is far too young to rule as yet. His mother is regent, and by all accounts a lot more biddable than her husband , God rest his soul." The Bishop crossed himself. "As far as I can see, your husband may well be more successful than myself. He is a man of great talent when it comes to solving such problems." He caught the look of worry that flitted across Edith's face, "And I would have no concern for his safety, my lady. He would not be travelling alone. There are groups of messengers travelling back and forth the whole time between the emperor and his vassals. Harold will be safe in their number."

Edith sat taller, as if a weight had been holding her down and had been raised by the Bishop's words. To know a little about what Harold was facing helped her picture it in her mind. The image of dark, lawless forests and ice blasted mountains was replaced with thoughts of elegant buildings and sophisticated company, at least for a little while.

The Bishop was a most entertaining guest with the knack of being able to talk to anyone on their level and to put them at ease. Even little Ulf was entranced, especially when Ealdred called him over from his seat to present him with yet another almond cake as a reward for being such a remarkably grown up young man. Godwin was so enthralled by the conversation he had with Ealdred that he swore intent to join the clergy and one day be a Bishop too. Magnus almost fell off the bench with laughter at Godwin's pious expression. His brother was already showing far too much interest in girls for that to be a reasonable choice of career.

CHAPTER 41

So sad it was, and so hard for his wife and little ones. Before Harold had even returned from Rome the king's nephew was dead, leaving a pregnant widow and two little babes to Edward's care in a country they had never seen and where they owned nothing.

Harold's mouth dropped open in disbelief. He had met Edith at Bosham, where she had brought the children to visit their grandmother as soon as word had reached her that the Earl was setting sail from Flanders within the month. She had stood by the landing, watching the rhythmical dip and rise of the oars on the dragon ship as it slipped easily through the water. Hardly had they tethered alongside before Harold had thrown his foot onto the gunwale and leapt up onto the dock striding to meet his wife with a grin on his face and a gleam in his eyes. As far as he was concerned he had accomplished what he set out to do. His eternal soul had been cleaned of blemishes and his earthly body had no need to worry about Edward's successor. It was time, he smiled to himself, to give some time to the family he had sorely neglected. He swept Edith into his arms, spinning her around as he always did until they were both giddy and breathless. Stepping back, he let his gaze take in just how beautiful his wife was. Her hair was still thick as ever, reaching almost to her knees, her eyes still sparkled like ice in the sun and they were only enhanced by the little crinkles he could see at their corners when she smiled. Slipping her hand in his, they walked along the landing, heading towards the manor hall.

All the way he had talked, telling her about the beauty of Rome and how he had travelled there with the Holy Father himself. Edith listened happily. It had been a long time since her lord had seemed so carefree and it delighted her to the core. He even spoke of returning to the Holy See and taking the family along with him,

"It is a wondrous place, Edith. There are buildings there that are a thousand years old! Can you even imagine that? Buildings that were standing when Our Lord Himself walked this earth! And now I don't have to worry about what will happen here should the king die then my time is almost my own. Oh, Edith, the plans I have! "

Suddenly he sensed an odd lack of enthusiasm from his partner. Her head had dropped and her fingers slipped from his. He grabbed her chin and tilted it upwards towards him and he was taken aback to see the unhappiness that was written in her eyes.

"You don't know? Oh my love, the Aethling died. When he landed here he was ill, he couldn't breathe. It was a problem he had ever suffered from, so his wife had said. In any case, his poor heart gave out even before the king could meet him. He was at the hall in Dover when he lost the fight, on our land. I took Godwin with me to the funeral in London. I thought it was the least we could do in the circumstances. Your sister has taken on the responsibility for the children's future. Oh, and Ralph de Mante's boy too. He was named for you so she stepped up to be his guardian when the Earl died."

The colour drained from Harold's face, leaving him grey with shock. It had never occurred to him that things would have changed at home while he was away. Edith could see his plans crumbling around him,

"So we are back to where we were before I left? "

Edith wrinkled her brow in thought,

"Well, perhaps not. You must have met little Edgar? He is a delightful little chap. "

"Little is the word. He 's only a babe, love, and it will be many years before he will be able to build up enough allies to be certain of the throne. Oh Hell and Damn! Am I going to have to groom him for the throne now? Please God that Edward lives a long and healthy life."

Harold was never one to wallow in self pity for long. He sighed, tightened his belt a notch, and grinned mirthlessly,

"Well, I suppose it will keep me out of mischief if nothing else. At least the boy will learn our ways and not have some ideas set from living at another court. And I suppose Edward is as like to live as long as anyone else, if not longer. It isn't as if he overdoes the food or the drink is it?"

Edith sniggered, "Or the sins of the flesh!"

Harold slapped her rear in mock disgust. "It is as well I am home, woman, if that is the depths your conversation has sunk to. Get thee to the hall at once, so I may remind you of how a dutiful wife ought to behave."

She gave him a look seductive enough to cause the heart of a Bishop to leap with lust, then lifted her skirts and scampered up the hill as fast as she could , Harold unbuckling his belt ready as he raced along behind her.

Contrary to Harold's worst fears, peace seemed to have settled on the kingdom for a little while, helped in no small part by Tostig's decision to follow his brother's lead and take a pilgrimage to Rome. Harold had always had his doubts about the wisdom of promoting Tostig to the Northumbrian Earldom and to say that things were not progressing entirely smoothly was a massive understatement. At least if he was out of the country perhaps there would be time to smooth the ruffled feathers of the wild northern lords.

Now there was a chance to return to Waltham, and to see how the building work at the Abbey was progressing. Alfred had promised a building as beautiful as the one he built at Walsingham, but Edith doubted that to be possible. Her Priory was so close to her heart that she could never imagine that there could be anything, anywhere so glorious. Still, she had to admit to herself, Waltham ran it a very close second. The great tower soared heavenward, square and strong, pointed windows piercing the flint fabric of the walls. Each one was filled with glass, such a luxury for any building but somehow just what fitted to perfection in this one. The great black flint cross had been placed on a platform outside, behind the apse, its shadow casting another against the wall . Inside, the church was equally magnificent. For such great walls there was a feeling of light and airiness. Heavy beams of oak criss crossed the vault of the roof. To Edith, it looked for all the world like the hull of a great dragon ship, tipped upside down. She squeezed Harold's hand in excitement. He had trusted her with this and she prayed that she had delivered to him what he desired.

"I have been to Rome, love, and seen the church of the Pope himself. As grand as the Archbasilica of the Lateran Palace might be, it has not an ounce of the beauty of this place. Not to me anyway. This is my vision become reality."

Harold moved slowly along the aisle, stopping eventually before the altar,

"When I die, and please God it will not be until I am old and grey, I can't think of anywhere that I would rather my body spent its rest than here, at this spot, in this church."

The Dean waited, in the shadows, for Harold to call him forward. He had the look of a pragmatist, happy to serve God, indeed, but with a weather eye to the secular needs of his community. Twelve canons, there were, and married ones at that, which might just take a little squaring away with Rome, but he could do that if needed. Just the man Harold needed to care for his beautiful building.

CHAPTER 42

It was an odd feeling, Edith pondered to herself. Now that the buildings at Walsingham and Waltham were complete and dedicated, she had nothing to distract her mind from the greater worries. The boys were growing now, becoming young men almost, and there would be all the fuss and connivance that was bound to go with finding wives for them. As for Gytha, heaven help the man that married her. The word firebrand must surely have been coined for her wayward daughter. It hardly seemed a moment since any of them had drawn their first breath and in no time it would be the turn of her grandchildren to do so. Time flew by far too fast, it seemed.

While Edith turned her mind to the problems of weddings, Harold found himself thrown back into the political mire. The Welsh had begun their poking and prodding again and the king had declared that this time

enough had to be enough. Harold gathered his men of
Wessex and marched to dispose of the problem one
and for all. For all Gruffydd was tough and experienced,
he met his match with Harold. Defeat bites, and
continual defeats bite hard. As Harold attacked from
the south, the newly returned Tostig lead his men into
the heart of Gruffydd's northern stronghold. He was
like an injured animal turned on by his own dogs,
ripped apart in the heart of the bleak mountains of
Snowdon. It was as if an aching tooth had been pulled.
Painful as the process was, the peace that followed made
it worthwhile.

Harold was standing by the well in the manor
yard, deep in conversation with the messenger who had
ridden in the evening before. Edith was puzzled. She
knew most of the heralds the king would dispatch, if
only by sight, but this man was not one of them.
Neither did he have the royal cipher on his apparel. The
scent of trouble was in the air, she knew it. Harold had
turned his back towards her, hiding the man's face from
view so she could not even lip read what was being said.
Her foot tapped in irritation. If something was going to
interrupt her existence then she would rather know

sooner than later.

"Edith, go to my treasury chest and bring one of the bags, would you?" This man must have brought information Harold was desperate to have, to consider giving such a reward. It did not take him long to share the news.

"That young man is from Flanders, Count Baldwin's court. He promised that he would find where my poor brother and nephew were, if they were still alive. I have to say I doubted it. The Pope himself swore to me that De Jumieges no longer had them in his charge and I had no reason to think otherwise. In any case, Baldwin has sent word of what he has learned. The boys are alive, and well it seems. They are captive still, but at the court of William of Normandy. He is married to Baldwin's daughter you know, and she has promised her father that they are being treated like the Earl's sons that they are and she has undertaken to ensure their safety."

Edith was perplexed,

"But Baldwin is Tostig's brother in law. Why did he not send news to him rather than you?"

Harold shrugged, "Would you? Baldwin knows Tostig and how volatile he can be. There would be no quicker way to cause trouble than telling Tostig anything."

"He will have to know sooner or later. So will the rest of the family. They have a right."

Sighing, the Earl nodded, "Which is fortunate timing, my dear. There is a meeting of the Royal council coming up, which we will all be attending. That might be the best time and place to tackle this. Everyone will have to be on their best behaviour."

Harold silently cursed Robert de Jumieges for the trouble he had brought down on his shoulders. The family were seated around a table in one of the guest chambers at Westminster. Carefully, measuring every word, Harold related what he had learned, making sure that he omitted any mention at all of the source of his information.

"The bastard!" bellowed Tostig, hurling his tankard at the floor. "If I caught hold of him I'd rip out his sorry Norman throat!" The queen rolled her eyes and tutted as she bent to clear up the mess.

"Just remember, brother dear, the king still has friends in Normandy. He might not take well to hearing that."

Tostig spat, "I care not. I have a brother and a nephew still separated from their family. You know how mother grieves over them."

It was exactly as Harold and Edith had expected. Tostig was full of fire and fury, ready to challenge anyone without a second's thought.

" Fighting amongst ourselves isn't going to get them back," Harold, threw a comradely arm across Tostig's shoulder. Huffily, he shrugged it off looking at his brother in disgust.

"I think that one of us needs to go over to speak with William. If we can negotiate with him we might be able to get them back without violence and without bloodshed." reasoned Harold but before anyone had time to react Tostig had squared up to his brother across the table. His hand reached for the dagger at his waist but Harold read his intent and grasped his wrist first, twisting it backwards until Tostig yelped in anger and pain. By now Gyrth and Leofwine had leapt up from their seats, knocking them over in their haste. Edith shrank back, horrified as Tostig tried to stamp his boots down her husband's shins. The two brothers grabbed Tostig by the arms and dragged him back, pinning him against the wall until he calmed down . Ealdyth stepped up to him, pulling his head down until she was staring him in the eyes. "This is my home, I do not have to stand this behaviour. Either calm down or get out. Either way, you will show me the respect that is deserving of your queen." Breathing heavily, he sat back down on the seat Edith had put back on its feet for him, never taking his eyes away from Harold's implacable gaze. Ealdyth bent forward and slid the knife from its sheath, tucking it into her belt. "I will give you this back when I am sure you will not use it against your own blood."

Everyone stood still for a moment, gathering their wits about them. Even in his worst temper Tostig had never been so quick to snap before. Harold waited a moment or two, then with his voice lowered he continued, "I do understand your feelings, Tostig, and I know why you want to sail over and attack the upstart Duke, but the truth it that it will cause trouble for you and the rest of us. Remember, he is married to your wife's niece and will doubtless call on Baldwin for help. No, the only way is to try to persuade William that it is in his interest to release the boys." Gyrth and Leofwine looked towards Tostig. They weren't prepared to let their brother have the chance to disagree. Reluctantly, he nodded his head.

"Now all we need is to decide who is best placed to try," Ealdyth spoke softly, trying to avoid any further upset but undoubtedly the one whose opinion mattered most.

"Well, Harold thinks this is a good idea, it should be him," sulked Tostig, his face twisted in bitterness. Harold refused to rise to the bait.

"I thank you, brother , for the faith that you have in me. I am head of the family after all so perhaps it would be best if it were me."

The others breathed a sigh of relief. Such a task would demand a man with experience of such sensitive dealings not some hothead who spoke with his fists and not words of reason. Ealdyth called Tostig over and handed back his knife, her eyes gently reproving her favourite brother,

"Your temper will get you into trouble one day. Remember, I will not always be there to stop you. Nor will the others." Tostig looked at her from under knotted brows but said nothing. He would remember this slight. One way or another he would make Harold pay for it.

To say that Edith and Harold were worried about Tostig's outburst would be a grave understatement. Edith had feared for her husband's life. If he had not been so quick to react then surely Tostig would have driven his blade home, and Harold would now be lying bleeding on the chamber floor.

"One day your brother is going to start some real trouble, my lord, and when he does it will rip the whole family apart."

Harold was rubbing comfrey oil onto his leg where Tostig had kicked it black. "I know. The older he gets the worse he becomes. For some reason he seems to think that I am the cause of all his woes, although for the life of me I can't think why."

Edith thought a little, "I think it's because you are so successful in what you do. Even now, in East Anglia, your name is spoken of with praise and Wessex is as settled as ever it was under your father. Added to that, the king relies so heavily on your advice and help and, well, Tostig has always looked up to Edward, if you know what I mean. He must feel as if you have pushed him out of favour."

"Oh yes, Tostig always was the jealous one. Although I fail to see what I can do about that."

Edith nodded. Only the Queen seemed to be able to bring him to heel now and who could now how long that would last.

CHAPTER 43

The salt tang sat soft in the wind kissing the faces of the little party gathered on the landing stage. The wind was whipping the water into choppy waves, tipped with white spume, which made the little ship bang and clatter against the wharfside. Mares' tail clouds rode across the dazzling blue arc of the heavens, leaving heavy grey billows of rain trailing in their wake, cresting the horizon, and causing the crew to wrinkle their brows in concern. Little huddled groups of men stood in discussion, pausing occasionally to scan the sky. Eventually there seemed to be some agreement. Hands were shook, orders were given and the captain prepared the ship for departure.

Harold climbed up onto the landing. His hair blew wild in the wind, whipping across his face and stinging his eyes. He nodded to his wife who stood waiting, sheltering in the lee of an upturned hull. She had pulled her cloak tight around herself and her hood was tugged firmly down over her head. "So you are going?" Edith's voice was muffled by the heavy woollen cloth.

"The captain thinks we should be in Normandy well before the worst of the weather hits. Hardly ideal, I know, but if I don't go now I can guarantee that Tostig will do something bloody stupid before I get the chance."

That was true enough. Ever since the argument at Westminster he had taken himself off to Tynecastle, taxing the lifeblood out of the locals and generally behaving like a spoiled child deprived of his supper and not a senior Earl.

Harold pulled Edith close to him, bundling her up within his leather cloak,

"You are shivering, love. I hope you are not worried for me?"

Edith leant closer, her head resting on his shoulder, "No more so than ever I am. I am just cold, that is all. This wind is bitter."

"And strong. But it will blow us across the Channel all the quicker. The sooner I can negotiate with William the sooner I can be home."

Edith was cautious, "He is a dangerous man. Anyone who can survive the way he has is no pushover."

Harold was well aware of that. William was a bastard born. Nothing wrong with that, from Harold's viewpoint. After all, in the eyes of the Church so were his handsome sons and beautiful daughters. William's problem was that his father had died when he was only eight, and the vultures began to gather around him. Time and again attempts were made on his life and so nervous were his guardians that he never slept under the same roof two nights together. He had to be tougher than ship's nails to survive that upbringing.

Harold kissed Edith, lingering, tasting the salt on her mouth as it mingled with that from his. She murmured softly, enjoying his hands stroking her back, his fingers strong against her yielding flesh. There was the sound of a subtle cough, and Harold reluctantly drew away from his wife, grasping her hand and squeezing it hard before tugging his gauntlets from his belt and sliding his hands into them,

"The Captain seems to think I delay too long, mistress. I shall be certain to send news as soon as I can and I promise to return as soon as possible, Wulfnoth and Hakon by my side. Besides which," he had dropped his voice to a whisper now, " I do not care to be away from your bed any longer than I have to."

Edith cuffed him, running her tongue across her lips and the smile she threw him let him know how much she was in agreement. Reluctantly, he pulled away and walked to the ship, leaping from the wharf down into the curved belly of the ship. He turned round and waved, eyes focused on hers. The ropes that tied the boat up were cast off, and the oarsmen began to dip and lift their oars ,slowly moving the ship out into the current where the sail was unfurled. It filled at once, curving outwards as it harnessed the power of the wind to move it sleekly through the waves. Edith stood, statue like, watching the boat as it moved further and further away, until finally it disappeared from view.

For months she waited for news. The storm that had blown up the evening that Harold left had been a herald of the weather to come. One followed hard upon another, dragging the country towards a cold and miserable winter. Edith saw no point in worrying. The chance of getting a message home when the conditions were so vile would be nigh on impossible. No, it was better not to fret and mope like some lovelorn maiden in one of the scop's stories. It was far more important to keep things running smoothly at home. She would not be accused of letting any of their tenants fail to fulfil every little item that they owed their lord.

It came as some surprise when a Royal Herald rode into the yard at Waltham in the early Spring. When Harold was away, it always seemed that Waltham might as well have been on the moon, for all the attention anyone from Court paid them. The young lad slipped back his hood and bowed, his message pouch clutched in his trembling hand. Edith snatched at her breath; how young he looked, young as her boys. It shook her to realise that her little ones were men now, Young, surely, but men all the same. She called to the herald to come to the solar to deliver his news, chatting to him along the way. Yes, he said, he was but sixteen years of age and it was the queen who had sent him. It was his first errand, he stuttered in embarrassment, and he was incredibly proud to have delivered it safely. Sixteen! She was married and a mother at sixteen! When Harold returned they really must do something about finding brides for Godwin and Edmond at least. Giving the boy a plate of honeycakes and a pitcher of mead, she took the message from him and sat by the window to read it, so the light would fall upon it.

She recognised the neat hand as that of Ealdyth herself. Whatever was in the letter must have been something she did not want anyone else to know, not even a scribe at the Palace. She read on, hands trembling,

"My dearest sister. Please forgive my sending you this news by note, rather than inviting you to court to inform you face to face. I would not have any others in the family know its contents, at least not yet.

Be still, for Harold is safely in Normandy, and will return to us soon. He made no mention of whether his mission had been successful, and I felt that he had written with someone watching every word he wrote. It was not filled with his usual jokes and japes, more something he might have written to one of his thegns rather than his family. Please do not let my mother know. I would not have her hopes raised for nothing. Nor my brothers. We shall keep this to ourselves. Even the King knows nothing of this. I pray that we shall be reunited soon with those across the Channel.

Ealdyth of Wessex, Queen"

Edith laid the parchment down on the window sill, before rolling it tightly and placing it inside her treasury chest, locking it away with a grim expression on her face. She was relieved that Harold was alive, of course, but the tone of this letter suggested that things had not gone altogether smoothly for him. She would not speculate, either to others or in her own mind. All that would achieve would be anxiety. No, she would dismiss it from her mind and concentrate on the news that her lord would soon be returning, God willing. That would be enough for her.

CHAPTER 44

"That's how I like to see a woman. On her knees!"

Edith spun around, livid at the words she had heard. She left the loom weights on the floor, where she had dropped them and marched furiously towards the figure standing silhouetted in the doorway then slowed, head cocked on one side in disbelief. Reaching out a hand, she stroked the face that bent towards her, familiar grin beaming. She found herself being kissed her so hard and long that she thought she might faint.

"Harold?" she whispered, hardly daring to believe it was true, "Is it you? My God, I didn't recognise you!"

Harold rolled his eyes upward, and self consciously smoothed his hand across his head, "The haircut? Don't remind me. The things I had to do to keep on William's good side you wouldn't believe!"

That night they dined alone, in the solar. There was so much that Harold had to tell Edith that he did not want anyone else to hear, not even the children.

"The whole thing was a disaster, sweet. We never even made it as far as Normandy before we were wrecked by that storm that was blowing up when we left. The Lord of Ponthieu had us captured, at least those who survived, and took every last penny I had taken to ransom the boys. Then he handed us over to Duke William. Oh, he seemed friendly enough, on the surface. We were treated well, don't misunderstand me, and I think he was genuinely grateful when I helped to rescue some of his men who got themselves stuck in quicksand. Well, we both know how wicked that can be. Nobody else seemed to know how to deal with it so up I stepped. When I think on it, it was funny, that, asking me to accompany him on campaign. It was almost as if he was trying to test my mettle. Anyway after I had managed to drag them out of the mire and ridden by his side, he insisted on knighting me. What could I do? I could hardly refuse him. That would have set all of us up to be treated as hostile. Trouble is, that left me sworn to be his vassal. Sworn, on relics let me say, to support him should he ever see fit to exercise his claim to the throne. I felt the cold of his blade at my throat when he dubbed my shoulders and I know, just know, he would have slit it from ear to ear given the chance. He is an ambitious man, Edith, and a greedy one too. He would delight in sucking this country dry, to support his Norman state."

He took a long draught from his beaker of ale, glad to taste the familiar flavour,

"And did you manage to release the boys? How were they? Did they remember you ?" Edith urged him, worry in her eyes for the little boys snatched away so wickedly and so long ago now.

"Fine, love, honestly. Hakon is even now snuggled up safe with his grandmother."
"But not Wulfnoth."

Harold grimaced, "Oh no, not both. William is far too canny to let both the pigeons out of the trap. He thinks he can twist our noses until we squeal as long as he has one of us in his claws."

Harold prowled over towards the window, swirling the ale in his beaker around and around. Something was eating away at him, something that he really didn't want to say. Edith waited, hands folded in her lap. She wouldn't rush him.

"The thing is, and this does frighten me, that

interfering, conniving, apology for a priest de Jumieges told the Duke, when he left the children with him, that Edward's desire was for William to have his throne after his death. He will swear to it, and if the king dies before little Edgar is ready to take him on then he will snatch the prize from under his nose."

Little Edgar. So young, so gentle and so unprepared to fight one of the most feared men in Europe.

Edith walker quietly to Harold, wanting to place a comforting hand on his arm but he shrugged it off and stalked away angrily.

"But that isn't the worst of it. God above I am so ashamed of myself for it! The Lady Matilda had got wind somehow of the fact that we are not wed in Church. Of course I played up to it, I had to, pretending that I always had my eye open for the next one to warm my bed. I can flirt and flatter a woman, of course I can. I am my father's son after all, but what I did then is unforgivable. I swore to become betrothed to their daughter. Poor little thing, no older than our Gunnhild. Desperate to please she was, and a wonderful wife she will make one day, but not for me! And what a selfish bastard I am, to feel sorry for myself when Adeliza will feel abandoned and you, my love...."

"I am old enough and wise enough to know that politics demands sacrifices of us all. Don't chastise yourself for it. Who knows, in time the child may make an excellent spouse for our Godwin, if not for his father. Betrothals are made and broken all the time. Good Lord! I never took you for such a sentimental old so and so."

Harold laughed bitterly, "Old seems to be the word. Look at me, Edith. My hair is getting greyer by the day, every morning I see more wrinkles and when the weather is damp my bones ache. I am not a youth any more and I am fed up with seeing people being hurt by decisions I have made."

Edith ruffled his hair with her fingers, rubbing the tips across the bristles that lead down to the nape of his neck. Her lips followed them, soft tender kisses as she nuzzled comfortably against his neck,

"You are an idiot, you do know that? I don't care how grey you might be, or wrinkled, or so stiff that you can't get out of bed in the morning. I don't care about any of it. You are my lord and lover, and when I look at you I will always see the sweet boy that wedded me and bedded me. As for the rest of the world, a bit of maturity gives weight to your words. People are more inclined to listen to someone who is speaking from experience. Besides which, that touch of silver in your hair is quite attractive. But promise me one thing, I beg of you."

Pulling her onto his lap, Harold took Edith's head gently between his hands and kissed the tip of her nose, "For you, my heart, I will promise anything. Anything at all."

She threw her arms around his neck, bringing his face so close she could feel his every breath, "For the sake of Heaven, never ever let anyone do this to your hair again, You look like a boar caught in a thicket!"

No one could deny that Harold had done his best in Normandy, nor did they, but he was left with a niggly feeling in the back of his head that it was an unfinished business. It was with that feeling of unease that he and Edith set off for Winchester to spend Yuletide at Court. It was a cold December but the atmosphere at the Palace was colder still. All the old Earls were gone now, and Edwin had replaced his father as lord of Mercia. Where Leofric had been pragmatic, his grandson Edwin was young, envious and as hot headed as his father Elfgar. He saw the position that Godwin's sons had and it irritated him, and the focus of his and his brother Morcar's ire was Tostig.

The king had, as usual, provided a wonderful feast, so expansive that it seemed to flow from one day into the next. Ealdyth was an expert hostess, seeing to every need of her guests even before they realised what it was they wanted. She flitted back and forth, jug in hand, filling every beaker when she was not seated beside her husband. It seemed that the whole affair was a wonderful success, but she could feel that something was deeply wrong.

Harold had noticed it too, as had Edith. Little knots of Mercian thegns were standing about the Hall, half in shadow, muttering amongst themselves. They were throwing looks like daggers, and the person on the receiving end was always Tostig. If he tried to move around the room they would jostle him, push him, trip him, trying to goad him into some rash act of retaliation.

"He is going to fly at one of them soon, Harold. I can see him getting more and more furious, even though poor Judith is trying to rein him in." Harold nodded in agreement, slowly stroking his moustache in thought. Then, he left his seat and went to talk to Gyrth and Leofwine. Edith could see a lot of nodding and gesturing towards the Mercian thugs, followed by the brothers all wandering across the hall to sit beside their brother. It said one thing to the Mercians; steer clear unless you want real trouble.

They managed to keep peace for a while, although it was obvious that Edwin and Morcar would rip off Tostig's head, given the chance. Edith decided to seek out his wife. She might be able to explain why there seemed to be such animosity between them. The chance occurred when they were both entering the guest block at the same time. Edith took her by the hand, and lead Judith into the chamber she was sharing with Harold. They sat, Edith on the bed and Judith on the little stool. She looked weary, deep black circles beneath her deep brown eyes. It was obvious why Edith wanted to speak with her but she would never have spoken without prompting. She was unfailingly loyal.

"Well, what a pair of men we have, do we not. I love Harold dearly but sometimes he gets himself into some real mischief. You have seen the state of his hair have you not? "

Judith smiled wearily, "Indeed so. I trust you have convinced him that he would best let it grow back?"

"Of course! I much prefer being able to run my hands through a man's hair rather than scratching them on stubble."

There was a sigh from Judith, "I wish I could get close enough to Tostig to do that. Or even that he could settle long enough to have the opportunity. Oh Edith, I don't know what to do. He's always been highly strung, touchy, but now he is worse than ever. He works so hard, trying to keep on top of everything but the whole of his Earldom seems to be against him. They speak in their own language in front of his face, knowing he can't understand. He thinks they are talking about him, laughing at him. I don't think it is the case but how can I persuade him otherwise? They complain at the taxes, but how else can the armies be paid for? Time and again the Scots cross the border, raiding and destroying and someone has to pay to keep them back. The Welsh too. The one thing I am certain of is that we are not welcome there. Tostig just can't adapt to their ways. If he had been Earl of Wessex it might have been a different matter but Northumbria... loathe as I am to say it, I fear it is beyond his skills."

Judith looked relieved, as if she had carried the world on her shoulders for too long and had finally put down the load. At least now Edith knew the full extent of the problem she could tell her husband, something she could not imagine Tostig ever admitting to. She threw her arms around Judith, hugging her tightly and promising to help however she could as she felt silent tears beginning to drip on her shoulder. They stayed there for a long time, Edith rocking Judith in her arms until the tears ceased.

Time to find Harold now. He was the head of the family and however old they were they were still brothers. He had to talk to Tostig, help him somehow. She found Harold deep in conversation with Aldin, the king's thegn that had helped Godwin when he had fallen ill. It was serious, she could see that, so she perched in the window recess waiting for them to finish. As Harold turned to walk away, she grabbed him by the sleeve, tugging him into the shadows.

"You are going to have to do something. Tostig is in such a mess! He's convinced himself that people are conniving against him. God knows if there is any truth to it."

Harold frowned, "I know. Aldin told me some of it, at least what he knew. Tostig needs a guiding hand but I have enough on my own plate. I can't tell him how to deal with these people. As far as I can see he needs to learn to listen and that was never his strongest talent."

Edith snuggled up to Harold, pulling his arm around her shoulders. He blew softly. When Edith wanted him to do something she had ways to make sure of it. He shivered as she began to stoke his hand, then gently tickled the inside of his wrist with her lips,

"Please, my love, just speak to him. Before he does something stupid that we will all regret. For me? Please?"

There was never any doubt about it. Harold would sort Tostig out, if only because he would be able to claim his reward from Edith that night.

CHAPTER 45

It would have been more worthwhile to spend the afternoon talking to the floor than his fool of a brother, Harold grumbled, frustration written large upon his face. He was angrily kicking a stone against the wall to the stable block when Edith finally caught up with him. The look on his face told her everything she needed to know.

"He won't listen to a bloody word I say. I told him to try to work with the local thegns rather than against them, let them see him as their protector not their enemy but I might as well have been talking to the birds. Be like father, I said, remember that however much trouble he might have found with the king he was adored by his people, because he was fair to them. He listened to their complaints. After all, weren't we all exiled because he stood firm for the folk of Dover? I told him to start again, to apologise even if he has to, but that was never part of Tostig's make up was it? Whether he pays attention or not is up to him. There was one thing he said that made me think though."

Harold had stopped kicking the stone about and was leaning thoughtfully against the stable wall, stroking his moustache. Edith was all ears. She recognised the signs when her lord was worried.

"He thinks that Edwin and Morcar have been dripping poison into the ears of anyone who will listen. According to Tostig they have been convincing people to believe Morcar should be their earl. by flattery and promises. I believe him, especially having seen what has been going on here. The trouble is you can only counteract that by proving them all wrong, listening to their fears and worries and acting to put things right, not by wading in with your sword drawn and terrorising all and sundry." He rubbed his nose thoughtfully, "The thing is, what plan are the Mercians hatching? They hate our family, I know they do, especially after the trouble in Wales with their father and Gruffydd. They will take any opportunity they can get to take their revenge."

That was not the news Edith had wanted to hear. Tostig and his faults was one problem but Edwin and Morcar was another thing entirely. They had always reminded Edith of a pair of greedy little pups, growing fat on their mother's milk while turning on the runt and seeing it starve. They plotted in corners, planned in the dark, and there was nobody to tug on their leashes since their grandfather had died. Harold was wise enough to watch and wait; even Gyrth and Leofwine had the sense to steer clear of acting out of hot blood, but Tostig?

"I will watch my brother as best I can and I will get the others to keep by him when I cannot. At least we might be able to prevent trouble under Edward's eye, but we can't always be there to pull Tostig back. And what will happen when he is back in Northumberland I have no idea."

Edith took a deep breath, "That is when he is there. According to Judith he spends more time with the king than ever he does in his Earldom. Any excuse and he flies to Edward's side like some lovelorn swain."

Harold turned away, punching the wall with disgust, "Well it's no wonder his thegns have had enough! For God's Sake! He might as well just hand over the keys to York now and have done with it."

Edith could hardly argue. No matter how much Tostig might complain of conspiracies and lack of gratitude he was master of so much of his own disaster.

Harold raised his eyes to heaven in despair as he blew hard on his painful knuckles. Blood was seeping from the grazes, like water from a spring. Edith brought a cupful of water from the well and poured it over his hand . She could feel the tension in his body and the effort it was taking him to calm himself. Harold did not like to lose control. He was too good a politician to allow emotion to take over his thought processes; he had to think of the bigger picture, like the fine chess player that he was.

" I need to go and find Gyrth and Leofwine. They must know what we are facing. I only pray that we can keep that fool under control between the three of us!"

" The four of us, love. I will do what I can."

The day after Christmas was always the day when Edward liked to take to the hunt alongside his Earls and closest thegns. He liked the informality of it all; everyone was equal when chasing the prey. It meant that everyone had to be up long before sunrise , ready to ride out when the king had finished his prayers. Harold was looking forward to the chance to relax. At least there could be no trouble for the hours they were all out riding to the hounds. The morning was a clear one, the sun rising bright and low in the sky, making it hard to see anything but the ground before him. He was so relieved to release the tension in his body that it took him a while to realise that someone was missing from the crowd . Worse than that; two people were not with the hunt. Harold swore, then rode up to the king to excuse himself , using feigned illness as an excuse. He spun his mount on its heels and spurred it back towards the Palace as fast as he dare. Please God, let him get there in time.

The screams pierced the morning air, like a shard of ice. Edith had been lounging in her room, taking the advantage of a little peace and quiet to sort through the clothing chest with Wilone. She leapt to her feet and cursed as she stumbled, trying to pull on her shoes as she half hopped half ran towards the doorway. Something was going in in the courtyard, and by the sound of things it was trouble.

The scene that met her eyes caused Edith to throw her hand to her mouth in horror. The queen was leaning against the wall, fighting for breath with blood dripping down her gown. Two groups of hugely muscled men seemed to be restraining someone. The air was blue with insults being spat back and forth and roars of anger echoed back from the walls. It took a moment for Edith to realise who the warring pair were and when she did her heart flipped in her chest like a fish in a sack. One was Edwin of Mercia, bloodied in the face and reaching for the sword the biggest of the kitchen hands had wrenched from his grip. The other, oh no. Edith prayed to God that she was mistaken but when she opened her eyes she realised she was not. He was hanging his head in shame, trying to staunch the blood that was dripping from a split lip and with his sword thrown to the floor. Tostig.

It did not take a genius to realise that Edwin had taken his chance to goad Tostig into action and Tostig thought he was solving his problem once and for all. That pair could go hang as far as Edith was concerned. What worried her was the state of the queen. She had gathered herself together enough to stand now, but she was as pale as a ghost. Edwin was sitting cross-legged, checking to see if Tostig's fist had broken his jaw. From the look on his face it was apparent he realised that he had underestimated his opponent. What a fool! No one could grow up in a family of five feisty brothers without learning how to use his fists. Ealdyth was able to speak now, dismissing them both from her presence in a voice colder than the day itself. The kitchen hands dragged the pair of them off to lick their wounds in private, just as Harold clattered into the yard. He threw himself from his mount and rushed to his sister's side, sweeping her up into his arms while his eyes spoke daggers at the two miscreants.

Edith followed behind as Harold carried Ealdyth to her room, accompanied by Wilone and the Queen's maid Cille. The poor maid was furious and terrified in equal measure as she pulled out the pins holding Ealdyth's veil in place to reveal a deep cut in her scalp, the length of her finger. Edith sent the maids to find some warm water and cloths to bathe the wound and to hunt out the king's physician. Whatever else, the king must not find out what had happened .

As the physician bathed the wound with herbal tinctures, Harold told his sister what had been going on. Edith was holding her hand, feeling her wince with each dab of the liquid but even more with every piece of information Harold revealed. It was hard for her to hear. She had been the one to convince Edward that Tostig was the man for the job, and he was her favourite brother; the quiet one, the one who always seemed so sensitive. She could hardly recognise the thuggish brute he had become. Perhaps, offered Edith, the best thing would be to let everyone calm down for a few days and then for Ealdyth to talk to her brother. He deserved a chance to put things right, after all. Ealdyth nodded, and called to her maid to bring a comb, gingerly parting her hair so that she could disguise the livid wound. "Thank goodness the king is unlikely to get close enough to spot this mess. For once I am glad that he is not the kind of man to notice when his woman changes her hairstyle."

CHAPTER 46

It was as well that Edith had conquered her jealousy. As the new year wore on, more and more of Harold's time was spent filling the role that should rightfully have belonged to Edward. The king had, he declared, much more important things to do than rule his country; every waking moment and many of his dreams were dedicated to his beloved Cathedral at Westminster. Someone had to keep the wheels of state turning and Edward trusted Harold, so that was that.

It tired him, though. He had to undertake his own duties, as Earl of Wessex, and now he had so many petitions to hear and laws to ratify on top of that he felt his head was spinning. The tricky part was in keeping the image alive that the king was in control. Edith saw it all, and it worried her. One of those jobs was difficult by itself but to do them both was a Herculean task. Sooner or later something was bound to slip.

The late summer sunshine cast a golden glow across the valley, bathing the town in sunshine. Oxford was nestled in the most beautiful of places, it had to be said. Even though Edith adored the wild open spaces of the fenlands even she could appreciate the rolling hills and peaceful rivers. Harold was smiling as he rode alongside her, the soft breeze flicking through his hair. It had grown back, whiter than before but still as thick and gently curling along his collar. The rode knee to knee, Edith having chosen to ride on her little bay jennet rather than in the carriage that followed them. They were happy in each other's company and not a word needed to be said between them for their thoughts to be clear to each other. There was nothing at all that could come between them.

Hooves rang out over the cobbled road as they rode between the huge wooden walls at the eastern city gate. The place could rival London itself, thought Edith in astonishment, in its business and lively air. The main square was marked by the market, swarming with people like ants round a honey pot. Cattle lowed from every corner, penned with wattle hurdles. Wool was piled high, for selling to the travellers and the townsfolk. Edith glanced at it as she rode by. It was good quality stuff, fine and clean, and she made a mental note to purchase some before they returned home. Stalls and booths were thrown up, higgledy piggledy, selling everything from cloth to sweetmeats to gloves to spices to horses. The noise was overwhelming. Finally, and with relief, they turned left , down towards the church of St Frideswide, leaving the hubbub behind. The king's compound lay ahead, and they passed through the gates into what seemed like another world.

""You do know don't you, what has been going on?"

Leofwine rushed across the courtyard, hardly able to contain himself in his rush to greet them. Harold slid from his mount, turning to lift his wife from hers,

"Know what? I know many things, idiot, so how am I supposed to know which particular thing you are referring to."

"Tostig, of course. You do know that he has come here at the king's request?" Harold nodded, brows knitted in puzzlement,

"Yes, as are we, but I fail to understand why that is such a cause for you to be running about like a tittle tattle fisherwife selling the latest gossip."

Leofwine had grabbed Harold by the arm now, and was dragging him across the yard to where a young lad was sitting, shaking. His hair was matted with blood and his tunic streaked with filth. He was clutching a cup of mead in his hands, but they were shaking far too much for him to lift it to his mouth without spilling. He was ashen faced, eyes staring out, unseeing.

"Talk to him, Harold, talk to him. He has just ridden in, not spoken to anyone who matters yet," Leofwine was shaking Harold now, in his urgency, "What he has just told me, oh sweet God I can hardly believe it, but yet I know it to be true."

Harold decided not to chide his brother for dismissing his own importance but crouched down, to be on eye level with the lad. He was even younger than Harold had first thought, fifteen or sixteen perhaps and barely away from his mother's teat. It was plain now that all the blood was not his own, covered in it as he was. Harold lifted his hand to the boy's face and turned it towards him. He wasn't even shaving yet. Slowly the boy let his eyes focus on Harold's,

"Tell me boy, what is this sorrowful news? Slowly now lad, and try not to miss out any detail. It may be important."

Edith had followed them over and laid her hand on the boy's slender shoulders in reassurance,

"Don't worry now, take your time. The Earl will wait until you are ready. Tell me, sweeting, what is your name?"

The boy turned to smile at Edith, glad to see a kindly feminine face,

"Durwyn, my lady. Durwyn of York."

Harold's ears pricked up at the word, "Come now, Durwyn, talk to me. You are safe now, and it would seem in the gracious protection of my wife. May I assume that something has happened in your fair city?"

The boy nodded, almost frantically, "It might once have been fair, but no longer. Bloodshed; *so* much blood has been shed."

Slowly, word by word, Durwyn told his tale. It seemed that despite Harold's advice Tostig had carried on his own sweet way, alienating enough of his thegns to mean that the moment he had left the area they took their chance. They had attacked the stronghold in the centre of the city, slitting the throats of anyone foolish enough to resist, including those poor fools still loyal to Tostig. The streets were sticky with the blood of the slain. His father had thrown him on to his horse and told him to ride hard for help, to ride for the king here at Oxford. He had no idea at all if his father still lived, let alone his brothers. All he did know was the the rebels were following hard on his heels, and that the man riding at their head was the one the pack had decided should be the new Earl of Northumberland. Harold didn't even need to ask. He knew straight away that it would be Morcar. Morcar Aelfgarson.

Harold ruffled the boy's hair, just as he would his own sons, to comfort him. He was staring from Edith to Leofwine and back again, eyes blazing with contained fury. How many lives had been lost because of Tostig's arrogance? And here he was, prancing about the place, fawning all over Edward while his own people, the folk he had sworn to protect, were lying dead in the gutters. It was time Tostig got a taste of his own medicine. Edith gently encouraged Durwyn to his feet and lead him in the direction of the guest chambers. If anyone deserved the chance to rest in a soft bed for a while it was he. Leofwine had hared off to find the physician and obtain a phial of poppy juice to help the lad sleep. Exhausted as he was, there would be no peaceful sleep with those images in his mind without some kind of help. Edith tucked him up, smoothing the covers like she hoped his mother would then sat beside him, stroking his hair and humming gently to him. Please God, never let her boys see the sights this poor lad must have seen.

She sat beside him, waiting until he dropped off into a fitful sleep. Her head was dropping, tired as she was herself and she felt her eyes closing despite her best efforts to stay awake. Suddenly she jerked wide awake. There was a commotion, and the racket seemed to be coming from nearby. Slipping from the chamber, she hastened out into the courtyard to see Tostig and Harold squaring up to each other. The change in Harold's brother was horrifying. He was thinner than a snake and jittery with it. His hair was just that much too long, unkempt, and a huge shock of white raked across his head. He was standing toe to toe with his brother, shouting at the top of his voice. He was trying to run to the stables, no doubt to ride off to face his usurper but Harold was restraining him by the arm. Tostig howled in fury, trying to shake Harold free and swinging at him with his free fist. That was the point at which Harold finally lost patience. He pulled back his right arm and let his fist fly, landing his knuckles firmly on the point of his brother's jaw and sending him spinning to the floor. A whole lifetime's frustration with Tostig was contained within that punch and it would have taken a much stronger man than he to withstand it. He was unconscious before he hit the ground. The whole awful tableau was completed by the sight of the king. standing on the steps to the hall as if stricken by lightning. The thegn Aldin was striding across the yard, sword drawn, and Edith ran to intercept him, eyes questioning,

"The king has instructed me to stand guard over the lady Judith, my lady. He fears my lord Northumberland may try to drag her away with him. And the children, of course. It seems that when my lord Wessex told him the dreadful news he threw himself into such a rage as I have never seen, nor had the King. It is perhaps as well that my lord Wessex decided to terminate the conversation, so to speak."

By now some of the king's men were picking Tostig up and dragging him across the yard, still unresponsive. He was to be confined and under guard until he showed some sign of returning to reason. Edith shrugged. This had been coming for a long time now. She spotted some of the stable boys struggling across to the guest block under the weight of the chests that had been transported in their carriage. Wilone was behind them, chivvying them along like some general marshalling their troops. Edith followed along behind them, glad to see something in the world never changed, even if it was only her maid's bossiness.

Harold slung his gauntlets down on the bed without a word. He unbuckled his belt and began to pull his tunic up over his head, throwing it down to join the gauntlets. He strode over to the pitcher and bowl which Wilone had placed on the chest top and, bending forward, poured the lot over his head. He stood unmoving, gathering himself as he waited for the drips to finish falling from his mane. Then , scooping up the water in his hands, he splashed his face, washing off the dirt from the journey and his fight with Tostig. He picked up the drying cloth from the chest and rubbed his head fiercely. Edith waved the maid from the room and sat on the bed. Not for the first time the sight of Harold's bare torso took her breath away. Every muscle rippled with strength as he towelled his hair and she smiled to herself as she saw the little scar she had left on his side. That blemish made him all the more beautiful to her. He threw the drying cloth down, and perched on the edge of the chest, eyes filled with exasperation,

"What a mess. What a bloody awful mess. I'm sorry, love, really I am, but I need to ride out at once. Somebody has got to try to pour oil on troubled waters before this gets any worse and before you say a word, how could I refuse?"

Harold had seen Edith start as if to complain,

"It was the king, you see. He looked dreadful. I can only assume it was shock, but he is not a young man any more and how could I cause him any more pain? I dread that he might succumb like father did, at least before the boy is ready to rule. Alright, I sound selfish, I know, but just for once I would like to be able to sit back and watch everybody else sort things out." He moved the bowl, then pulled out a clean tunic from the trunk, his best one, and tugged it down, smoothing the creases then refastening his belt.

"But so soon?"

Edith was downcast. She had hoped he could wait until the morning at least. It seemed that every time she tried to grab some time together it was snatched out of her hands. Harold took her in his arms, his damp hair caressing her face as he kissed her apologetically.

"Honestly, I'm blaming myself for this. I could have given Tostig more help, kept my ear to the ground for trouble." Now Edith was cross.

"And how could you have found the time to do all that then? You barely have any time to yourself as it is.

Aside from that, Tostig is an adult and sooner or later you have to let him succeed or fail on his own account. You can't protect him forever."

Wearily Harold got to his feet. His back was aching after the ride and in truth all he really wanted was to have a good meal, drink far too much of the king's best wines and sleep for a week. Thank you so much for this, brother, he muttered to himself as he headed out to mount up, I must remember to pay you back for this one day.

CHAPTER 47

To ride out alone and face the gathered forces of
Morcar took strength , bravery and the coolest of heads
and Harold had those qualities in depth. This
insurrection must have been a long time in the
planning, he gauged, as he saw amongst the crowd of
armed men faces he recognised. Danish men, men he
had met when he had travelled abroad on the king's
business, men who would go anywhere and fight
anyone for a price. How ironic, he seethed inwardly,
that Baldwin's men were hell bent on destroying his
brother in law.

He thanked God he had not waited for the king to
gather his husceorls to accompany him. The mood of
the Northumbrians was such that the slightest
provocation would have been enough to cause all out
war. As he listened to the ringleaders his heart sank
lower and lower. It was soon apparent that there would

be no way back for them. They hated Tostig and that was that. Even Harold could find no way of negotiating a return to the way things were. Tostig ought to be glad that he had escaped with his life, if what he saw was anything to go by. Morcar was smirking at him, arms folded and a look of smugness spread across his face. He and his brother had outmanoeuvred the mighty Godwinsons and he was full to the brim with self satisfaction. Harold got the impression that Morcar was not to be trusted as far as he could spit. He filed the impression away in his memory for future reference. Straight faced, he announced Morcar to be the Earl of Northumbria in the name of the king, and promised to relay the concerns of the folk of the north back to their ruler. Then, wearily, he climbed back into the saddle again and turned his mount towards Oxford.

"So, the upshot is that Tostig has been ousted and Morcar has planted his backside firmly in his seat. The mood that lot were in, if I had said otherwise my head would have been on a pike on the city walls of York by now. They were in no mood for negotiation."

Edith scratched her head thoughtfully, "That is as

maybe, but how do you suppose Tostig is going to react when he finds out. From what I have heard the poor soul is not himself. He is utterly convinced that everyone is out to get him. Judith is at her wit's end. The Queen has been trying to reassure her that everything will turn out alright but she isn't an idiot. She fears for her boys, and rightly so."

Harold stretched, trying to ease the knotted muscles down his spine,

"Well I have asked Ealdyth to talk to him, to try to prepare him for what has been decided. I guarantee that he will blame me for the mess he is in and I fear he might be right, to a degree. I should have made sure to get him together with the thegns and hammer out the problems long before now." Edith shook her head, "It was his place to know what was happening, not yours. And who knows? Maybe it will be a relief to him, not to have to struggle with it all any more." Whether he would or not, Harold was not relishing having to give his report to the council in front of the haunted eyes of his brother.

The table on the dais at the end of the Great Hall

was full of familiar faces. Bishops and thegns, Earls and royalty sat shoulder to shoulder , anxious to hear Harold's report. As Tostig walked through the double doors the mumbling from the council stopped, almost as if in embarrassment. A stool was placed in the centre of the hall and the king gestured to Tostig to be seated. Meekly, he complied, clasping his hands around his knees as he waited, and gently rocking back and forth. All eyes turned to Harold as he stood. He cast a sideways glance at his little brother and felt his heart break. Tostig looked a broken man, dishevelled and not in possession of his wits. Harold had to stop himself. So much of this was of Tostig's cause. He steeled himself and began.

Calmly as he could, Harold explained the events which, in his opinion, had lead to the current crisis. He tried not to apportion any blame, but it became more and more obvious to the observers that Tostig had been woefully unsuited to the task he had been given. Indeed, Edwin and Morcar had been quick to take advantage of the situation by organising the rebellion but as things stood it would have happened anyway, sooner or later. Out of the corner of his eye, Harold could see that his brother was getting more and more agitated. Now he had come to the point where he had to relate the agreement he had been forced to make in

Northampton. Harold closed his eyes. So far Tostig had been able to keep himself more or less under control. He could hear him muttering under his breath and he could see the twitching and fidgeting but he had so far neither done or said anything that might jeopardise his future. Please God let him not react now. "The situation was such, given the representations from many parts of the Earldom, that I could see no way to avoid war unless , on the king's behalf, I acceded to their request. That is to say, that Morcar Aelfgarson should now be known as Earl of Northumbria." Harold felt as if he was giving a death sentence and waited, breath held tight, for the earthquake that must follow.

Tostig shot to his feet, "And what about me then? Me and my family and the good people these bastard reivers killed? Do you think that you can just forget about that, pretend it never happened? Christ Jesus!" He picked up the stool and hurled it viciously across the room. It shattered as it hit the wall, splinters of wood flying in all directions. Before anyone could move to stop him, he had leapt towards Harold. He thrust his hands out before him, howling and grabbing at his brother's neck. Harold was quicker though and brought his own hands up between them, thrusting them apart then pushing Tostig hard in the ribs. Furiously, Harold threw himself across the table and he pursued Tostig as he staggered backwards. This fight had been a long time coming. Fists flew from both men. Harold felt his fist slam into his brother's face, smashing his nose and sending blood spattering down his tunic. Tostig kicked him, and tried to bring his knee up into Harold's groin but he wasn't quick enough. Harold grabbed his thigh and pulled it up, sending Tostig flying backwards. He landed on his back on the floor, Harold standing over him with fists clenched in fury. He wanted to kill him, brother or no. The only sound in the room was the panting of the two protagonists as they gasped for air.

"**Enough!**" The voice of the king rang out , cold with anger. "This is a Royal Council not a bear pit! Wessex, get out and calm down. I shall send for you later. Harold snapped a bow and left the room staring his brother in the eye with every step as he stalked to the doorway. "Tostig Godwinson!" Tostig pulled himself up from the floor, groggily trying to wipe away the blood that was trickling from his nose. He raised his eyes to the council without raising his head an inch. "Never has such a display been seen by this council." Tostig mumbled a half hearted apology through broken teeth. "Had you accepted the situation with good grace, which I would have expected from any of my Earls, then perhaps we might have been able to come to some sort of accommodation. As it is, I am not prepared to risk having you cause more trouble for my subjects. I will give you a week to set your business in order, then you will be exiled from this country. "

Tostig stumbled as if he had been stabbed through the heart, "You're all in this together, aren't you? You and that thieving bastard I called a brother. He did this to me. He stole my land and gave it away. I'll go, my lords, I'll go but remember this. That is my Earldom and I won't give in that easily. I will take what is mine!" He stormed out through the doors, slamming them closed as he went. The noise echoed sharp and final around the room, finally ebbing away to leave only empty silence.

CHAPTER 46

Edith had heard much of what taken place. She had positioned herself outside the hall, ears straining to catch the words that were spoken. The sound of the fight had made her wince, and the manic anger in Tostig's voice had filled her with dread. If she had believed in such things she might have said that he was possessed. As it was she was certain that something in his mind had snapped under the strain of trying to do a job he was so obviously unfitted for. She hustled back to the guest block, wanting to avoid being caught out.

Harold said nothing. He walked into the chamber, stripped to his undershirt and climbed into bed as if all his strength had been stolen from him. He shut his eyes and slammed his head against the pillow as if he was trying to knock out the memory of that awful scene. The side of his face was sliced open, and obviously someone had dabbed on something to staunch the blood. My poor love, thought Edith as she tucked him up.

Outside, Tostig was wasting no time and within the hour had his belongings and family stashed on carts and on the road. What irony that they should be headed to Flanders, to Baldwin's court, when his men were part of Tostig's downfall. Now there would be nobody to try to stop the paranoia. Heaven alone knew what Tostig's next move might be.

Harold refused to leave the room that night. His head was thumping and his face was not a pretty sight, bruised and bloody as it was. Edith went to the kitchen and begged a bowl of pottage and bread for him. Sitting on the bed, she spooned the soup to him like a sick child. He dipped the bread, putting it in his mouth when it had turned to mush. It wasn't just that it was painful to eat. He felt sick every time he thought of his fight with Tostig. "I never thought he had quite such a punch in him," stated Edith, trying to lighten her lord's mood, "I only hope you gave him back as much."

Harold yawned, testing his jaw as he did so, "I'm only glad that someone had seen fit to remove his knife. I would have been dead, there's no doubt about it."

"They've gone already, you know. Tostig didn't hang about where he wasn't wanted. Hopefully that will be an end to it."

Harold raised a cynical eyebrow and winced, "You think so? I doubt it. Even when he was a kid he wouldn't let go if he thought someone had wronged him. Always had to have the last word, if you know what I mean. And I think he really does love Edward, you know. It will have broken his heart for him to be the one to exile him. Oh why can't everyone be like you Edith, and just be happy as they are? There is far too much greed and selfishness in the world if you ask me." He was right, of course. Tostig would never be able to admit defeat. Edith gathered up the bowl and spoon and leant forward to kiss Harold ever so gently on his swollen lips. If anyone was going to be the target of Tostig's anger they both knew that it would be Harold.

Cursed. That was the only word Edith could think of to cover the events of that week. Edward really couldn't care less what Earl ruled where but everyone at court knew how upset the King had been by Tostig's behaviour. It was as if he had suffered a personal betrayal. Harold had decided to leave Oxford at first light, before anyone was about. He did not want to

have to explain himself to anyone, nor to let them see
the mass of ugly bruises he was sporting. He had
decided to take Durwyn along with them, much to
Edith's pleasure. The lad couldn't return to York, at
least not until all the fuss had died down, and there was
always room for a keen young groom in his retinue. The
sky before them was smeared an angry red as they rode
through the East gate, "Red sky in the morning,
shepherd's warning,"Edith heard Wilone mumble in a
foreboding voice. She huffed, and spurred her jennet up
to the front of the column where Harold was riding, his
hood pulled up over his head to keep away prying eyes.
This was a journey neither of them was looking forward
to. Neither were Leofwine and Gyrth, who had decided
that their surname would not be the most popular at
Court for a while. Their road lead to Bosham, where
Harold would have to tell his mother what had
happened with Tostig. There would be wailing and
railing at the Gods and he, Harold, would doubtless get
the blame for not looking out for his brother and,
worse than that, the family interests. Thank goodness
Edith was with him. She could distract Gytha with tales
of their children and the story of poor Durwyn. Under
her fiery exterior, Gytha could be a soft touch for sob
stories.

The sun had barely reached its height when Edith

heard a horse being spurred along the road behind them. She turned in the saddle to see the horse and rider pushing their way through the column of travellers, shouting angrily for them to move in his urgency to reach the riders at the front. Edith grabbed Harold by the sleeve and gestured towards the frantic horseman. They could see now that, under his cloak, he was wearing the king's colours. What now?

The poor boy was almost in tears. Trembling, he fumbled in his saddle bag, looking for the letter he had to deliver. Edith spotted the Queen's seal holding it closed. She was perplexed. Why on earth would Ealdyth need to send a Herald after them at breakneck speed when they had left Oxford so recently. Please don't let it be Tostig. Don't let him have harmed himself, or even worse his poor wife and little ones. She scanned Harold's face as he read, trying to find a clue as to what was so urgent.

"We return to Oxford as quickly as we can."

The husceorls turned their mounts and readied themselves to ride back. They needed no urging from their lord. They were his men and they would follow him to their deaths if they had to. Harold summoned his brothers, gesturing them to take the carts, carriages and the women on to Bosham. They would have to deal with the fallout from telling their mother. He had to get back to Oxford as quickly as he could. Edith made to turn her horse, but Harold grabbed the reins. His face was white, eyes wide with shock and fear. "Don't. You aren't coming with me. Go to Bosham with the others." Edith was livid. She was not going to play the meek little woman. If Harold wanted her to leave him here then he had better have a very good reason, She folded her arms, implacable, and refused to move an inch. Harold heaved a great sigh and lead her horse off the path and under a tree where they could not be overheard.

"The note is from Ealdyth. Do not tell anyone about this, but the king is ill. Ill like father was." Edith felt sick. The last thing that anyone needed was for the king to die at a time of such upheaval.

She looked Harold in the eye, face filled with concern, "He still lives? Please tell me that he still lives!"

The Earl nodded. It seemed that the king had collapsed, unable to use his left arm and leg and he was muddled in his thoughts. Ealdyth wanted him back, just in case the worst should happen."

Edith grabbed her lord's arm, in great earnest, "Then I shall come and do *not* try to stop me. The Queen will need someone should that be so, someone who she can share her grief with." It was true. If the king should pass then Harold would have enough to do trying to hold the kingdom together until the Witan could convene. Ealdyth would need a woman to support her. He nodded, whistling softly through his teeth as he kicked his mount into a canter and sped back along the Oxford road with his heart in his mouth.

CHAPTER 47

Ealdyth grasped her sister in law hard by the hand, eyes full of gratitude. The days where they would avoid each other were long over now. They seated themselves in the window recess, whispering for fear of waking the king from his fitful sleep.

"Harold did not mean to upset you. You know how clumsy men can be with words. He is just afraid of what might happen should, well, you know. He saw the greed in the eyes of Edwin and Morcar. They would ride down the hounds of Hell itself if they thought they could snatch the throne. There will be civil war, you can trust me, if there is no clear candidate for succession. You know whomever the king should choose the Witan will agree to."

The Queen nodded in sad agreement. Her husband was dying, a slow death it was true, but he was no Earl Godwin; he would not fight it. All he wanted was to get back to Westminster, to have one more Christmas and to see his beloved Minster consecrated. Edith could understand that. He would feel that the Minster was a part of his body and his soul, like she did about Walsinhgam; like Harold did about Waltham. Somehow they would have to keep the illusion that the king was well. There must be no sign of his weakness.

They decided to take a walk in the fresh air. The warmth in the King's bedchamber was overpowering and making them both drowsy. The physician would stay by Edward's side, even if he could do so little. As they rounded the corner to the physick garden they almost collided with the king's thegn, Aldin. He was grinning from ear to ear and carrying an object which reminded Edith of the basket seats the children had used when they were too small to ride properly. A look flashed for a brief moment across his face, almost too quick to be seen, but Edith noted it with a little smile to herself. It seemed Aldin had made a support for the King to use when riding back to London. He trotted off , anxious to see if it would sit properly on the saddle. Edith turned to look at the Queen, whose face had flushed rosy and wore a little smile.

"He's a handsome man, that Aldin. If I wasn't so

loyal to Harold then I might try to snare that one. He isn't married is he?" Edith was prodding.

"No he's not married. He has been a loyal body servant to the king for many long years now."

"Forgive me for saying so, and this is just between sisters, but I think he has loyalty to you too." There, Edith, that should do it. If she had gauged things wrongly then she would find her behind being booted in the same direction as Tostig. She waited for what seemed hours for the Queen's reply.

Ealdyth blushed a deep crimson now, and clutched her hands together as if she was trying to hold something very dear to herself tight and safe.

"You are right to say so. He has been my loyal friend ever since we met, even before I met the king. He says he loves me, Edith, and I truly believe it. I love my husband, lady, and he has ever been like a kind father to me, probably kinder than I deserve, but Aldin lights my days with sunshine. Just to hear his voice makes my heart skip a beat."

Edith raised her eyebrows, "But what about matters of the bedchamber? You are without a child of your own."

"Because, sister dear, I have never known a man.

Oh it is not for the wanting, believe me. I would take Aldin to my body in a heartbeat were it not for the king. I would not hurt him thus. He doesn't deserve it."

"But Edward has not taken you in all this time?" Edith was incredulous. The thought of Harold as a celibate was beyond her imagination.

"It is true. At first it was because he wanted to spite my father, and then we just became like father and daughter somehow. In any case he is a most saintly man, and I don't think he has ever wanted to commit the sin of Adam."

It gave Edith pause. How strong must their love be to wait all these years for each other. How terrible that their union could only ever come with the death of the King.

They made it to London, and through guile and good fortune no one saw the state the king was in. It was an illusion, of course, and to maintain the image took all the ingenuity that the family could muster. The problem would come when the Christmas Court was to take place. Nobles and men of God from every corner of the country would descend upon Westminster, each of them watching the other for the slightest hint of weakness, real or imagined.

Edith and Harold had hurried to Bosham once the king was safely tucked up in his Palace. At least Gytha's fury had had time to settle by the time they arrived. Leofwine and Gyrth had taken the brunt of her fury, but they just let it roll off them, like water off a duck's back, the same as they always had. They were glad, they said, to have taken young Durwyn with them. When he had related the horror that he had experienced she had flapped around the lad like a mother hen. Maybe she had realised just what Tostig had caused through his ineptitude. As soon as they dared, they excused themselves and rode home to Waltham, to try to grab a little peace before the storm that would soon erupt around them.

"Tell me, love, what will happen when the king dies?" Edith had waited her moment before asking Harold the question which sat heavy in her heart. They were curled up together, in their own bed, just enjoying the chance to be alone together in their own house. She was stroking his chest, her touch soft as snowflakes on his skin. He grabbed her hand, kissing it,

"Well, the Witan will gather together to choose

the candidate from among the Earls that they feel will make the best leader. Then whoever they choose will be crowned, probably in the new Cathedral if the king holds on till it is consecrated."

"You know that wasn't what I meant. There will be trouble, won't there?"

Harold eased himself upright, leaning against the bed head.

"There will. I fail to see how it can be avoided. If Edgar is chosen then every lord in the land with husceorls to their name will be trying to grab him for their own purpose. Duke William will see his weakness and be over here before you can blink. Not to mention the kings of Norway. They think this country is theirs by right anyway. The Witan will have to chose carefully from among the other possibilities to defray all that."

Edith looked up, her eyes glowing in the rushlight,

"And you? Will they light on you for their choice?" The thought of it made her feel sick, and it felt as if just to speak the words made the idea real.

Harold threw back his head, bursting into a peal of laughter that made the rafters ring, "*Me?* Oh Edith, how can you even *think* such a thing! What nonsense!

I'm no leader my love. If someone gives me orders I will carry them out and I do it to the best of my ability but to be the king? No, no, I am far too old for any of that nonsense. Let a young man with no ties take that on. I have enough work to do controlling my brood of children and that wickedly attractive woman I am proud to call my wife."

Edith settled down, her head on Harold's chest. She prayed that he was right.

CHAPTER 48

Christmas. The celebration of the Saviour's birth. What hypocrisy was all around the Great Hall, then. Edith sat in her place, halfway down the hall, and watched those around her. It was like watching a flock of crows circling a dying lamb, at least that was the image that sprang into her mind as she surveyed the expressions on the faces of every noble she looked at. The food, succulent as it might be, tasted like ashes in her mouth.

Harold was seated at the king's side. She could see the dagger-looks being thrown in his direction. Assumptions were being made among the chattering lords and their minions. Everyone could see now that the king was one step from his death bed. If only they realised that Harold was only seated there as a favour to his sister and in gratitude to his honest and fair lord. It looked for all the world as if he was marking Harold as his heir. Edith felt as if her worst nightmare was coming true as she watched little huddles of the greatest men in the land whispering together.

Harold was terrified. The king had retired before the end of the feast and Harold himself had carried him up to his chamber. The man felt lighter than a feather in his arms as he lifted him onto the high bed, kneeling to undo his shoes and removing the stockings himself. He wanted to do it as an act of respect and love, to serve the king as a thanks for the kindnesses he had received through the years and the way that he had always been judged on his own account, not as an extension of his father's arm. It was then that it happened, the one simple act that threw Harold into a state of fear. Ealdyth had reached to take the crown from the king and to place it on his treasury chest. He only wore it on Holy days such as this, and his wife had always been the one to slip it back into the silk bag that it was kept in, but this night he lifted his hand to stop her. Instead, he beckoned Harold to his side, his hands shaking violently with the effort. Edward lifted the golden circlet, the great sapphire at its centre glowing bright in the light of the candles. Then, with the last of his strength he leant towards the Earl of Wessex, placing it between his reluctant hands. Their fingers touched, and Harold could feel how icy Edward's fingers were. The meaning in Edward's eyes was obvious. Here, my lord, is the crown of England, and I am giving it to you. Keep it safe, care for it, for you are my chosen heir.

The Earl slipped back into the chamber, and gestured frantically to his wife to join him outside. She drained her glass of mead and excused herself from the Bishop of Winchester, who she had been chatting with about their daughter Gunnhild and how much she was enjoying her life at Wilton Abbey. The night air was crisp, studded with crystal starlight, and Edith wrapped her cloak tightly around herself as she hunted out her husband. He was pacing back and forth by the Western end of the new Abbey building and it looked for all the world as if he was arguing with himself. Dear God, he wasn't suffering from the same affliction as Tostig was he? As she got closer, she could see that he was trying to decide about something, weighing up the for and against of it. Spotting Edith, he ran towards her, tugging her into the shadows of the Abbey.

"What on earth is the matter? Is it the king? Has he passed already? Oh not before he sees his Abbey consecrated!"

Harold twitched, looking about him as if he feared

being overheard,

"Yes and no. Yes, it is the king but he still breathes, my love. He has such strength of will within himself that he will see his building made sacred, have no fear. It is worse than that, if it can be so. He handed it to me. He said not a word but I could read the meaning in his face. Ealdyth was there too; she saw it, and Aldin. I don't want it! I never wanted it! But what am I supposed to do if an anointed king made it so clear. What am I going to do, my love? Tell me, please, what should I do?"

Edith stared in absolute confusion. He was babbling, spitting his words out so fast that she could make no sense of any of it. She took his face between her hands, forcing him to look at her,

"What did he give to you, Harold? What is it that has upset you so?"

He looked at her as if it were she that had gone mad,

"Why, the crown of course. He handed me the crown. Our hands touched and I knew it. He wants to name me his heir."

The shock turned Edith's legs to jelly. She slid to the frosty floor, trying to make sense of what she had heard. It was madness, surely. Harold didn't want this; had he not said so? But the king, the king anointed with chrism from the land of Christ himself and blessed by the highest priests in the land, he wished it. And even in her scrambled mind it all made some kind of terrible sense. Her man was proven. Had he not shown himself to be an efficient and effective general over and over again? Aside from that, he was respected by men of power both far and wide. He had been trusted to do the king's work for so long now that he had been like a king in all but name. But he did not want this and perhaps that was the most telling thing of all. He had never sought this power; everyone knew his opinion on that score. Would that not make him the perfect choice? Well, Edward was no fool, even ill as he was. He had made the right choice for the country in Harold.

"I have to think, Harold. You can't expect me to say anything until I have thought it all through. I need to sleep on it"

Neither of them did sleep though. Harold was tossing and turning, muttering and cursing. Edith lay stock still, eyes closed and mind churning. No matter how she played it out in her mind, she was the loser. If Harold wore the crown he could hardly seat what amounted to his mistress beside him. Whatever deals he would have to make would scupper that straight away, be it with the Church or the world at large. Should he refuse then the country would be torn apart, earl against earl and invaders against them all. She sighed to herself as she watched the future they had both yearned for crumble into dust.

Edith sat up in bed, running a comb through the length of her hair. She looked down at her lord. He had fallen asleep at last, his hair tousled with sweat, despite the chill of the night. Poor boy, she mused, your life has never been yours to choose, has it? Feeling her kiss, he turned over, bleary eyed, shaking his head as if hoping that last evening had just been a dream.

"About time you were awake. There is much to do today and you want to spend it lounging in bed." If there was one thing that Harold had never liked about Edith it was her ability to have the most awful night and yet be awake before the lark looking as fresh as a summer daisy.

"First of all, we need to meet with your brothers. They should know the fullness of it. Depending on what they have to say, you will make your next move."

Harold groaned, rubbing his hands through his

hair in an effort to tidy it up. He crawled from the bed and pulled on his tunic and stockings, as Wilone swept in through the door. Ignoring him completely she lifted Edith's gown from the peg in the wall and began to aid her mistress to dress. Where had she been at this time in the morning? The thought slipped into Harold's mind but it was soon driven out by a regiment of others.

The Queen had allowed them the use of her private room for the family meeting. She herself was sitting with the King, keeping company as he dozed what was left of his time away. Harold recounted to his brothers what had happened, his voice almost less than a whisper. They were speechless which, thought Edith, was probably the first time in as long as she had known the pair.

"And you will do it? Take the crown?" Gyrth was incredulous. The magnitude of the decision horrified him.

"That is why I have asked you here. I would do nothing without discussing it with those closest to me. The Queen thinks I should. She trusts to Edward's judgement. My wife, I know not," he looked imploringly at Edith, "And now I ask you."

Leofwine looked to Gyrth. They really ought to have been twins. Every thought, every action, was a joint one,

"Father would have snatched it with both hands and what a mistake that would have been. It shows the mark of you as a man that you even ask for our advice. The country could do a lot worse." Gyrth nodded in agreement at Leofwine's words, "But," he added as an afterthought, "I do not know how the Earls Mercia and Northumbria would take it, one of the sons of Godwin in the seat of ultimate power." They all fell silent. If they thought it looked like a grab for power then what was to stop them doing the same thing.

"Marry her." Edith felt as if she was standing beside herself, watching the drama unfold, " The sister, Aeldgyth. Marry her." The words felt like glass in her mouth but they had to be said. She closed her eyes, unwilling to see the pain in Harold's face. "It is the only way to keep that mercenary pair under control. You have to make them family."

Harold was shaking, "But Christ above, Edith, I killed her husband! What makes you think she would consent to it, even if I did?"

The words were spilling out now, like water from a broken dam, "Because she will do as she is told. They are no fools. They will see the benefit to being the king's brothers in law and won't let her finer feelings get in the way. Besides, she is no blushing virgin. She has been bartered before."

There was silence, a thick and heavy silence that hung on the shoulders of each one of them.

"But, Edith, what about you?"

Gyrth had mouthed the words that Harold had not dared to. Smiling ruefully, she knelt by her lord's side and fixed his eyes with hers,

"Oh my sweetest love, I am a mother and a mother of sons at that. I would give my life to see them safe from harm. If cutting out my heart would protect them from the hell that is war then hand me the knife to do it now. All I have to give you is my release from your vows to me. Let me do this, Harold, for I know that you will make a strong and upstanding king. You will be a king I shall be proud to say I knew." It was too much now. To look in his beautiful eyes was to feel her resolve breaking. She ran from the room before Harold could change her mind.

She had reached the carriage that Wilone had

procured for their departure before he caught up with her, grabbing her wrists as he forced his mouth against hers, "I will never be free of you Edith. You run in my veins, in every beat of my heart, every single breath. If I were never to see you again in this life you would still be the only woman I could call my own." He pulled her back into their chamber, throwing her onto the bed and loving her with more sorrow and bitterness than she had ever known.

"I shall go home, my love. It would be best if I were not here, like a spectre at the feast, while you are making your... arrangements. I will try to explain it all to the children, although goodness knows how they will take to the idea. Please God let there be enough time for them to come to terms with it all." Edith had it all sorted in her head. Harold nibbled at her ear, making the hairs on the back of her neck tingle with delight. It never failed to astound her just how quickly he could change his mood after he was satisfied. He was more relaxed than he had a right to be, "Many a lord takes a mistress. After a while, who knows? You might well find me back in your bed, lady." Edith was in no mood for humour. She climbed from the bed and straightened her clothing, tucking away her belongings in her trunk, ready for travelling. Wilone knocked on the door to ask if her mistress was ready to leave. How odd that was, as if there had already been some subtle shift , thought Harold. Last night the maid would have had no compunction about striding into the room if he and Edith were stark naked and in the full throws of lovemaking.

"It won't work!"

Harold sat up in surprise, "What won't?" Edith threw her hands in the air and looked at him as if he were a dolt.

"The plan, you idiot. Edwin and Morcar will no more believe that you have just given me up like that than that the moon rises in the morning and the sun at night. After all they are more devious than a fox tempting a hen to become his bedwarmer. No, we have to give them cause to think that you have had enough of me. They have to feel they are close enough to the throne to see their kin on it one day, like Godwin did, and you said it yourself; that you could be back in my bed before the end of the nuptial feast and their sister as like to breed as that bedpost."

"Can't you think of anything? After all, I have no experience of casting a lover aside, never having felt the need." Harold was pulling her back onto the bed again but she swatted his hand aside impatiently.

"Wilone, ask the carter to wait. There is something I need to attend to before we leave"

The serving dish glanced against the side of Harold's head, splitting it deep enough for the crimson to run like a flood down the side of his face,

"You bastard!" A beaker honed in toward his head which he dodged just in time, It thumped against the wall and dropped to the floor with a clatter.

"You see! That is exactly why I am ridding myself of you, harpy! I will not put up with you, or your temper, or your moods, or your bastard offspring any longer. I would rather spend my years with a woman who knows her place," another trencher flew by his head, "Even if it were an arranged marriage it could hardly be any more loveless than this!"

By now a crowd of onlookers was beginning to gather. There was nothing more titillating than someone else's domestic warfare. Leofwine and Gyrth had arrived, alerted by Wilone to potential trouble. They were trying to restrain Edith from assaulting their brother any further.

"As if anyone would have you. Have you looked at yourself lately with your paunch and your bald patch? Ha!" Edith was loving this. It was more fun than she had enjoyed in many a year.

"I think I shall marry. Someone younger and prettier and less like a Gorgon than you are."

"Is anyone desperate enough? Really?"

"Hang desperate. You forget I am Earl of Wessex and that will bring the women flocking. In fact. I might find some young maid looking for a healthy, fine figured lord." Harold was enjoying himself too, all apart from the cut over his eye, that is. He could feel all the tension flowing out of his body.

"You've as much chance of that as you have of marrying that Mercian girl, and you cut her last husband's bloody head off!"

"Don't dare me, woman. She is much prettier than you could ever be and she has kept her figure!"

"Oh, bless my soul. Harold, the great lover! You're smitten with her, that's what you are!" A stale loaf hit him in the solar plexus. Harold gave a theatrical groan, and motioned to Leofwine to get rid of her. He dodged another beaker and hoisted her over his shoulder, She hooted like an angry owl, thumping him in the back as he carted her back to her lodging.

By the time he reached the chamber door she was helpless with laughter. Leofwine dragged her through the door and dumped her without ceremony on the bed where she curled up, unable to move for laughing. Harold was not far behind, supported by Gyrth, sniggering fit to burst and dabbing the bloody laceration with his sleeve.

"Did it work, my lady?"

"Oh yes, Wilone, like a dream!" Harold pulled Edith into his arms and kissed her. Then he did the same for her maid who blushed beetroot and scuttled from the room in alarm. The two brothers looked at each other in utter confusion.

"We had to make it look real, you see, so we couldn't tell anyone of our plan, apart from Wilone. Edwin and Morcar would have been less inclined to fall in with marrying their sister to Harold if they thought that it was just a short term price for their cooperation. Who would want their sister to be left alone in the marriage bed, to be mocked, while her husband was casting his seed in another field. Oh I am sorry, though. I misjudged that first dish."

Gyrth and Leofwine grinned at each other. Their sister in law was a bigger prankster than they were. Then, putting on straight faces, they went back to the hall to indulge in spreading some gossip.

It was time for Edith to leave. She could not stay after her little performance, and Harold had some hard days ahead. "I wish I could be here with you. When the day comes , for the king, you will need to take care. There will be much jealousy and even more flattery."

Harold kissed her fingertips, "Have no fear. I know who can be trusted and who cannot. What about you, though? I do not know when I will be able to see you again. It will not be easy to travel to Waltham without prying eyes." He lifted her into the carriage, his face suddenly serious, "Look after her, Wilone. She is the most precious jewel I shall ever possess. And try to make sure the children understand why I am acting as I am. It is only to secure their futures." Edith reached forward and caught the hint of a tear on the hem of her veil. "God be with you, my love."

CHAPTER 49

It made no difference. No matter how many different ways Edith had tried to phrase it, in her head, she couldn't square the circle. The boys would be livid; she knew it. As the carriage pulled up towards the gates to the compound at Waltham Edith couldn't help but cry. Without the hope of Harold trotting up one day, with a grin across his face, the place seemed as if it had lost its soul.

The steward ran out to hand Edith down from the carriage as the head groom grabbed at the reins. He looked out through the gate, as if searching for someone,

"The Earl will no longer be resident here, so do not look for him." It felt so final, to actually say the words. Godwin and Magnus had sauntered across the yard, hailing their mother with a wave. Oh, they were both so like their father, in their looks and their mannerisms. Their temperament was all the old Earl though. It would take a great deal of tact to explain away the change in circumstances.

"I'll kill him!" Godwin had flown into an incandescent rage, much as his mother had feared. He was buckling on his baldric and forcing his sword into the scabbard. The others were not far behind. Even Ulf was running around gathering weaponry as if they were about to be besieged. Edith dropped her head into her hands. It was wonderful that they wanted to protect her and her name but it was really so unfair.

"STOP IT!" The boys jumped with shock; their mother never, ever shouted, "Listen to me, and put those swords down. You will not go to confront your father. He has done nothing that deserves such behaviour."

"What, lady mother? He is allowed to cast you off like an old sock, is he, so that he can wed himself to some crone who will bring him the throne? Not to mention throwing us off like some embarrassment conceived the wrong side of the blanket? I shall have it out with him, on my life, and when I do he will regret ever causing you pain!" Godwin was within his rights, at least in his mind. He adored his mother and hated to see the pain etched on her face and he would do something, even if it meant causing a rift with Harold. The Haroldson boys had all been brought up with a strong sense of right and wrong.

"Your father has been put in a terrible position; one that means he cannot avoid causing hurt and, by the way, the whole thing was my idea. He is not just your father, or my lord, but one of the greatest Earls in the kingdom. A man of such power has to make decisions for the good of England and as awful as it seems, our needs have to come a very long way down the list."

EdmUnd sat down on the floor, throwing his sword down in disgust. The others followed suit. Thank heavens she had managed to head off their revolt. The last thing Harold needed at this moment was a phalanx of angry youths descending on Westminster.

"I thank you for your understanding."

Godwin huffed, "Only because of my respect for you, lady mother. At the first opportunity I shall inform the Earl of our feelings." The others nodded in agreement.

"There is another reason that you would not be

welcome at the moment. The king, well I know no other way to say this: he is dying. Your Aunt Ealdyth will not want silly fuss at this time. She does not deserve to deal with your nonsense at such a time of loss. " An icy silence flooded the room. Change was uncomfortable, uncertain. It was like rolling dice and not knowing if the number you come up with is a winner or a loser.

"So this is all about that, isn't it? About who gets the crown?" Magnus was no fool, and it was pointless to try to pretend he was wrong. Edith nodded, casting her gaze across each one to be sure they understood the magnitude of what had been said.

"Well I suppose we shall just have to bit our lips, although I am still not happy about the way you have been sent off home like some errant hound dragged back to the kennel." Dear, brave, foolish Godwin. He would always want to solve an argument with the point of his blade.

It was actually a relief to be away from the claustrophobia of the Palace and back to the slower country life. For a while Edith immersed herself in the tasks it required to run an estate. It was surprisingly satisfying, she pondered to herself, to do something as simple as counting how many barrels of grain were left to see them through until the harvest. She visited her Priory at Walsingham and spent time in prayer and contemplation. It refreshed her mind and spirit, and by and by she came to terms with her changed life. Occasional visitors would drop by at Waltham, bearing with them all the gossip from court. Harold had been declared king after Edward's death, but he had caused something of an uproar by being crowned the very afternoon of Edward's burial. Edith frowned. It looked disrespectful at the very least. He had married Aeldgyth, and that had been pretty quickly too. At least he had tied together the two great houses. Hopefully there would be peace now.

Sour Winter began to melt away, and the buds of Spring began to open, soft pink and white against the pale blue of the sky. Edith was standing by the drying grounds, overseeing the washing of the bedding and taking the opportunity to breath in the clear warm air. That was one of the things she loved about the flat lands. The sky seemed to carry on for ever. She blinked, rubbing her eyes then stared upwards again. Yes, there it was! At first she thought that she was imagining things, or that something was in her eye but no. There was a strange streak across the sky, glowing bright in the light of the sun. The longer she stared, the more surprised she became. Surely it was moving! By now the other women were staring too, shielding their eyes as they stared in a mixture of horror and amazement.

"My lady, what is it? I have never seen the like!" Wilone was shaking in fear. She was a country lass who believed deeply in signs and symbolism. To her this was a great portent, although whether of good or evil she could not decide. It bothered Edith too, although she would not admit it. She had been thinking, mulling over the past, and something tucked away in the back of her mind had surfaced and it frightened her to the core. When he had been in the care of Duke William, Harold had sworn on Holy relics to be the Norman's loyal vassal. Harold had dismissed it with an airy wave of his hand. It had no substance, he said, as it was done under duress. Even Archbishop Stigand was in agreement. And that was where it might have ended but for the fact that William was cousin to the dead king. And he was a very, very ambitious man who did not like to think someone had tried to make a fool of him. Now this, this omen. She shook her head, dismissing it all as superstitious nonsense, or at least trying to.

As Edith spread out the woollen cloth along the floor ready to cut it up to make a gown for Gytha, she was faintly aware of a figure standing in the doorway behind her. She snipped carefully along the outline she had draw, tongue between her lips in concentration,

"Do I ever find you other than on your knees woman?" She stopped, frozen in shock. How could it be? Hands, cold from the chill evening air, had rested across her eyes now, "Guess who!" The scissors fell to the floor with a clatter as she threw them away, the better to take the hands she knew so well in hers.

"I thought I had been put aside, that you were happily married in the sight of God?"

"Oh that! Don't! Surely you knew I couldn't keep away from you for too long."

His kiss was just as she remembered it, warm and sweet. He sat down on his familiar seat and Edith curled up by his feet, content to lay her head on his knee. "I cannot stay for long, love. I have made the excuse that I wanted to visit the Abbey, to see how my endowment is being used. It is just a coincidence that our home is en route." Our home!

"Tell me, your Highness the king, will you have the chance to speak to your offspring before you must leave? There are bridges there that need to be rebuilt."

"Of course, sweet, whatever you command, but not until I have carried you off to bed and shown you just exactly how much I have missed you."

Harold held his woman in his arms, close enough that she could feel his heart pounding against the wall of his chest. He had loved her as he always had; it felt no different, just more precious.

"Do you hold her like this, afterwards?" It was an itch that Edith had to scratch despite herself.

"What, Aeldgyth? Oh please, don't make me laugh, heart, not at a time like this!" Harold was shaking with suppressed laughter. "I can tell you now, and I will swear it on the Holy Cross, that as far as that lady is concerned I might as well be a virgin. It is not that surprising, really, given that when I was presented with her first husband's head it was very much detached from its body. When we climbed into the marriage bed she lay there like a bar of iron. And there was I, in my undershirt, trying to convince my body of the need to perform. Anyway I couldn't and she didn't want to so that was my wedding night. The same every night since, too, as you must want to know." Edith giggled, snuggling up and stroking the scar under his ribs. Still their secret, seen by no-one.

CHAPTER 50

As the sun came up next morning, Edith stirred contentedly in bed. She was watching Harold as he dressed; her favourite secret pleasure. His clothes finer now as befitting of his rank. He seemed reluctant, as if he was being dragged back from a dream into an uncertain reality.

"Why did you really come home? It was not just to satisfy your lust, I know that. Tell me, before you have to face the children." Harold sighed and sat back down on the bed,

"If I asked you to think of two names in the whole of the universe that were giving me trouble, who would you think of?"

Edith thought for a moment and then bit her lip in thought. One name jumped straight to the front of her mind, but the other evaded her for a moment. Her eyes widened in surprise as she realised who it might be,

"Duke William, I'm certain. But.. surely not Tostig?"

"Oh the very same. He has been sniffing around every court in Europe looking for support. Of course Baldwin had to make some concession. Seems the little sod thinks the king wanted him to have the throne and I have usurped him. Yes, I know he is ill, his mind is lost, but that doesn't stop him being dangerous. And the word from Normandy is that William is pulling in every favour ever owed him to build a fleet for invasion. It never rains but it pours, does it?" Weariness settled on Harold's face, "I took that stupid ring of gold to try to keep some sense of peace and here I am facing not one but two invaders. I'm not doing much of a job, am I?" For a fleeting second he looked as if he wanted to run, as far and fast as he could. Then, resignation settled back on him. "Listen, when I have gone, I want you to take the children to Bosham. My mother is getting old now and it would be good for her to have some company. Stay there. It is closer to the coast should there be need to flee. I'm not saying it will happen, but I want to make sure that you are all safe. Promise me!" Edith lowered her head in agreement.

"Good!" Harold grinned his familiar grin, "Then lead me to our children and let me take the punishment they think I deserve."

CHAPTER 51

If Gytha had told the tale of when Tostig went swimming in the river and Gyrth had stolen and hidden his clothes, leaving him to walk the mile home through the village stark naked, she must have told it twenty times. Edmond laughed politely, tucking the rug across his grandmother's knee as he did so. Since Godwin died she seemed to have shrivelled into herself. Her cough was terrible, racking her body with each spasm. It had to be admitted, though, seeing the hall filled again with young folk seemed to bring back something of her old spark.

Gyrth and Leofwine had joined their brother, taking their husceorls with them. They had left their fyrd positioned along the coast, trying to give some protection against Tostig's raids or, worse, the Normans and their dragon ships. Even in Bosham, word drifted back of Tostig's adventuring. He had been nipping at the coastline, raiding here and there, from Wessex to Lincolnshire, causing carnage wherever he went. He had even taken on Edwin and Morcar, filled with hubris, and been sent smartly on his way. Things settled for a while, and Edith prayed that he had at last seen sense. It came as a surprise, therefore, when the steward rushed into the hall, declaring that the Queen had just ridden up through the gates. Edith bridled. How dare she show her face here. She might be married to Harold but never would she be family. She pulled herself up to her full height, ready to boot her bony backside back to Westminster, then her face split into the widest of smiles. Yes it was the Queen, the old Queen- Ealdyth. The two women hugged in greeting, both relieved to see a friendly face. Edith looked behind her, "Where is your handsome thegn? Don't tell me you have tired of him! If you have, there is always a place free in my bed."

"I know you, Edith Swannhesa. You would no more sleep with any other man than my brother than fly to the moon. As for Aldin, he is with Harold." If that was the case, then there was trouble, bad trouble. Harold would never have pulled away his sister's sworn thegn if things weren't falling apart. The steward brought them both a beaker of mead and they sat together at the furthest end of the hall, well out of hearing.

"Tostig has really done his worst this time. Baldwin had finally had enough of him and told him to go. Judith and the boys are safe in Bruges, thank Our Lord, but now the fool has bound up his future with Hardrada, that vicious Norwegian Viking. Aeldyth's brothers have shown themselves for the useless wasters I always suspected and were walked all over when they faced Tostig and Hardrada's men. So, now, Harold has had to march North to try and remedy the situation. He won't get away with negotiations this time. One or other of them is going to end up dead, and now I have to tell our mother about it." Ealdyth was white-faced. Her man might well die too, before they had even had chance for a life together.

The howl that Gytha set up rattled the hall to its foundations. Edith felt it through to her bones. The thought of losing her boys was more than she could bear. That was why their father was in this awful position now, to save them. She sat down next to Ealdyth, where she was hugging her mother and stroking her thick white hair. "I know, we did not exactly see eye to eye over our marriage. But you know what your brother is like. He could talk the birds out of the trees with that charm of his. And your father wished it. I could have left if I wanted and nothing said but he means the world to me. I hope you understand." Ealdyth looked at how her gown was stretched across her belly. A child who may never know its father.

"Don't try to stop me. I have as much right as anyone to be there when they come home." Not if, never if. Ealdyth shrugged and pulled her jennet up short, waiting for the other woman to mount.

"The lads have been told exactly what to do while I am away and what *not* to do. They will keep Gytha from worrying as best they can." They set off, accompanied by the Royal Steward for protection. The conversation was jolly, too jolly, casting around any subject they could think of that did not involve Tostig. He would never be welcomed back, even if he trampled Harold into the dust.

Riders were pouring through the gates exhausted. They slid from their saddles, like dead men. The acrid smell of blood hung in the air, metallic and vile. There seemed so few, and each looked shattered by fatigue. The king had dismounted beside his sister and stood unable to move. Misery was written large on his face, misery and shock. She took his hand in hers and squeezed it hard. "Swannhesa is here, my lord. She insisted she wanted to see you." Before she could say any more, Edith shoved through the crowd and, spying Harold, let out a scream of relief. He was here, he was alive! She ran towards him and threw herself into his arms, tears of relief washing her face and his. He pulled her close, smelling the comfortable familiarity of her hair, her skin. He could feel the swelling of her belly against his own. A child! Something bright and new and unsullied. Cheek against cheek, he whispered his sorrows into her ear. She had always listened, always been the one to tell him everything would be alright. But even her tender words and softest kisses would never put right the carnage that had been wrought at Stamford Bridge. Suddenly he felt more tired than he had ever felt before in his life. He wanted to go to bed and hold Edith close long into the night. He staggered towards the Great Hall, clinging to his woman like a drowning man might cling to a branch. His eye caught that of his wife, the queen. She was staring horrified at the tableau before her. The king shrugged, and went through the doors then left and upstairs to the royal bedchamber, taking the only woman he had ever wanted with him.

Harold pulled Edith towards the bed, desperate to do something, anything, that would take away the images in his mind. He had been in battle before but never anything so blood sodden as that day in Stamford. Worse of all was the memory of Tostig, his little brother, lying sprawled on the ground, his guts spilling onto the grass beside him. He had fought with honour, like a lion, but in the end he had been felled, like an oak in a forest. Harold had knelt and crossed himself as he closed his brother's eyes which were staring unseeing at the skies. Harold couldn't erase that image from his mind. He only hoped that making love to Edith would block it out, even if only for a little while. She could feel his misery and despair in every touch, letting him work out his pain on her body and when he had finished, collapsing into a sleep borne of total exhaustion, she cradled him in her arms and wondered if he would ever find peace again.

The sky was an angry red when he finally awoke. For a second it seemed as if the world was wonderful as he gazed down at his sleeping love. Then the memories came back, assaulting every sense until he screamed out, hands over his ears to drown out the sound of men dying.

"I took him to York. It was his church you know, he founded it and loved it as much as ever the king did with the Abbey." Edith was holding him tight now, swaddled in her arms, "I washed him and bound up his body. I didn't want anyone else to touch it, the state it was in. It was the least I could do for him."

"His mind will be at peace now, my love. There will be no more fear for him."

"But don't you see? The sin I have committed is one of the worst. He was Abel and I Cain. I was the one that struck the fatal blow! I killed my own kin and God knows I will suffer for it!"

There was a nasty air of anticipation hanging over the Palace at Westminster. Queen Aedgyth had cosseted herself away, surrounded by her ladies in waiting, refusing to even accept Harold's messages, let alone speak to him. That suited him fine; let her go her own way. If he should survive this mess then he would see their marriage dissolved and he would marry Edith ; properly this time, with monks chanting and censers burning and holy writ. Since Hardrada and Tostig scythed through their armies Aedgyth's brothers were in no position to complain.

The waiting seemed endless, as if every single soul was holding their breath. There were whispers, rumours, but nothing solid. That was until an unexpected visitor was ushered into the solar by Robert the Steward. There was a slight whiff of distaste on his face,

" There is a young.... gentleman .. to see you, my lady. He insists that he must speak with you immediately. He would not be put off." It was obvious that Robert did not like being ordered about in what he viewed as his own domain. Edith raised an eyebrow, putting down her sewing and positioning herself in the window niche with as much calm as she could muster, "Very well, show him in." Of all those she thought might enter the room, the last she expected was Durwyn. Edith jumped to her feet, wrapping her arms around the boy in welcome. Rather than reciprocating, he stood stock still, clutching his hood in his hands and staring at the floor.

"I asked if I might see the king, my lady, but that gentleman would not allow it. The lady Gytha sent me, she said whatever happened I had to speak with the king and that my message was for him alone." His eyes were a picture of torment. Edith took his hand in hers,

"Well, then, we had better find him, hadn't we?"

Harold was in the armoury, overseeing the repairs to equipment that had been damaged during the fighting at Stamford Bridge. Hammers rang out on anvils; grinding wheels threw out sparks in glittering arcs as swords were re-edged. The noise was such that he could not hear their shouts and when Edith tapped his shoulder Harold he jumped a foot into the air with fright. His nerves were balanced on the edge of a knife. He ushered the pair out into the quiet of the the upper court, away from hearing.

"I rode as fast as I could, my lord. The lady Gytha said I must not stop for a second of rest. They are here, the Norman fleet. Word came from Hastings; the people were fleeing in all directions from their ravening hordes. My lords Godwin, Edmond and Magnus have begun to organise the fyrd. Their men will join you if you wish it, or stay to defend Bosham."

Harold was whiter than a fresh fall of winter snow. It was too soon. There had not been enough time to rest, for those souls who had marched the length of the land to recover. He gathered himself, becoming the general again, "Tell me boy, how many ships? Do you know?"

Durwyn took a deep breath, as if remembering to the word his message, " Seven hundred ships, my lord, with maybe ten thousand troops." God, what a force William had gathered, but if he chose the right ground for the fight than numbers would be meaningless; they would just be tripping over each other if the battle ground was narrow enough. Harold's brain kicked into gear. He summoned his brothers and his senior thegns to meet him in the great hall. Durwyn turned towards Edith, looking for confirmation that he had done well. She patted his shoulder. At least now they all knew what faced them.

Harold laid the position out before his loyal men. It seemed as if a dagger had been plunged into every heart. To live through the hell that was Stamford and then to have to battle again so soon was bitter news.

"My lord, I will ride with you and fight to my death, willingly so, but my men are exhausted. They have not the strength to fight such troops as the Duke will have at his call. They might run, through mental exhaustion as much as fear, and that would be disastrous." Harold knew it, but he had thought this out,

"Indeed so. And because of that I will send most of them back to their homes. If we fail then they are better served defending their manors and if we succeed then it is no loss. I have sent messengers to call up as much of the fyrd as we can, from those who we set down from watching the coast. Any man his commander thinks fit can join us, the rest can be released with our heartfelt gratitude."

Gyrth had been thinking. He stood slowly, waiting to speak. Harold's eye let on him,

"But what if we should fail at Hastings? We need a force here, in London, to defend it from the invaders. That will give time for reinforcements to gather and give us a second chance. You should command that force, my lord and king. To lose the anointed ruler at Hastings would be to lose the country entirely. If you are safe here at least there will still be hope. I shall head our army, and I shall be proud to march with them." Dear, sweet, innocent Gyrth. Everyone always thought of him as a clown, and here he was, wiser than any of the wisest clerics Harold had ever met. But this was his battle. He had broken his promise and he was the one who had to answer for it,

"I thank you brother for your suggestion, and I would gladly follow your lead ,but William is as cunning a bastard as I have ever ridden alongside. I have stood shoulder to shoulder with him in the line of battle. I know his tactics; the way his mind works. Aside from which, it would look as if I was running and hiding from him, and that would mean the battle is lost before we even engage forces. I will stand with you all, within the shieldwall. If we stand together how can we lose?" Fists hammered on the table and cheers rattled the rafters. Harold knew his people and what they needed to hear at a time like this. He had rolled the dice. Please God his number was the winner.

Edith sat quietly, dressed for travel. The sun was just lifting above the rooftops and she listened to the sound of the chorus of birds which would always greet the day. Harold had thrown on his cloak over his mail coat. It felt strange to be here at Waltham without the family bustle all around them. Troops were waiting in the courtyard, ready to ride for Hastings. Harold had wanted to return here, to see his Abbey and to pray for his soul within it. He gave the Dean a bag of coins to say masses for him if need be, "Should the worse happen, my heart, I want you to see to it that my body is laid here, before the altar, so that I can spend eternity in its peace." Edith did not like it. To her, it sounded as if Harold knew defeat was coming. Harold saw the look on her face and threw his head back in a fit of glorious laughter. "Do not take it so, woman! Any commander worth his salt makes such arrangements beforehand. It means such worries will not be distracting when I need all my wits for the job in hand. You do see that, don't you? Besides, how could I lose if my lucky charm is with me."

Edith insisted that she accompany him, at least as far as the camp they would set up before the English armies came together and for once Harold hadn't bothered to argue. She could see the change that had fallen on him. His mind was already on the field at Hastings. She had been given instructions. Stay at the camp until news of the outcome. If disaster befell, then she had to get the boys out of the country, away from any desire for revenge. Get them to Dublin; to Diarmid . They would be safe there. As for the girls, Gunnhild was safe at Wilton, Ealdyth would see to that. Gytha needed a husband, but far from these shores. He walked over to his chest and lifted an object, long and slim, from within. It was wrapped in purple silk, the colour of kings. Edith slowly unwrapped it when he placed it on her knee. She already knew what it would be.

"It's Gudbrandur! My father's sword!"

"Polished and sharpened until it can split the length of a hair. I oiled it myself." The blade shimmered, the damask folding in the steel beautiful as the summer sun on a river, "I hope, pray, that I will be here to give it to her on her wedding day. If not, you must do so for me. Tell her how much I loved her, and how she reminds me of you. Tell her I polished this for her, myself." Edith felt panic rising in her throat. Harold had been everything to her for her whole life. Without him, how could she carry on?

"You will be fine, my love. You are stronger than ever I could be. Find refuge somewhere, if it comes to it which I sincerely and devoutly hope it does not. Wherever you are, whatever happens, I shall always be with you. Know that."

Edith swallowed. The horror Harold had to face was a hundredfold worse than anything that could happen to her. She smiled then threw herself at him, kissing him so hard that she would always be able to remember the feel of his lips on hers.

"Come now, my love. Men are waiting. We must go." Edith followed Harold to the chamber door, taking one last glance around the room. It felt oddly empty, even though not one item had been removed. She slid the door to, then, in a flurry of panic, she flew back inside, pulling up the lid of her chest and rummaging deep within for something. Clothes were cast everywhere in her desperate search and then, yes! Here it was! She slipped the object into the scrip at her waist and walked, head high, through the door without a second glance. Whatever should happen now, she was ready.

The air was thick with the sickly sweet smell of blood spilt and rotting bodies. Clouds of flies had started to descend, looking for somewhere to lay their eggs and feed their young. Carrion crows sat in the branches waiting for an opportunity to sate their appetites. The dead had been stripped of everything of any value, leaving them anonymous in the sea of misery. If Hell was real, it must have been like this.

The woman stepped over the crest of the hill and was confronted by the charnel house that besmirched the meadow. Her face blanched and her eyes, already red rimmed with tears, grew large with horror. Making an effort to control her emotions she began to make her way across the filth, forcing herself to look at each body in turn. So many faces, so many she recognised even as ravaged as they were. Not one face looked at peace. Fear lay across each visage, like a death mask. Solemnly she continued her journey. At one moment she slipped in the gore, leading the man who shadowed her to reach forward to catch her . Twisting her head towards him she gave a scowl of such anger and hatred that when she shook her arm loose he did not offer again.

By her feet were two that she knew so well. She knelt down beside them, filled with sorrow. Hope for the two brothers was gone. Leofwine and Gyrth, always together in life and now in death. Hardly ever before had she seen them without a grin on their faces; always laughing, always joking. And now here they were , faces sliced, eyes open, staring at the sky but never again to see it. Her hand slipped across their eyes, closing the lids to give them what peace she could. She whispered a prayer and, crossing herself, bent down to kiss them adieu. The metallic tang of their blood sat bitter on her tongue.

Conscious of the impatience of her escort she stood and continued the task that she had undertaken. Wherever she trod, she stood on mangled limbs, viscera, puddled and congealed gore. The hem of her gown trailed in it, her shoes were soaked with it. It seemed that she searched for hours, forcing herself to look and look again, trying to find the one she sought. Dusk was wrapping the coast in mist, adding to the unreal feel of it all, when she spotted him. Her heart shrunk within her. She wanted to howl, to cry, to scream with anger for the stupidity of it all but she did not. She would never give the satisfaction of the sight of her tears to those who had ripped her life apart.

The mark was there. It was on his beautiful chest, where she had made it so many years before when they were little more than children. A cross, a little cross. Such a small thing, but everything to her. Not caring any more ,she sat down among the bodies and ran her fingers across the torso she knew so well. One last touch that she could remember on the dark nights that would surely follow. She curled over and laid her head against the body. It felt oddly unfamiliar without the warmth and the heartbeat she had lain beside so recently. Reaching for her scrip, she fumbled with the strings which held it closed. She struggled with the knot, her fingers numb with shock and pain but eventually she managed to pull open the pouch. Inside was a little pouch made of leather , old and stiff to open. Unfastening it, she pulled out a rose petal. It smelled sweet, sweeter than anything on this earth and was redder even than the blood which lay all around. Forcing open the dead man's hand, she thrust it against his palm, letting the reflex curl his fingers around it, holding it safe for eternity.

She could sense her escort restlessly moving from foot to foot. He must be horrified by his surroundings too, she mused. It was one thing to be involved in the heat of battle, another surely to stand in the aftermath and face the destruction you had been part of. Giving one final kiss goodbye, fingers lingering against the scar she had made, she looked up and held the knight's eye with hers,

"This is he. This is my lord. Harold Godwinson, king of England."

Printed in Great Britain
by Amazon